I0824005

Disney

TINKER BELL

AN ENCHANTERS TALE

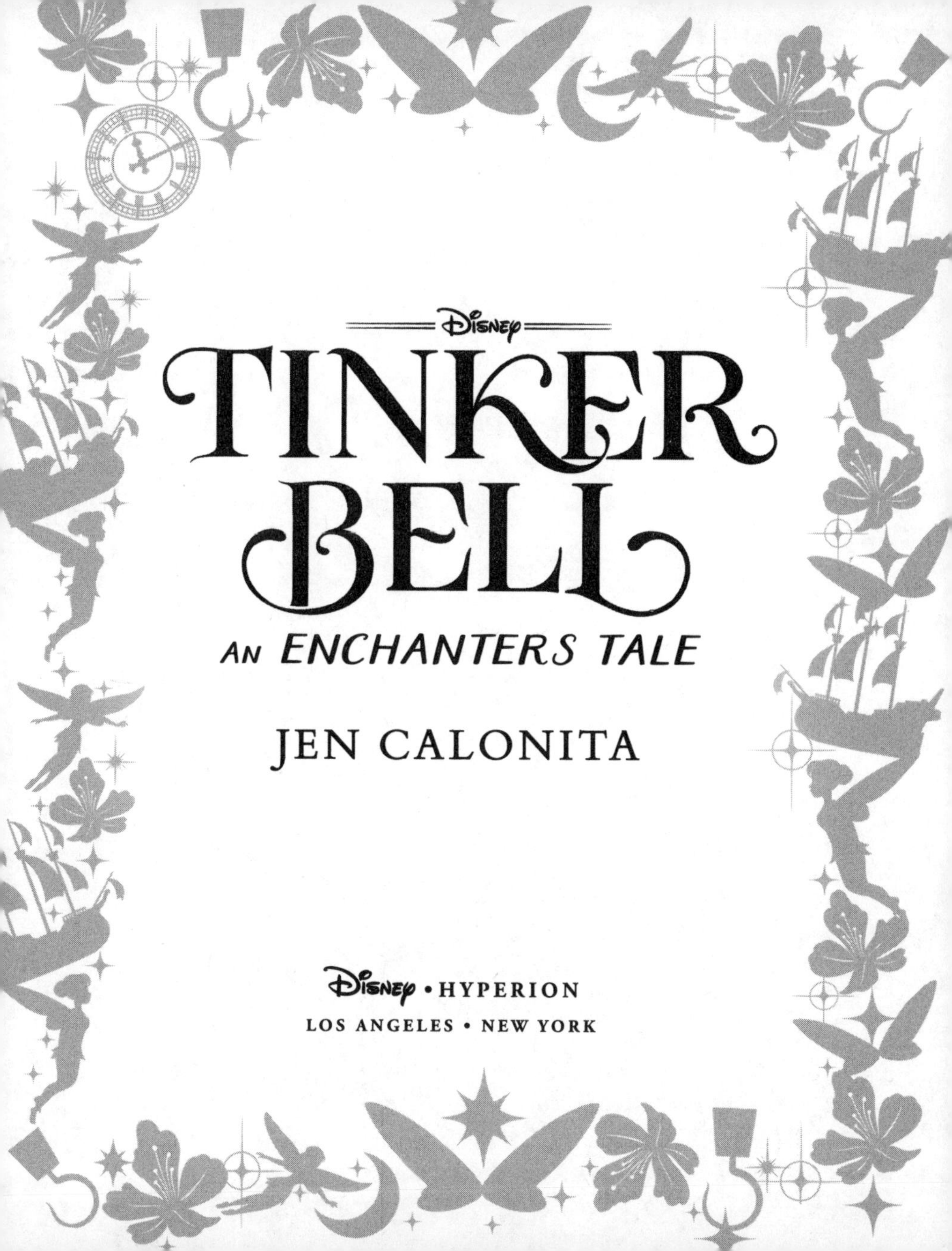

Disney

TINKER BELL

AN ENCHANTERS TALE

JEN CALONITA

Disney • HYPERION
LOS ANGELES • NEW YORK

Disney

TINKER BELL

AN ENCHANTERS TALE

For information address Disney • Hyperion, 7 Hudson Square, New York, New York 10013.

First Edition, September 2025
1st Printing ode
FAC-004510-25170
Printed in the United States of America

This book is set in Garamond/Monotype
Designed by Marci Senders

Library of Congress Control Number: 2025930348
ISBN 978-1-368-08977-7
Reinforced binding
Visit www.DisneyBooks.com

For Heather Verreault, Tinker Bell's biggest fan

PROLOGUE

TINKER BELL HAD NEVER BEEN FOND OF THE WORD *NO*.

Or *can't*.

Or *impossible*.

They were useless sentiments, really. They certainly never served Tinker Bell well. Not when she was creating a (revolutionary) pixie dust replenishment system. Nor when she was fixing a rain collector. Not lately, as Tink explored Never Land, searching for wonders, uncovering secrets. To Tink, *impossible* was just a problem to be solved. So, whenever the fairy encountered a block, Tinker Bell found a way to fly around it.

And right now, that block was Ash.

"I'm sorry, can you repeat that?" A surge of heat shot through Tink; she felt like she might burst into flames. A blue jay watching their interaction from a fallen tree took to the air, but not before whistling a warning to Ash.

Ash, however, was oblivious. "Tinker fairies don't travel to the Mainland," he said, as he tended to the acorns they were roasting. "It's just—it's not done. It wouldn't be right."

"It wouldn't be *right*?" Tink flew over the campfire now, putting the full weight of her stare on him. It was amazing how quickly their excursion had turned. One minute it was all, "How lovely was that deer and her fawn grazing near Mermaid Cove?" And now Ash's opinion on her pipe dream had soured everything. "What exactly does that mean, Ash?" A pair of squirrels eyeing the acorns sensed Tinker Bell's ire and scurried away.

The garden fairy finally looked up. Noticing Tink's pinched expression, he dropped the poker, tiny embers rising into the cave. "Don't get your wings in a twist. I didn't mean it like *that*."

"Didn't mean it like what?" Tink countered, flying closer now. "Didn't mean to insult every tinker fairy on Never Land?" She raised her voice, her wings fluttering fast.

Ash sighed and placed his hands in his tunic pockets. "Here we go."

"Excuse me?"

"Aw, come on, Tink. Everything doesn't have to be a fight. You look like you're ready to throw an acorn at me. While it's on fire."

Well, that part was true. Warily, he met her gaze. And then she couldn't help it. She let out a little chuckle, her anger deflating as quickly as it'd started. "Throw a flaming acorn at you," she repeated. "Can you imagine?"

Ash shook his head then turned back to his work with the acorns. "Do you want lightly toasted or blackened?"

"Blackened, if you please."

Ash was both Tink's fiercest ally and greatest adversary. Her fairy confidant, conscience, and the only one she trusted to pick debris out of her wings. He also drove her mad with his hovering. Sometimes he flew so close, Tink couldn't tell if the sound of flapping was her wings or his.

But it was his talk about returning to Pixie Hollow that irritated her the most. She knew he missed home, but as she told him repeatedly, he was welcome to go back anytime. Ash wasn't the one who'd felt this longing to explore Never Land beyond the fairy village. It was Tinker Bell who knew deep in her gut that there were other flights to take, other inventions to be made, other—non-Hollow— methods to be investigated. Perhaps non–*Never Land* methods.

"Anyway, I just meant tinker fairies don't have permission to go to the Mainland. Forget Pixie Hollow. The Never Fowl wouldn't allow it." Ash pushed a tuft of brown hair off his sweaty brow. "Only nature fairies get to go and even I haven't been on account of my—"

"Debilitating allergies," Tink finished drolly. Ash claimed to have an intolerance to any object that washed up from the Mainland, sputtering and wheezing whenever Tinker Bell hauled one in and started to take it apart. "Though you didn't seem bothered by that tomato-shaped pouf. Especially after it became your new bed. I bet you could make a quick Mainland trip."

Ash's olive brow pinched, his nose scrunching like it did whenever he tasted a sour berry. "The pouf was barely recognizable after your tinkering. The chamomile made it smell divine."

Tink tried not to flush under the praise. That would completely undermine her point. But, as usual, Ash was far from finished.

"Anyway you wouldn't be able to redress *all* the Mainlander things while we were there. I've heard they rid themselves of all natural greenery and flora." Ash sniffed. "Besides, what if something went wrong? What if I had a coughing attack? What if I couldn't breathe well enough to fly home?"

Tinker Bell rolled her eyes at the familiar argument. She knew it would do no good to counter that the hay fever and congestion was all in his head. Another useless block. No, Ash insisted he had been born that way.

Of course, like all fairies, he had been born of a human child's laughter. Or so the lore went. Tink wondered who that child was. And who the child was whose laugh created her own fiery nature, her temperament, which jumped all over the place most days. Only this morning she'd been on a high after finding a new lost Mainlander thing washed up on the shore from the Never Sea (which resulted in a violent set of sneezes from Ash). And now her mood dipped low.

"Don't you want to know what this is?" Tink pointed to the gold circular object lying nearby. It sported a blue face and delicately painted numbers. That wasn't even the most exciting part about it. No, the most exciting part was the lost thing *ticked* like magic, two arrows on the face moving slowly with each second that passed.

Except Mainlanders didn't have magic, so how did this contraption work? And what was it meant to do?

Tink couldn't wait to study the mechanisms inside. It seemed especially intricate, and she feared it breaking so she'd have to do it in the morning, when there was more light. Tink jiggled the chain the lost thing was attached to, which lent heft to the item.

"No," Ash said, motioning to the rocky ledge in the cave they'd claimed as their own. They were slowly fixing it up, making it a suitable place to stay till Tinker Bell "got this wild idea out of her system and returned to the hollow." At least, that was how Ash saw it. Secretly, Tinker Bell wasn't sure if she'd ever live full-time in Pixie Hollow again.

"We don't know what any of those lost things are," Ash said now. "And we don't need to." There were several unidentifiable objects Tink had collected, from a glass bottle with strange labels, to a large pair of spectacles, to a long black scope that extended when Tink pulled on one end and brought the view into much closer focus. "All they do is collect dust."

"But what if we knew what they could do?" Tink dangled the thing in the air, her determination growing. A plan forming.

And Ash knew it.

"Hey, turn off your tinker brain, will you?" He sounded panicked now. "I've heard the nature fairies talk. The Mainland is unpleasant. It's dangerous. Besides, what are the odds we'd even find more of your ticking lost things there? What if we got discovered? We can't risk the trip."

We. Tink smiled sweetly now, changing tack as she touched down on the ground, placing the round lost thing carefully on the shelf. "You're right. We can't."

Ash eyed her warily. "You won't do anything foolish, right, Tinker Bell?"

"Me, foolish?" Tink said innocently. "Never."

Ash will forgive me, Tink thought as she darted into the night sky high above the Never Sea several hours later. *Besides, I'll probably be back before he even wakes up. That pouf* is *ridiculously comfortable.*

The water looked like a sheet of glass from this height, the moon reflecting off the still sea below. Tinker Bell relished the quiet. It calmed her, even if competing thoughts jockeyed for space in her brain. She had never flown this high before. She wondered what she could encounter up here. Tink shivered, thinking of the dreadful Never Fowl.

Shifting course, Tinker Bell zoomed through the sky, searching for the legendary star, the one the garden fairies had spoken of. She flew higher, rising to where the wind was strongest, her pixie dust lighting up the night sky like a trail. *I'm not being foolish*, she told herself as she fought the wind. *This is what tinkerers are meant to do. Find answers.*

The thought needled at her. She'd long wanted to understand the connection between their two worlds. There was the other side of that origin lore—not only were fairies born of a child's laughter, but every time a child claimed they didn't believe, a fairy would fall dead. Most didn't like to talk about such things, but Tink held a secret morbid curiosity about this other, magicless place, where one's temperaments were so powerful. How else were the Mainland and Never Land linked? And why?

Tinker Bell needed to understand it.

Ash said she was a bit obsessed with Mainlanders and maybe that was true. Could she help wanting to know what else was out there beyond the Never Sea?

The questions went on and on, piling up in her mind, growing with each lost thing she collected, keeping her up at night while Ash snored. Sometimes she really didn't understand why she seemed to be the only one who cared.

A flash of light brought Tink back to the task at hand. There it was. The star. It had to be. She glanced back, seeing Never Land so small and distant below. Then she looked back at the star with a new longing burning inside her.

Her heart started to pound. Was she really about to do this?

Go.

The single thought was all it took for the fairy to zoom forward, her wings fluttering fast through the airy clouds to reach the star. The anticipation to get to the Mainland was killing her now. Look at her making her own rules, with no one to stop her. Was her hearing heightened as well? It felt as if she could hear whispers on the wind calling to her. Urging her forward. She wished Ash could see this.

The wind began to pick up, shifting and pushing her forward without even a flap of her wings. She felt her whole body being pulled forward into the light. And then, when it was almost too bright to stand, the whole world seemed to stop for a moment, and it felt as if she were suspended in midair.

Her heartbeat quickened as she reached out to touch the mirror-like wall in front of her and it actually waffled like a wave. Then *boom*! She felt her whole body get sucked through to the other side. Tink blinked, trying to get her bearings. Did she make it?

The sky was brighter here, as if it were already daytime, which would be impossible if she were still on Never Land. Something had definitely changed. She dared to look down and grinned when she realized her view had been altered as well. Her small feet were hovering high over a large piece of land where structures suffocated the landscape and greenery was sparse.

The Mainland. I did it! Tink jingled, flipping through the air, pixie dust glittering around her. *See, Ash? Traveling between worlds isn't that hard! And there is some green space here!*

Tinker Bell couldn't wait a second longer to see it. The closer she got, the more the structures seemed to grow in size. The buildings were larger than anything she'd seen in Tiger Lily's village, and they were made with very different materials.

And then she spotted them: Mainlanders! Their sizes, shapes, and skin tones varied—and their clothes were markedly different—but they also reminded her of Tiger Lily. Tink landed on a building roof to watch them. Curious how everyone seemed to be rushing somewhere, their eyes fixed straight ahead. *Where are the children?* she wondered. Everyone here appeared to be older. None of them seemed to look up at the warm sun peeking through the clouds above them, which was good in a way. No one noticed her. Itching to see more, Tink flew on.

A flash up ahead made her shield her eyes. She stopped short and gasped. *Is that a gold man?* Tink flew over to the large, ornate figure. It appeared to be a golden monument of sorts. There was an obelisk above a tiny structure that encased the golden man. Below him, there was a platform on which Mainlanders stood, admiring, some laying flowers at the base.

Tink was so busy people watching, she almost missed it.

"Catch me if you can!" a small voice cried.

Children! Several of them, Tink noticed with delight. She watched them race over the platform and down a path of green. One child caught another, grabbing their arm as the pair burst into laughter. The sound made Tink's whole being come alive.

So this is what a child's laughter sounds like, Tink jingled dreamily. *How beautiful!* Her mind seemed to calm. Her disposition brightened. No wonder this was how fairies were made. Was there a better noise in all the world? Tink drifted along, following their laughter, wanting to soak it in. Then she spotted a grown Mainlander among them.

"Come along now, children!" the woman said, sounding annoyed. She walked briskly, eyes straight ahead like all the other Mainlanders. (Busy! Busy! Busy!) "We can't stay long at the park."

"Only an hour?" The smallest child stomped his feet. He was holding a tiny boat in his hands. "I want to stay in Kensington Gardens all day!"

"Well, we can't, Oliver." The woman reached into the folds of her dress to produce something small and round hanging from a gold chain. The Mainlander opened the top of the circular item and Tink gasped.

The ticking round lost thing! Just like the one she'd shown Ash last night.

"We only have an hour," said the woman. "See how the hands on the clock are moving? At two we need to meet your father at the shoemaker. What time is it now?"

"The clock is pointing to the one," Oliver told her, scrunching his face up tight as he studied the numbers.

A clock, Tink thought reverently. The lost thing had a name! And apparently it tracked Mainlander time?

"Yes, now let's hurry along if you want to race your boat in the pond." The woman rushed ahead again.

The children followed, as did Tink, watching the clock till the woman placed it back in her dress. Tink tried not to let her disappointment get to her. What she wouldn't give to look at that clock more closely! Was it the same as the one she had? Did it work the same way? How did one tell time? Did every Mainlander own a clock such as this? Why were they all so concerned with the time anyway? Didn't they just rise with the sun and rest when it went down?

Her brain was practically buzzing again. She could hear Ash's voice in her head. *Take a breath, Tink.* It took her a moment to realize the woman and children had disappeared around a bend in the trees.

Wait! Tink jingled in alarm. She zoomed around a tree and up and over a pond spying Mainlander after Mainlander, some sitting in the grass, one atop a horse, another flying a piece of paper attached to a string. But she couldn't find the children again. *How could I have gotten so distracted?* Tink chided herself, growing moody again.

Suddenly, there came a strange wailing sound. It reminded her of the mermaids filing their nails against the rocks. Tink's whole body twitched.

The cry was different from ones she'd heard animals make. And it was very different from the sob Ash gave that time he'd accidentally sat on a porcupine. This was high-pitched and hoarse, and it sounded like it was coming from a small (for Mainlander standards) bed on wheels. *(Why would one need a rolling bed?)* Tink flew closer and peered inside the contraption. Something was thrashing violently, knocking the white bunting it was wrapped in clear off its body. Tink jingled in surprise.

A baby!

The child wailed louder now, its eyes closed tight, the sound so piercing Tink thought her eardrums might burst.

How ghastly was her first thought, but her next was kinder. Why was this helpless child all alone in Kensington Gardens? (She was very proud of herself for remembering the name!) There wasn't a grown Mainlander anywhere. The child wailed on, flailing and kicking, and finally, Tink found she couldn't take it anymore. She dropped down onto the edge of the small wagon and whistled.

Now see here! she jingled, her right eye twitching. *Stop this caterwauling at once!*

The baby stopped crying and looked at her.

Very good, Tink jingled, satisfied, as the baby stared at her with interest. *I don't see what you have to cry about when you're riding around comfortably in this lovely green area.*

The baby hiccupped, its small chest moving up and down fast as it tried to calm itself. Up close, Tink could see a single red curl sticking out of the baby's white bonnet that was tied around its little neck. The child's dark eyes still brimmed with tears, but now that it was no longer yelling, she found the baby was rather sweet-looking. The baby wriggled its small fingers, reaching out to grab her. Tink jumped back.

Oh no, she thought, taking to the air again. *I'm not a toy!*

The baby's wails restarted and Tink felt a strong headache coming on. Did babies cry like this all the time? No wonder an older Mainlander had walked away. Tink pursed her lips as the little one reached its arms out to her.

Tink sighed. She was no Mainlander; she couldn't just leave the defenseless baby here all alone. *All right*, she jingled, flying down to the rim of the wagon and landing on it. *Stop that now and I'll stay for a moment.*

At the sound of her jingle, the baby quieted again, almost as if it understood. But that was impossible, wasn't it? Mainlanders couldn't understand fairies, yet the way the baby was looking at her, its eyes so keen with observation, she felt as if it were memorizing her face. *Hmmm* . . . Tinker Bell was as fascinated by the baby as it seemed to be with her.

And then, instead of more tears, the baby started to coo . . . almost as if it were trying to communicate with her.

That is a much nicer sound, Tink jingled, and the baby's face lit up, the child showing its gummy mouth. Drool pooled down the side and landed on its chest, and Tink let out a peal of laughter before she could stop herself. The baby, delighted, mimicked her, giggling too.

Tink inhaled sharply at the gurgling high-pitched sound of the baby's laugh, soaking it in. This was even better than the bigger children's mirth. It felt warm, pure.

Aren't you something? Tink jingled, her voice softened. Who knew babies could be so delightful? At least this one was, when it wasn't blubbering. *What are you doing out here all alone?*

The baby murmured as if trying to tell her something. It reached out its hand again. This time, Tink didn't fly away. Instead, she used her hand to touch the baby's pinkie finger. *Hello there.*

The baby cooed some more as if to say, *Hello to you, too.*

The pair smiled at one another.

"Peter? Peter, where are you? Someone help! I've misplaced my pram!"

Tink heard the woman's voice and started, as did the child, his dark eyes widening. So the baby was *Peter*. What a nice name. His small mouth started to wind up again, the cry different this time, as if to say, *I'm here.*

Tink felt her wings deflate slightly. She had rather been enjoying their moment together, but it was already over.

Tink lifted into the sky again as a woman rushed into view to grab the *pram* (she liked that word far better than *bed on wheels*).

"Oh, Peter, I'm so sorry!" said the woman, while the boy continued to stare at the sky as Tink fluttered overhead.

Tink gave a small wave. *Goodbye, Peter*, she jingled.

And then she was off.

Tinker Bell tried not to let herself grow too melancholy as she headed for home. She'd only planned on coming to the Mainland for a short while, of course. And she had done what she set out to do. Learned her lost thing was a clock. It would be foolhardy to stay and push her luck further, even for her.

She wondered . . . What would Ash think of it all? He couldn't possibly be mad at her when he heard what she'd learned. (And she was perfectly safe! The park was lovely!)

She frowned. Then again, maybe this particular adventure was something she should keep to herself. At least until she had a better understanding of what it all meant. Plus, there was always the chance she'd want to return . . .

Shooting through the sky, Tink embarked on the mythical journey in reverse, her mind whirling. When she finally arrived on Never Land, dawn was breaking over the island. She hovered high above for a moment and sighed as she stared down at the island she called home, her eyes focusing on Prism Falls, the magical water source that fueled the island. As she got closer, she swore she could hear the faint echo of the song of the falls—a hypnotic ballad produced by the rainbow water hitting the tide pools. Never Land's original lullaby.

Her wings felt lighter somehow after such a long journey, and Tink hummed to herself, adding a melody to the adventure replaying in her mind.

Her thoughts buzzed around so rapidly she didn't even notice the slate-colored clouds swarming below.

Nor the large ship with the black skull-and-crossbones flag thrashing in the breeze.

PART ONE
WANDERER

ONE
Many moons later . . .

"We went to Mermaid Cove last week," Ash said. "Do you really want to sit and listen to the mermaids drone on about hair treatments again already?"

"Hey! Don't knock self-care!"

Tink watched as a conch shell flew across the cave and came dangerously close to hitting Ash.

The garden fairy flew out of the way, landing on a plant hanging high above. "You almost killed me, Blair!"

"Please." Blair examined a strand of her pink hair. The mermaid was lounging in the shallow end of the cave's pool, her glistening tail in the water, her top half perched on the sand. "If I wanted to do that, I would have aimed."

"She's got you there!" Mimic's laughter echoed in the cave. The amiable shape-shifter flickered as if he might shed his human shape at any moment. Around the group, he often appeared at least *part* person (minotaur and mermaid among his favorite forms), much to the confusion of others in his herd.

"Watch and learn," Blair said, tossing a sea star in Mimic's direction. Immediately, Mimic transformed into a red hare, leaping across the cave and catching the star with his mouth before taking it back to his cozy corner, turning human. He draped his large legs over one of the nets Tink had converted into hammocks.

"These two," Ash muttered, looking at Tink for backup.

Tink tried to hide her smile. Yes, Blair could get cranky, especially when her hair kept knotting from the salt water as it had today. But Tink loved listening to her friends bicker. She also embraced the sound of their laughter, their tears, hearing them share their deepest fears or have heated debates about things like sea versus land travel. ("Mermaids have to circle the island, whereas I can turn into a falcon and go as fast as the wind blows," Mimic had argued just the night before.)

As different as they were, over the last several years they had become the fiercest of friends. Finding them had cured the itch Tink had been feeling that something in her life was missing.

For the most part, a small voice in her head said, but Tink pushed it away. Warring thoughts were always competing for her attention. She didn't have to listen to *all* of them.

Tinker Bell loved being a Wanderer. That's what the friends had taken to calling themselves. The group comprised the four of them, as well as Tiger

Lily from Never Land's Indigenous people, and a pirate called Caiman. Their mission? To explore without restrictions. No being forced to stay within their designated parts of the island or strictly interact with their own people. Free to do what they wanted, when they wanted. To roam the Never Woods one day and stay up talking about their findings all night.

They'd christened the hideout a few moons ago: Wanderers Cay, or "key" as Ash liked to say. The sandy inlet near the coral reef was nestled in a small cove on the south end of the island. Its cave opened to the beach, giving them a perfect view of the sparkling Never Sea. The low rocky ridge that surrounded the cay provided a good amount of shade midday and protected them from the island's southerly winds that had picked up in recent years. The reef was rife with fish to eat and had two sunning rocks that Blair favored, and there was a lush soil patch just a few paces away. Tiger Lily liked that it was a short ride away from her village and Mimic and Blair often spent the night.

To Tink, it was utopia.

For Ash—not so much, but he was still here instead of back at the hollow, and he hadn't tattled on them to the Never Fowl. So he couldn't hate it that much.

"We could stay here and help Caiman with the garden," Tiger Lily suggested. The young woman's dark tresses were loose except for one long braid on the right side of her face, which rested comfortably on her collarbone. She was brushing her horse Pony's white mane near the cave entrance. "My tribe lost half our potatoes during the flooding."

"You did? Why didn't you tell me?" Tink asked, alarmed.

"I'm telling you now." Tiger Lily's smile was kind. "We were prepared. We harvested enough early that we should be all right. But it can't hurt for us to store some away for those who might need it. Just in case."

"I wish I could say the same about the salmon," said Blair, her pink lips puckering. "I'm seeing less and less of it in the waters of the Never Sea."

Tink's stomach churned. There had been a lot of strange disturbances on the island as of late. From storms that seemed to blow in more frequently to the island's rapidly rising and falling temperature. Conch shells, which had always served as the best trumpets, disintegrated when touched. Trees rotting, their insides hollow as if they'd been scooped out. Just this week, two enormous cyclones had blown in, and lightning had scorched a patch of wheat growing in the Indigenous Never Land peoples' field. The disasters seemed to only be getting worse. . . .

The fairy stole a glance at the Wanderers map they'd fashioned near the entrance. Mimic, with his talent for drawing, had added tiny renderings of different parts of the island—from Prism Falls to the Never Woods. They'd add a mark wherever they observed distress to the land or sea that couldn't be explained. Tink swallowed, taking in all the new Xs.

"Did I hear someone say they want to help me in the garden?" Caiman called into the cave. Tink's mood improved quickly. Was that a bounce in his step?

He looks happy here . . . finally, Tink thought. When she'd first met the pirate, he was clearly adrift. Never Land was not a place he set out to find, and pirate life didn't suit him either. It took some time, but slowly they had earned Caiman's trust, and he'd begun opening up to them. She hoped today's surprise would please him.

"I brought fruit seeds," Caiman added. "They're actually really fascinating. There appear to be a bunch of species variants, depending on how they're planted."

Blair suddenly grew very busy with her nails. Mimic studied a rock. Still Caiman waited, his green eyes hopeful.

Tinker Bell watched on; she couldn't help but be fascinated by the Mainlander. Sure, the pirates had brought nothing but trouble ever since the *Jolly Roger* blew into the Never Sea. But, of course, Caiman wasn't like the others.

"I'll join you," Tinker Bell offered. "I'm dying to see how the witches' hair is growing. That should fix the pulley on that food basket that keeps coming undone."

"I'll go, too," Ash jumped in.

Tink glanced around, willing one of the others to volunteer as well. She *may* have already snapped at Ash for flying too close to her several times that morning. Honestly, Tink wasn't sure she could take more time together without a few friendly buffers.

Alas, it seemed Mimic and Blair were now giggling in the shallows, and Tiger Lily was busy with Pony, giving the horse fresh water she'd brought in a canteen. "I'll be there soon," her friend called.

"Great," Tinker Bell replied, trying not to sound miffed. She led Ash and the young man out to their makeshift farm.

"I have to admit, you've done a marvelous job with the new crop. Look at these squash blossoms," Ash said, zooming over the lush blooms and crawling vines. "You'd make a great garden fairy if you weren't a pirate."

"Erm, thanks," Caiman said, wringing his hands.

Tink rolled her eyes. While she was grateful Ash had finally seemed to warm to the human (his "Mainlander allergies" mysteriously improved shortly after Caiman had demonstrated his penchant for botany), sometimes he had all the tact of a hedgehog.

"Caiman, what needs watering?" Tinker Bell asked.

"Oh, the hemlock would be great. And the herbs," Caiman replied. Tink saluted playfully then grabbed the watering device she'd fashioned out of an old oak trunk.

"What are you using for the fruit trees?" Ash asked.

"Well, Mimic grabbed me some clay from Shifters Beach, and I've found it's worked wonderfully for . . ." Caiman prattled on happily.

Tink snuck a glance at the human's face as the two talked soil enrichments. He had filled out nicely, his round face was smudged with dirt, his nails black, his clothes worn and starched from the constant sunshine and earth. What a contrast from the sickly husk he'd been when he'd first arrived.

Tink shuddered, thinking of all that still haunted her from that time. From the storm that had swept in all their woes.

Little did anyone on Never Land know it was all her fault.

TWO

"YOU STARTED WITHOUT US?" CAME BLAIR'S VOICE. THE MERMAID TREADED along the waterway lining the garden. Mimic followed, his own purple mermaid tail splashing water up at them.

"Hey, I'm the one watering here!" Tink said crossly.

"Uh-oh, duck and cover, everyone," Blair said. "Tink's getting fiery."

Tink narrowed her eyes.

"Perhaps it's time to give Caiman his gift?" Tiger Lily asked, walking toward them.

Caiman's eyebrows raised. "A gift? What, you mean besides the mud? And Ash's watermelon seeds? If they take like the potatoes and sugar beets did, think of the bounty we'll have."

Ash preened, picking a bit of dust off his tunic. "I told him you like watermelon."

"Oh, the mud was a *gift*?" Mimic teased. "I thought you'd wanted it to give those pirate piggies a night's bath."

Caiman swallowed hard, seeming to shiver at the very thought. Every evening, he'd return to the ship to bring food and supplies to the pirates. And when they went to sleep, he'd stay up to tend to his seedlings and plants—the ones Captain Bartholomew held hostage. Tink was determined to find a way to get both Caiman and his precious atrium on the island for good.

"Tinker Bell, will you do the honors?" Tiger Lily smoothly cut in, handing the leaf-wrapped package to the fairy, who flew it over to the young pirate. Caiman uncovered a small book, made of grapeseed parchment and bound with thick, curled roots.

"I modeled it after some of the books you snuck over for us," Tink explained. "A thank-you for all your work on the produce. We've recorded everything we know about Never Land's plant life. And Tiger Lily had the Elders from her village contribute a lot of their knowledge, too."

"A guide to Never Land flora?" Caiman clutched the book to his chest as if it were made of gold. "This is the most thoughtful gift. Thank you." His lower lip quivered. "My mum would have loved it."

"Personally, I thought Blair's anemone top would've been more fun, but I was overruled," Mimic joked as Blair splashed more water at him.

"Look at all these entries," Caiman breathed, flipping through the book and pointing out pictures of plant life. "Arrowhead leaf, grows near the Never Woods. Oh, and look at this! Sea salve, which is only found near Mermaid Cove." He turned the book around so Blair could see the drawing.

Blair yawned. "I've never heard of them, but if the book says they're there, they're there."

Caiman sat down on the nearest rock, mesmerized. "I didn't realize the island had fig leaves. Their stems have sap that can fix any rash. I should find some for the ship. We're running mighty low on tonics." He grinned over at her. "You're a gem, Tink."

She placed a hand on her right hip and posed. "I know."

They all laughed.

"I almost forgot." Caiman reached into his pocket and produced a long black rod with a feather. "I brought you something, too. From the *Jolly Roger*. It's called a quill. You use ink to write with it."

"A quill!" Beside her, Ash sniffled darkly. Tink shot him a look before holding it up, committing the name of the new Mainlander lost thing to memory. "I can keep it?"

"Aye. Captain won't know it's missing. We have loads." Caiman had already gone back to perusing the guide, brow furrowed.

"Do you have a moment?" Tiger Lily asked softly, moving closer to the fairy.

Tink carefully set the feather down on a nearby tree branch. "Of course."

"I was thinking about taking Pony to the north side of the island. Some of our villagers saw something there that concerned them."

"Listen to this!" Caiman's voice drifted over them. "Beach burs survive well on sandy dunes. Maybe we should plant some of those around the cay. Might make the whole area homey."

Tink lowered her voice, not wanting to worry the others. "More disturbances?"

Tiger Lily shook her head. "No, that's the odd thing. They stumbled upon some overturned ground, torn roots, trampled bushes. At first, they thought maybe it had been made by a wounded animal, but they saw the same hack job over and over again, all over a particular grove. Almost like it had been done purposefully."

"Huh," Tinker Bell said. This was much different than the disasters that had started to befall the island. This felt like an intruder. . . . "Well, I'll go with you. To check it out."

Tiger Lily smiled. "I was hoping you'd say that."

"Oh, and the red gillyhooks! Their leaves are good for bug bites and for removing the stench of a skunk if attacked and . . . their leaves also taste good in hot water," Caiman continued, his voice getting louder and more jovial with each passage.

"Caiman." Blair pinched the bridge of her nose. "You don't have to read us the entire book. We know what grows on Never Land."

"I know, but there are so many interesting plants I've never heard of," Caiman said. He paused, his chapped lips moving as he whispered to himself. "Hey, what are these? By—by that enchanted waterfall? What was it called again?" He pointed to a page in the book that showed a drawing of the falls and some dense foliage behind them.

"Prism Falls," Tiger Lily told him. "Its waters are the magical source of the island."

"And that's the Forbidden Side behind it," Mimic said, peering over Caiman's shoulder. "Nobody goes there. Not even the bears. Looks like there must be some sort of forest or something. Probably not plants you'd want to mess with, mate."

Caiman shivered. "No, no, I can see that."

"Yeah, if you're scared of visiting Pixie Hollow with me," Ash started. "You definitely wouldn't like—"

SQUAWK! SQUAWK! SQUAWK!

An obnoxious sound drowned out Ash's next words. Everyone tensed as massive shadows darkened the sky. Then wolf-size birds swooped low, brushing up dirt and rumpling Caiman's neat rows of vegetables with the flaps of their wings. Tinker Bell shot a look at Tiger Lily, remembering what her people had found on the far side of the island.

The birds' screeched at the top of their lungs, demanding Tinker Bell's full attention. She felt her insides tighten.

The Never Fowl had found the Wanderers' hideout.

THREE

The Never Fowl should have been called Never Not There. Or the Always Atrocious because that's what they were—humongous blue birds with long beaks they stuck in everyone's business. They sat in the highest trees on Never Land and watched the island's inhabitants like hawks. When anyone attempted to do anything uncharacteristic—like confide in their best friend about leaving Pixie Hollow, for example—the Never Fowl swooped in squawking, needling, making it clear that sort of talk was not to be tolerated. They seemed to think themselves the island's guardians and wouldn't let anyone infringe on that very important role. Mimic had heard that they'd once driven out a family of rabbits because they'd eaten more than their fair share of the spring bounty.

Noooo, Tink thought, her stomach dropping. She grabbed the quill as though it were a shield. Tiger Lily turned to face the birds straight on.

SQUAWK! SQUAWK! SQUAWK!

A herd of blue circled the area like bats, knocking the plant book out of Caiman's hands before heading inside the cave.

"Um, excuse you," Blair said, swimming for the waterway entrance. "I don't recall sending you an invitation."

The Wanderers followed the intruders into the common area. Dried flowers and knit bags of fruits and vegetables they'd collected hung from the stalactites above, sunlight creeping through holes in the rocks. Jars of shells and other lost things they'd found together lined the rocky ledges where the hammocks blew in the breeze.

Tinker Bell had designed the cave with changing tides in mind. The Wanderers always deferred to her when it came to logistics. Who else could find an acorn cap and turn it into a flowerpot for Caiman's seedlings? Or mend one of their cooking kettles when it cracked? Tink was the one who figured out how to purify their drinking water, which had become more and more polluted as the moons went on. From what, exactly, was anyone's best guess.

But now the Fowl were jabbing at the lost things sitting on the ledges and swooping low over Blair's head. Ash tried to block the Fowl from moving any farther, but they barreled through, screeching and snipping until the fairy fell back in horror. Mimic quickly transformed into a bird himself—shape-shifting as close to a Never Fowl as he could (which was a pelican)—and tried to lead the birds out of the cave. But none would listen. One of the birds clipped a shelf with a blue bottle on it (a lost thing from the *Jolly Roger*), and it smashed to the ground.

Tink felt a flash of anger. "Stop!" she shouted. She knew the birds could understand her, even if they rarely felt the need to speak with anyone directly. "Who said you could come in here and touch our things?" Two birds flew in front of her, blocking her path to picking up the fauna book that had once again flown out of Caiman's hands.

Caiman reached down to grab it, and a bird pecked his arm. Caiman slipped and fell, clutching his arm in a panic. "Oww! My book!" Caiman squeaked, crawling backward on his hands to get out of the bird's path.

"Give that back!" Tink said, diving at the Never Fowl now, trying to get them to abandon the book. Instead, the birds squawked louder, one towering over her small frame, another landing on the book and digging its gnarled feet into the thick pages. Up close, Tink could see the Never Fowl could swallow her whole. One nipped the quill right out of her hands. Undeterred, Tink rushed at the bird. Ash flew in and dropped down in front of her.

"Are you mad?" he asked, grabbing her around the waist, trying to yank her away.

"No, Ash, let me go! They're going to ruin everything. I'd rather be eaten than stand by—" She kicked her legs out, jingling in fury as the bird came at her, book hanging from its talons.

"Breathe, Tink, breathe," Ash urged, quickly moving her out of the way of the tome headed straight for her head.

Thankfully, at that very moment, Mimic managed to swoop down and grab the flora book with his beak. He dropped it into Blair's waiting arms. In the mayhem, she swam over to one of the ledges and hid the book behind a pile of netting Tink had been using to make a few new hammocks. The birds darted around in a huff.

SQUAWK!

Tink and Ash jumped, wondering if Blair had been caught. Instead, she realized one of the Never Fowl seemed to be calling to the others from the back of the cave. The rest flew to the bird's side and landed in front of the Wanderers' map of Never Land, the Xs crawling over it like bugs.

"Is this about me saying there was a lack of krill in the Never Sea?" Blair called to the birds, sounding agitated. "Because it's true! Whether you like it or not."

The birds ignored her as they squawked at the map, chattering at one another in their ancient language. Tink watched from Ash's arms (for some reason, he hadn't let go) as one bird pecked at Prism Falls. The others started pecking the spot now, too, even though it was the one area that didn't have an X on it yet. Their chatter scared Pony, who raised his hind legs, trying to pull free from Tiger Lily.

"What do you want with our map?" Tink yelled to them.

The Never Fowl ignored her, too.

"What are they doing?" Blair hissed, covering her head as a few continued swooping around the cave to prevent anyone else from moving. "If one of them tries to nest in my hair, I swear I will—"

"Never Fowl!" Tiger Lily's voice was authoritative and loud, echoing through the cave. "This is Wanderers Cay and you have no business here."

The birds quieted somewhat, only a few still squawking.

"Unless there is something you want to share with us about the island, I suggest you leave at once," Tiger Lily continued. "We have done nothing wrong."

We haven't. But maybe I *have*, Tink thought guiltily.

The majority of birds took flight, and everyone ducked, including Tink who untangled herself from Ash and tried to rush out of the cave to see where the birds were going. The largest one flew in front of her.

His eyes zeroed in on hers as he started to squawk again, and, to Tink's surprise, she could understand him: *"THERE ARE DARK FORCES AT WORK HERE, FAIRY. BE CAREFUL."*

"Dark forces?" Tink repeated, dazed. But before she could get her bearings, the Never Fowl was gone.

FOUR

"IS EVERYONE ALL RIGHT?" MIMIC TRANSFORMED INTO HUMAN FORM AGAIN. He spit a feather out of his mouth.

"Yes." Blair stared at her reflection in the water, pulling at a few wayward strands. "And if anyone was wondering, my hair is fine, too. Prickly birds! What did they want?"

"I don't know," Tiger Lily said, watching the creatures fly away from the cave entrance. "The Never Fowl don't appear without a reason."

Tink found herself breathing heavily, the twinge of guilt she felt turning into a suffocating wave. Or maybe that was Ash, who was still practically on top of her, trembling with fear. *Dark forces.* "Did any of you hear what the bird said to me?"

"I thought the Never Fowl can't talk," said Caiman, rushing to the other side of the cave to retrieve the flora book from the netting. "Thanks, Blair."

"Of course," the mermaid replied brightly, leaning her elbows on the sand.

"The Never Fowl don't communicate with anyone but each other. Not even with me and I was just a bird." Mimic scratched his jaw, which had a small, jagged scar barely visible running down to his neck (supposedly from the time he tussled with a bear). "Why? Could you understand their squawking, Tink?"

The other Wanderers looked at her, and Tinker Bell felt rising panic.

"I guess I must have been hearing things," she said hastily, trying not to let her nerves get the best of her. She glanced at Ash, who swooped downward, quietly surveying the feathers that had been shed on the cave ground and in the water below. She wondered . . . had the other fairy heard the Never Fowl's message too?

"I don't understand why they grabbed the book," Caiman said. "It's harmless enough. Really, it's a celebration of Never Land, if you think of it."

"And why did they keep squawking at the map?" asked Tiger Lily, who turned and headed over to the back wall. "Did you notice how they kept using their beak to jab at Prism Falls? Did they overhear our conversation in the garden?"

"Maybe they just didn't like it that we've marked disturbances," Blair suggested as Caiman sat down on the rock near the water and went back to reading. "They hate that we're snooping around, right?"

"They do consider themselves the island's protectors," Tiger Lily said, turning back to the group. "And they get especially worked up when anyone tries to instill panic."

"But we're not trying to cause panic," said Tink quickly, flying over to the map and gesturing at the glaring Xs spread across the land. "We're just trying to get everyone to wake up and realize something's *off.* Those birds spy on everything. How can they not see it?" Then again, maybe the Fowl finally did see. And had their own theories about the strange occurrences. *Dark forces.* Tink swallowed hard, playing with a frayed edge of her leaf dress.

"Maybe the Never Fowl have witnessed what's happening," Tiger Lily echoed Tinker Bell's thoughts, her dark eyes pensive. "And that's why they were motioning to Prism Falls. They want us to check on the waters. It *is* the source of all magic on Never Land. If something is out of balance there, the whole island could be in jeopardy."

Blair held up her right arm. "You're giving me goose bumps, Tiger Lily."

"I'm sorry." Tiger Lily pursed her lips. "It can't hurt to check. Pony and I will take a ride up there and see if anything is amiss."

"And we'll go to Pixie Hollow," Ash suggested. "Right, Tink? We can check if any of the fairies have started to notice anything."

"Nope, no thank you, I'm sure the hollow is fine. If it wasn't we would have heard. No need to go there," Tink said hastily. The group stared at her. Clearly her rejection of Ash's idea hadn't been as smooth as she'd hoped. Tink coughed. "I just think Tiger Lily shouldn't go to the falls alone."

Blair groaned. "That's so far. I'd have to swim around the whole island to get to them." Her violet eyes brightened. "Can't I just pull an Ash and go talk to the merfolk? See if they've heard anything about other disturbances? Have them keep an eye out?"

"Tink isn't wrong," Mimic admitted. "She should join Tiger Lily. The rest of us can ask around the island to see if anyone has heard anything strange about the water source. Blair to the cove, Ash to the hollow. Shifters Beach will probably be empty at this hour, but I haven't been to the Never Woods in a spell."

"That's clear on the other side of the island," Ash reminded him.

"So?" Mimic stretched both arms out, making his elbows crack. "I've been itching to be a centaur and that would get me there quick."

"Why not a crocodile?" Caiman suggested, looking up from his book. "They're fast on land and can regenerate teeth if they lose any in a brush-up. I've seen 'em in these waters. Mostly near the Rock."

The Rock was a freestanding cave in the middle of one of Never Land's many coves. Tink had no clue why there was a cave in the middle of the water—one that flooded depending on the tides—but the pirates seemed to like it. Their ship was anchored close by.

"Eh. Never really wanted to be a croc before. Centaur it is. Catch you all later." Mimic did a few lunges before taking off at a run, halfway out of the cave before his whole body transformed from man to half horse. With a toss of his hair, he was off.

"Blimey, I would be a croc in a second," Caiman said wistfully. "Imagine being able to glide from land to water, as easily as you'd like. Immersed in the green. Blending in with the scenery."

"Yeaaaahhh . . . I'm good with mermaid. See you all back here later," Blair declared. With a flick of her tail, she dove below the clear blue waters, her glimmering tail visible as she gained speed and started racing out of the cave.

"Caiman? Did you want to join us?" Tiger Lily asked as she mounted Pony.

"Um . . . do you mind if I stay and read some more? Might be a useful bit we can use in here." Caiman held up the book happily.

Tink and Tiger Lily shared a small smile. Typical Caiman. He much preferred to spend his time with the Wanderers in the security of the cay.

"Of course," Tiger Lily told him. "You can let us know if there is anything in there that could help us."

Ash looked at Tink. "I guess I'll head to the hollow alone. Will you meet me after? Everyone was asking for you last time I was there."

Tink felt her stomach tighten. It wasn't that she didn't love everyone in the fairy village. She had good friends there. But whenever Tink visited the other fairies, she felt an overwhelming sense of guilt for moving away.

She reached down to pick up the quill the birds had stolen and held the broken piece in her fingers. Her mind flashed back to the Mainland and that night she'd visited so long ago. "Probably not," Tink told Ash, "I have a lot to do here. But tell everyone hello for me."

"If you're sure . . ."

"I'm sure," she insisted, her voice tightening. *I know I should want to, but I don't! Does that make me a terrible fairy? Is Never Land out of balance because of me?*

She could feel her chest rising and falling and she tried to calm herself so she said none of those thoughts out loud. Better to let them live in her head where they did most days, waking her up at night, worrying her. She took a deep breath—just as Ash always told her to do—and her heart rate slowed.

She softened. "In fact, you should stay there a while, have a good visit." Ash started to protest. "We'll come get you if there's anything urgent. Otherwise, we can fill you in on anything we learn in a few moons."

Ash flew a little higher, a reluctant smile tugging on his lips. "All right then. See you in a bit." He flew off without another word.

"Well, that solves one problem at least," Tiger Lily teased. She went over to Pony to saddle the horse up. "Enjoy the silence, Caiman."

"Huh?" Caiman looked up from his book. She could see his lips moving. He had a quill in his other hand and the jar of ink he left at the cay.

"Happy reading," Tink told him.

"Oh. Thanks."

Tiger Lily clicked her tongue. Pony's ears twitched and the horse galloped out of the cave, Tink flying alongside him.

FIVE

The friends rode in silence for a while. Tinker Bell took in the land that she loved with a deep sigh. The air was warm, the wind was light, the scent of fresh morning dew mingling with the honeysuckle that grew near the coast carrying on the breeze. She kept up with Pony and Tiger Lily as they raced across the wheat fields, passing the turn-off for Mermaid Cove, and Tiger Lily's village where the grass was still green. They rode by the gnarled tree the Wanderers had nearly used for their hideout (the tunnels of caves beneath it had been neat, but it had lacked a water entrance for Blair).

"Let's go to the falls first," Tink suggested. "Clear our minds and all that. We can hit the north side after."

"Good idea," Tiger Lily said. "I haven't been to Prism Falls since I was small," she added wistfully.

Tiger Lily was the only one among the Wanderers who could *choose* whether or not to grow up, aging in increments. Her people were as old as the island itself, and once someone in her village chose to move forward, they'd go to sleep one age and wake up another. For a while now Tiger Lily had been comfortable at sixteen, roughly the same age as Blair and Mimic. They'd figured out Caiman was only a year older. Tink and Ash seemed to be the only ones who didn't mark birthdays.

"Maybe song of the falls will give us some new clarity," Tiger Lily added.

"I hope so." Tink paused, looking to the water and finding the *Jolly Roger* in her periphery. It was anchored in its usual spot next to the Rock. She sighed heavily. "Those pesky pirates. What an eyesore."

"Ooh, I have a new theory about them, actually," Tiger Lily said.

Tinker Bell landed on the young woman's shoulder, eager to hear more. She loved Tiger Lily's theories. "Go on."

"At its core, Never Land is a creative place, right? One that makes things, grows things. It creates."

Tink nodded, dodging a dragonfly that zoomed by.

"Well, maybe Never Land won't allow most of the pirates on land because the pirates are so *destructive*. And that would be counter to everything the island's about," Tiger Lily explained. "Didn't Caiman say Captain Bartholomew had been known to be pretty ruthless?"

"That's putting it lightly. I believe Caiman said he was known to murder hundreds. And only hired crewmembers that matched his bloodlust."

"Exactly," Tiger Lily said. They'd reached a division in the path, and she guided Pony inland. "So perhaps any beings who have taken life—or intend to take lives—aren't allowed here."

"That would certainly explain why Caiman's allowed on land. I saw him try to rescue an injured spider the other day," Tink said. She patted her friend's shoulder. "I think you might have cracked it."

Tiger Lily smiled while Tink tipped her head up to the sun to soak the moment in. A moment later, she felt cold as a shadow crossed their faces.

Dark clouds, thick and wide, stacked on top of one another like they were trying to form a chain. They whipped across the sky, blocking out the sun and making Tinker Bell shiver and think of the Never Fowl again.

Tink couldn't take it anymore. "Can I say something?" If she didn't share her thoughts with someone, she might go mad. "Something we keep just between us?"

"Of course," Tiger Lily said without hesitating.

Tink took a deep breath. "I think the pirates being here . . . and all the terrible things happening on Never Land . . . I think it might be my fault." Despite her best efforts, tears pricked the corner of her eyes, freezing almost instantly in the wind. *Ugh*.

Tiger Lily pulled on Pony's reins and stopped for a moment. "Oh, Tink. Why would you think that?"

"Because it all started—the pirates' arrival and the bad weather and droughts and disappearing sea life—it all started right after I . . ." She looked around to be sure no one was listening. "Snuck off to the Mainland." Her mind went to the baby—Peter—in his pram. "I was so thankful I got to see it with my own eyes, but what if I was never meant to go?"

"What? No. Of course you had to go," Tiger Lily said wholeheartedly. "Everyone wants to know where they came from."

Tiger Lily was the only one Tink had told about her secret excursion. She'd originally thought she'd gloat about it to Ash, but the minute she'd arrived back on Never Land, a fierce storm had blown in. The one that caused the *Jolly Roger* to appear on the horizon. The island hadn't taken kindly to the Mainlanders' arrival, and it made Tink wonder. Was *she* the one who'd made it happen? Had she brought them back with her somehow? Was she the reason the island had been off-kilter? Because she'd broken the rules? Because she hadn't been content with her life to leave well enough alone?

"Except, I'm from here," Tink said, feeling more confused than ever. "But I'm also tied to the Mainland." She looked out toward the mountains in the distance. "And sometimes I feel guilty." Her cheeks warmed. "Because I'd give anything to go back."

Tiger Lily stroked Pony's mane. "Oh, friend, you still feel unsettled, don't you?"

Tink feared the tears wouldn't stop if she went on. She swallowed hard. "Yes."

A wind gust pushed in from the west, sending Tink off-course and she forced herself to stay steady. Tink tried to avoid rain whenever she could. Wet wings made for poor flying conditions.

"I don't know what's wrong with me." Tink sniffled. "I thought leaving Pixie Hollow was what I needed to find myself. Then when we met the other Wanderers, I was sure that would satisfy the empty pit in my stomach. But it's still there, and I fear it's growing bigger and as it gets bigger so do the problems on Never Land. Like when the Never Fowl arrived, I thought they were there to take me away for what I'd done. I was afraid to tell the others, but Tiger Lily, I could swear I heard them speak to me," she whispered, frightened. "They said 'dark forces' are at work. What if . . . What if those dark forces are me?"

"Oh, Tink . . ." Tiger Lily put out her palm for her to fly onto and sit for a moment to rest. And cry some more. "This is not your fault."

"How do you know that?" Tink blubbered, hating how pathetic she sounded.

"Because what you did, visiting the Mainland, may not have been a tinker fairy's job, but it was important for you to figure out who *you* are. Never Land would never be upset about that." Tiger Lily looked around at the clouds blowing in faster now. "What's happening here is bigger than any of us. I actually agree with the Never Fowl. I think dark forces *are* at work."

Dark forces on Never Land. Tink rubbed her arms to keep warm as the sun disappeared behind the clouds. No one would have ever used to describe the weather there as ominous. For the longest time, every day was the same. Perfectly beautiful. The sun shone bright. If it rained at all, it was predawn, drenching flowers and keeping the landscape vibrant, but never affecting anyone's plans. The sky was always a vibrant blue, dotted with light clouds that drifted by and thickened in the late afternoon on the rare occasion a storm blew in. Sunrises were glorious, the sky a mixture of purples and pinks that helped greet the day. Sunsets were equally a delight, with colors that glowed orange and made the sky look like it was on fire.

But there was a reason the Wanderers marked Xs on their map in Wanderers Cay. The shift from Never Land's utopian nature had been gradual, but all the more dramatic.

"If I had to guess, I would say the pirates' arrival disturbed the balance of the island," Tiger Lily said. "I don't know if a ship of foul men could cause all these things to happen to the land, but I do know my people say the ship is not a welcome sight."

"Ash doesn't trust the pirates either," Tink confessed, dabbing at her eyes. "I don't even think he likes Caiman sometimes. And he's as docile as a lamb."

"Ash may have other concerns when it comes to Caiman." Tiger Lily gave her a knowing look. "That fairy is very fond of you, Tink."

"Ash?" Tink flew into the air now, her tears gone, a new emotion emerging. "As friends, you mean."

"No, I think he wants to be more than friends," Tiger Lily told her pointedly, and Pony brayed as if in agreement.

Tink turned away, her cheeks burning again. This couldn't be true, could it? "I think maybe we should go back to discussing murderous pirates." She softened once more. "Or the falls. If you don't mind." Tink took to the air again.

"Of course," Tiger Lily agreed, and clucked her tongue to get Pony to start moving again. "The falls are definitely more important than Ash's feelings for you." They both chuckled till a fierce breeze blew through, threatening to hold them back.

Tink's wings beat against a rising gale. "I really wish this wind would let up."

"Yes, though it's also sort of fitting," Tiger Lily said as Pony picked up speed. "Wind's how we got Prism Falls in the first place."

"What do you mean?"

"Legend has it, a powerful gust once blew over the island and whispered stories of the Mainland, knowing how much the island loved tales. Prism Falls became the well where all the stories collected. And all the magic."

"The island's magic came from stories." Tink liked the idea. She reached down and her fingers skimmed sunflowers blowing in the field.

"And more than that," Tiger Lily told her. "My grandmother says the magic in those tide pools doesn't just fuel Never Land. They can also grant a heart's desire."

Tink felt her interest pique. "How so?"

"She says those waters can empower and transform any being with a single drop. Apparently, this is how the mermaids came to be. The wind longed to be a mermaid and the waters made it so."

Waters that could make one anything their heart desired? How could tide pools be capable of such a feat? "Now you've made me want to get to the falls faster than ever."

Tiger Lily gave her a wry smile. "Race you?"

Tink felt fire rip through her. "You're on!" She took off like a shot, Pony and Tiger Lily keeping up with her as they sped across the earth for what felt like the longest time. And then, finally, the landscape changed again, the mountains so close, she was flying through the cracks between the pair that led to where they needed to go. *Here we go*, she thought as she entered the shadows of the mountains to reach it.

This time with the sky as her friend, and Tiger Lily navigating a narrow path, Tink reached the entrance first. A deluge of water gushed down the mountainside and she faltered for a moment, taking in the falls' beauty. She never got over the fact that they were so large; the water cascaded from the top of the mountain peak all the way to the valley below, where large pools of water churned, their white foam bubbling up along with a mist in the air that could easily be fog. But there was no mistaking the unique appearance of the water. The spray was rainbow-hued, water every color of the spectrum swirling together in a vibrant display that could only mean one thing: *magic*.

Tinker Bell strained to hear the famed sound of the falls; the melodic tune that made people weep. A siren's song, Blair had heard it said. Tink waited a few yards away for Tiger Lily so they could experience the moment together.

"Want to give your wings a rest?" Tiger Lily pushed her hair behind her so that her shoulders were clear for a perfect seat.

"With pleasure." Tink zoomed in for a gentle landing.

The horse only made it a few feet farther before he reared up on his hind legs. He seemed startled by something on their path. "Pony? What's wr—?" Tiger Lily started before a sharp sound rent the air.

REEEEEEEEEEEEEEEEEEEEK.

Tink started to tumble backward before righting herself, flying forward a few feet where she stopped short and held her head in agony.

REEEEEEEEEEEEEEEEEEEEEEEEEEEEEEEEEEEK.

She couldn't think. Couldn't feel. All she could do was clutch her ears as if trying to stop someone ripping them from the inside.

Tiger Lily cringed, clutching her head with one hand and Pony's mane with the other. Quickly, she turned the horse around, forcing him to trot back the way they came, yelling over the din that Tink follow her to the safety of the chasm again.

REEEEEEEEEEEEEEEEEEEEEEEEEEEEEEEEEEEEEEEEEEEEEEEEEK.

The fairy fought the pain in her ears to get there. Seconds felt like hours.

When she reached Tiger Lily and touched down on her friend's waiting palm, both young women struggled to catch their breath.

"What was that?" Tink panicked.

Tink could read the worry lines etched on Tiger Lily's face as she stared back at the water. "I think that was the new song of Prism Falls."

SIX

Days passed, and Tink found herself alone at Wanderers Cay. It was strange how there had been times she'd longed for peace and quiet, when Ash was breathing down her neck, Blair was prattling on about sea-festival mishaps or Mimic flickering in and out. But sitting alone in the cave, listening to the echo of the tiny waves of water hitting the cave floor was making her pretty melancholy. Maybe she didn't want to be alone after all.

After their journey to Prism Falls, Tiger Lily had dashed off to tell the Elders in her village what they'd heard, and Tink had headed back to the cave to tell the others. It didn't occur to her they wouldn't be back yet. Of course, Blair tended to linger when she met up with the other mermaids, and Mimic was clearly enjoying his stay in the Never Woods, probably reconnecting with some old pals. Ash, of course, was still in Pixie Hollow.

The odd thing was that Caiman wasn't there either. He always spent nights on the ship and came back to the cave first chance he could during the day. So where could he be?

Tink sighed, the sound loud enough that it actually pinged against the walls.

"Hello? Tink?"

She flew up in surprise. "Caiman?" she called, rushing out of the cave to see him pulling his rowboat onshore. Her mood improved ten-fold. "I was worried. Have you been on the *Jolly Roger* all this time?"

"Aye," Caiman said, using the back of his hand to rub his sweaty brow. "Sorry. Captain wouldn't let me get away so easily the past few days." He rubbed at his right arm. There was a purple bruise running from above his elbow to his wrist.

"What happened?" she demanded, flying to his arm. "Did they hurt you?"

"No, Tink, it's not like that."

She registered the worry written on his face, and suddenly she understood why there was a shadow under his chin as well. "You're lying."

"I'm fine," Caiman said, a sudden growl to his normally timid tenor. "Was just getting my knocks for shirking my responsibilities. I had to do much swabbing of the deck for forgetting all the produce I'd meant to bring. Got distracted by, you know, everything." He shook his head, as if shaking out his thoughts (a move Tink knew well herself). "But forget about the captain. I found something that might help us." He pulled the fauna book out of his pants pocket. "Come on, let's tell the others."

"Oh, they're not—"

"Where is everyone?" Blair demanded, her form breaking through the water inside the cave. She pulled herself up on a rock and tapped her fingers impatiently, looking like a queen. Noticing Tink and Caiman, her expression changed. "There you are! I've got gossip! Come in here."

Whoosh! Mimic flew past them, a majestic harpy for a few moments till he landed in the cave, transforming into a human who stuck the perfect landing on the sand. "What did I miss?"

"Tink! Tink!" Ash flew into view now. He wore a necklace of flowers and a crown of daisies on his head. "Everyone wanted to know where you were. You have to come next time. I swore I'd find a way to convince you and, hey—" He looked around in surprise. "You're all back." He looked at Tink. "How was Prism Falls?"

"Not good," Tink said. She felt like a storming tide; her mood cresting and falling without warning. "They were . . . out of key."

"Out of key?" Blair repeated. "What does that mean?"

"I don't know. They sounded awful. Loud and piercing. And not at all like they usually do."

"Well, that's not good." Mimic sat down and plucked a feather off his chest. "Not good at all, especially with what I saw in the Never Woods. Trees are dying from the inside out. Apples are falling off trees completely rotten. Food is growing scarce. The creatures there are worried." He walked over to the map and added an X mark over the Never Woods using the red coral Blair used as lip stain.

"Same under the sea," Blair said, her mouth set in a thin line. "I spoke to so many merfolk that are hearing the rays are trying to migrate to a new part of the ocean. The sea turtles as well. Something has spooked them all."

Mimic added an X over the Never Sea now as well.

"I found something useful in the plant book," Caiman tried, but the tenor was so sour in the cave, no one could muster a response, let alone match Caiman's enthusiasm.

Tink had a sudden thought. "What did they say in the hollow?"

Ash looked at her blankly. "No one really said anything. They were too busy celebrating the new season."

Tink resisted the urge to roll her eyes. Typical. If something wasn't happening directly in front of a fairy's eyes, they tended to ignore it.

"I saw something odd though," Ash admitted. "Some of the trees in the hollow—the leaves were already turning and falling even though that doesn't usually happen for another moon cycle or two. Felt early, but when I asked some of the other nature fairies, they said they hadn't noticed."

That doesn't sound good, Tink thought.

"I've got some good news," Caiman tried again, pointing to a page in the book. "Listen, I—"

"Hey, Caiman." Blair sat up straighter and frowned. "What happened to your face?"

"And your arm?" Mimic asked.

Caiman's face clouded over. "I fell. It's nothing."

Tink tensed. The thought of the pirates hurting Caiman made her burn inside. She had to convince Caiman to stop going back to the *Jolly Roger* at night.

"It doesn't look like you— Oh! Tiger Lily!" Blair said, getting distracted at the sound of galloping.

Tiger Lily rode into the cave high atop Pony, her long, dark hair pulled back in a braid. She dismounted in seconds.

"Sorry I couldn't return sooner," Tiger Lily said, her voice measured and low. "After I told everyone about the falls, the Elders wanted to hold a meeting." She looked at Tink. "Between the waters' discord and the new disturbances, people are worried."

"I've never seen mermaids care about anyone other than themselves, and even they were concerned," Blair noted. "That's when you know Never Land is in trouble."

"Great." Mimic groaned. "So, we've been right all along. Never Land is falling apart. Which is why the Never Fowl paid us a visit."

Tink sank down onto one of the hammocks. She didn't even mind when Ash joined her. "What are we going to do?"

There was a low rumble of thunder in the distance, and they all looked out the entrance of the cave. Wind was rustling through the trees, bending palm trees easily. Tink rubbed her arms to keep warm.

"Another storm," Mimic murmured.

"What did your Elders say, Tiger Lily?" Tink asked. "Do they have an idea of what's causing all these changes? What it means?"

Tiger Lily shook her head. "My grandmother says the magic of the island has always been steady. Like a beating heart—sometimes it slows, sometimes it quickens, but now Never Land seems to be skipping beats. Something is definitely interfering with the island's magic." She looked at each of them one at a time, her words clear. "A terrible evil is sweeping across the land."

"A terrible evil?" Blair repeated. "I don't like the sound of that."

Neither do I, Tink thought, her mood darkening like the sky.

Caiman whistled loudly through his teeth, and everyone stopped and looked at him. He waved the plant book in the air. "That's what I've been trying to tell you! I think I found something that could save Never Land!" He rushed the book over to Mimic and Caiman, who huddled near the shore where Blair was resting half in and half out of the water.

Ash looked at Tink curiously and she shrugged. Something in the plant book that could save the island? She doubted it. But there was no harm in hearing him out.

Caiman pointed a dirty finger at a drawing of a small deep purple flower that looked somewhat like a hydrangea. "You ever seen one of these before? It's a penumbra."

"What's a penumbra?" Tink flew over, now curious.

"It's a flower. With very interesting powers by the looks of it. And look where there appear to be a bunch of them." Caiman flipped back to the page with an illustration of Prism Falls, resting his hand on the foliage behind it. Tinker Bell landed on the page, squinting closely. Yes—in between the thick, thorny bushes—she could just make out small lotus-shaped blooms.

"The Forbidden Side?" Mimic looked at the book curiously.

"Nope! I'm out," Ash said, dusting his hands.

"Not a good idea. Not a good idea at all," Blair agreed.

"Well, hang on, we did say the vegetation that grows there would be very powerful. Maybe that it was even connected to the falls somehow," Tink said. She thought of what Tiger Lily had said about the tide pool's power to transform.

"Wait, so actually *go* to the Forbidden Side? All for some flowers? No way," Blair said. "Not happening."

"I agree!" Ash said, getting upset.

"You don't understand," Caiman tried, but the others all began talking over him. Tiger Lily listened to the exchange quietly. "If you would just hear me out!" he begged, but everyone was too worked up.

Tink tapped her foot impatiently. This was getting ridiculous. She followed Caiman with a very undignified whistle and the others looked at her. "Would you all let Caiman speak? He said this penumbra was important and I want to know how."

The pirate beamed, turning red at the attention. "Thanks, Tink." He opened his book again. "The penumbra is important because the sap is an antidote that can sever the 'dark parts.'"

"So you want to use plant sap to heal the island?" Ash sputtered. "How exactly are we supposed to do that?"

"No clue," Caiman said. "But it seems like this flower is powerful. Maybe—maybe it's worth collecting a bit of it and using it to save Never Land. Worth a try, no?" The group was quiet. "Does anyone have a better idea?"

A clang of thunder rumbled across the island and seconds later, sheets of rain fell outside the cave. Mimic and Blair rushed to the opening to check for damage.

"What do you think?" Tink whispered to Tiger Lily.

"I want to know why I've never heard of this bloom before," she said quietly as lightning lit up the cave. "Unless my grandmother kept it from me. Something that can overcome darkness is a bloom my people wouldn't want many to know existed. What if it fell into the wrong hands?"

Tiger Lily had a point. A flower that powerful would be kept hidden from Never Land. That could be why it grew on the Forbidden Side.

"But it does make sense if you think about it," Tiger Lily went on. "The island would want to protect its magic for a situation such as this. Never Land is smart. If someone is tampering with its magic, the island would find a way to correct the balance."

Tink's heart beat faster.

"But which of us is going to risk crossing to the Forbidden Side?" Ash asked nervously. "It's forbidden for a reason. What if the moment one of us sets foot on sacred ground, we're *bam!* Zapped! Dead. Done for."

The group was quiet again.

"It's risky," Tiger Lily agreed. "We don't even know if this penumbra will work."

"Could be a fool's errand," Mimic agreed.

"*Or* Caiman just found us a way to restore the magic of Never Land. I don't think we can ignore this," Tink pressed.

"Exactly!" Caiman crowed, his eyes bright. "Maybe that's why the Never Fowl were here in the first place—they were telling us to go to the Prism Falls and continue on to the Forbidden Side to find a way to . . ." He peered down at the passage in the book, his thumb holding the page as if it were a life raft. "*Sever* all the bad stuff that's been happening."

"Sever the bad . . . like the pirates," Ash pointed out. "No offense."

Caiman shrugged and looked away, his bruised chin in full view. "You're not wrong."

Ash looked at Tink now. "What if we could use that sap to get rid of the pirates on the *Jolly Roger*?"

"How in the gods' names would we do that?" Blair asked.

"I dunno. We get this penumbra and we feed it to the pirates somehow and then they disappear! Never Land saved. Problem solved." Ash puffed out his chest triumphantly. "Maybe this *is* a good idea."

"I told you," Caiman said happily.

"All right. I say let's go!" Mimic said, raising his fist. "Tink and Ash—you take the air. Tiger Lily and I will bring Caiman. Blair, we'll meet you near on the falls' side."

Tiger Lily frowned. "I'm not sure that's a good idea. We don't want to hurt the landscape, especially in such a sacred space."

"Yeah!" Caiman chimed in. "You heard Tiger Lily. We can't go trampling the flowers. Maybe a flier should go and get me a sample or two."

"I can be a flier," Mimic said.

"I was thinking Tink and Ash," Caiman said. "Fairies are small and light. If they go, they don't even have to land."

"But we don't know what the penumbra looks like," Ash pointed out. "You're the plant expert. Why aren't you the one going?"

The pirate looked slightly ill. "Me?"

An idea began to form in Tink's head. "I'll take Caiman!" she jingled loudly. She smiled at him encouragingly. "I can give you some pixie dust. You know what the penumbra looks like and can identify it from the air, then I can go down and pluck it. No vegetation ruined. No harm to the falls." Caiman still looked uneasy.

"I don't know. We really don't know what happens over there," Tiger Lily said, concerned. "What if you're flying into a trap?"

"We'll be fine. If we see anything amiss, we'll change course," Tink said.

"You don't want some backup?" Ash asked worriedly.

"To Tiger Lily's point, the fewer people we endanger, the better," Tink said. "And to Mimic's, we need an expert. Caiman and I will go tomorrow at dawn. Right, Caiman?"

Caiman swallowed. "I . . . all right."

Tink felt empowered now as she flew higher. This whole mess felt partially her fault, no matter what Tiger Lily said.

She needed to be the one to fix it. And if she helped Caiman face his fears in the meantime, so much the better.

SEVEN

"I DON'T LIKE THIS!"

Caiman flew alongside her, his eyes closed as he glided through the air, his arms and legs out like a starfish. The pixie dust circled around him like beams of the sun, making his whole body glitter. Tink tried not to laugh. The pirate was afraid of his own shadow.

"You're missing out on the most incredible view of Never Land you'll ever see," Tink said.

"I feel sick. And dizzy. Is this what flying is like all the time?" Caiman asked, huffing and wheezing now as he tried to control his breathing.

"You're imagining it," Tink said. "Your balance would be a lot better if you opened your eyes."

Tink looked up and out over Never Land, the mountains in the distance. They'd had a later start than they'd agreed upon. Caiman didn't arrive till well after the sun was up and before he'd go anywhere, he wanted to check on the garden. Captain Bartholomew had given Caiman a welt on his right arm to match the one on the left, which Caiman tried to cover up with a handkerchief tied around his forearm.

Tink felt so furious, she wanted to fly over to the *Jolly Roger* and give those pirates a piece of her mind. But she had to focus. All morning, she'd been itching to just get to the Forbidden Side and fix things already.

"You know, if you're nervous, you don't have to do this," Ash had reminded her when he saw her flying back and forth across the cave. "We could just go back to the hollow where things are pretty much the same."

But pretty much was not good enough as far as Tink was concerned. She saw Tiger Lily watching their exchange and tried to respond kindly. "I'll be all right. I promise." Ash had just nodded and then hugged her.

And now, she and Caiman were in the air. With Tiger Lily's directions, Tink hoped she'd remember how to get to Prism Falls and then beyond it. What if the sound of the falls was worse? What if Caiman couldn't identify the penumbra when they got there? What if there was no way to access the Forbidden Side, even from above? What if Ash was right and the Forbidden Side killed them both?

What if. What if. What if.

Tink's mind was constantly working. She couldn't shut it off. Sometimes she'd wake up in the middle of the night, hear Mimic snoring, or look below the surface of the water to see Blair fast asleep. And instead of being comforted by the fact she wasn't alone, her brain would immediately kick into high gear.

Sometimes it was about tinkering. What if she could create something that would tell them if the water level was rising in case of flooding? What if there was a way to build a shelter on the beach so they got more of a breeze, especially as the temperatures rose? What if they could create some sort of catch-all to grab fruit from the fruit trees near the beach so that none of it was wasted?

But right about now, all she could think about was ridding Never Land of the intruding evil forces.

"How much longer?" Caiman moaned. "Please tell me we are almost there."

Tink saw the mountains growing closer and the chasm that lead to the falls. "We are. Now open your eyes. Just for a second. I bet it will make you feel better." She couldn't help but stare at the bruises on his arms. Why was the captain taking his ire out on poor, helpless Caiman? But if the penumbra worked, the pirates would be gone and Caiman could finally be on land for good.

"Fine. But only for a moment!" Caiman adjusted his pants. They were held together by a threadbare belt that had seen better days and Tink wondered how she could make him a new one. Caiman opened his left eye, then his right before his eyes widened fully. "Blimey, would you look at this view." He glanced over at Tink flying beside him. "Tink, we're flying! Flying!" He crowed now, his voice echoing out and carrying on the wind.

She laughed, a feeling of joy rushing through her. "Yes, we are!"

Caiman looked down at the pixie dust circling his hand. "If my mother could only see this!"

Tink felt her happiness dip. But when she looked at Caiman's face, he didn't seem sad. He was euphoric. Her mood soared once more, as did they, flying through a cloud.

Caiman gave a small squeak. "This dust will last, right? I'm not going to go tumbling, am I?"

"I hope not," Tink said innocently, and Caiman blanched. She laughed. "Kidding! I brought more than enough to get here and back to Wanderers Cay." She flew ahead of him. "Now follow me. We need to go straight on to the chasm and over the falls and if Tiger Lily is right, we should be right over the Forbidden Side."

They flew on quietly for a few moments, enjoying the ride till the chasm came into view. Locking her eyes on the top of the trees, Tink took a deep breath and slipped into the opening. A shadow fell over both of them as they flew on, making her instantly cold. When she looked back to check on Caiman, she saw his eyes were open (thank the fairies!) as he trailed her through the mountain range.

ERREEEEAAAAAAAAAAAAAAAAAAACCCCCCCCCKKKKKKKKKKK!

Tink winced. They heard the falls before they saw them. The high-pitched wail was worse than it was the other day, all ting-y, like a giant bell clanging out of tune. Caiman covered his ears, which caused his whole body to dip downward.

"Caiman! Let go of your ears! You're going to crash if you're not careful!" she jingled.

"That is horrid!" He looked down at the water gushing over the edge of the mountain into pools below. "I can't stand it!"

Tink looked down now, too, and paused. The water had been clear the other day, but today it was cloudy and filled with debris. Was that normal? She'd need to remember to ask Tiger Lily. "We're going to go up and over it. Hopefully the sound will let up. Ready?"

"Ready . . . I think!" Caiman called over the terrible wail.

Tinker Bell flew forward, rushing over the top of the mountain and the stream that lead to the falls and approaching the mist rising above the falls. Was this water or was this a cloud? The air felt thick and ominous and all her senses were on high alert. *This doesn't feel right.* She couldn't see a hand in front of her face.

"Tink! Tink! Where are you?" she heard Caiman call.

"I'm here!" she shouted, but she found she couldn't see the pirate. *We should turn back*, she thought as the air around her seemed to spark. Was Ash right? Were they going to get fried? Just then, the wind began to swirl, blowing her off-course . . . whatever that course was. "This is too dangerous. We should turn—"

Swish! A gust of wind sent Tink feet over head, spinning, tumbling through the air, her cries of fury getting snuffed out by the sound of the wind. She tried not to panic, but her wings felt like they weren't working. She was falling, falling, falling and couldn't stop it. And then: *boom!*

Her body froze feet from the ground. Tink blinked in surprise as Caiman's did the same thing. Wait! She could see him again! The fog had lifted and they were . . . Where were they?

"Are we dead?" Caiman asked, his eyes closed tight again.

"No!" Tink exclaimed, spinning around now. "We're *here*!"

Behind them was a wall of fog that crackled—that they'd just survived—but in front of them was a mountaintop paradise. Flowers as far as the eye could see, in every color of the prism she could imagine, growing tall and lush. Here no grass was burned. Every apple and pear on the trees surrounding them looked lush and perfect to eat. In the distance she could see the Never Sea shining with brighter blue than she'd remembered. The sun was warm, the sky clear, and the smell of honeysuckle and jasmine instantly calmed her. "Open your eyes again."

This time Caiman listened immediately. "Oh my stars . . . look at this place!" The pirate reached his hands out, as if swimming through the air to explore the field of flowers in front of them. "Look at all these beauties! They've got moonflower and lavender, and ooh! Ooh! Is that dianthus?" He gasped. "There's even wisteria." She saw his chin quiver. "I wish Mum could see all this. She loved wisteria."

"Did she?" Tink felt a tug on her heartstrings. She wanted to tell Caiman to snip some and bring it back to grow at Wanderers Cay, but they had to be smart. The Forbidden Side had let them through. They should take just what they needed and go back. "We should find the penumbra," she said gently.

Caiman wiped at his eyes. "Aye. Right-o. Let's see." He flew slowly over the field. "That's not it. No, that's not it either," he said, exploring bloom after bloom.

"What does it look like again?" Tink asked.

"Purple so bright it glows, like pixie dust, I guess. But I don't see any, anywhere."

"It has to be here," Tink said, trying not to let the frustration creep into her voice. They'd come all this way. She zoomed over the field, making lines in the sky as she went up and down each row of flowers and searched every tree. But there was nothing like what Caiman was describing. She tried not to panic. *Breathe, Tink* came Ash's voice in her head. *Get some air*, she told herself, flying closer to the edge of the mountain over the sea.

And that's when she saw a small patch of something fuchsia. "Caiman! I think I found something. Is this it?"

Caiman rushed over. He peered down, then gasped with glee, holding his chest. "Oh my, you did it, Tink! You found it! That's penumbra. I'd bet my right arm it is."

The patch of bright flowers glowed so bright, Tink thought they were on fire. Together, they looked like one giant bloom, but when she narrowed her eyes and peeked at the plant through her fingers, she could see there were dozens of small flowers that looked like purple pom-poms. Below them, the flowers had gleaming yellow stems. "Do you think you can reach down and grab one?"

"Yeah. Better take several to be safe," Caiman said. He produced a small knife from his pocket and hovered over the blooms, determination etched on his face.

"Are you sure?" Tink worried. "Maybe I should do it. Just tell me where to make the cut."

"No, Tink," he said. "It's all right. It's like you always say—I don't have to let my head block the way. I can do it." He lowered himself slowly, till his whole body was over the flower bed.

Tink watched as Caiman lowered the knife. "Hold it steady."

"I got it," he said, and she held her breath as he sliced at the stem. The whole patch glowed brighter, vibrating as Caiman pulled out half a dozen stems at once. "Got them!" He held the plants up in triumph.

Tink cringed, waiting for the Forbidden Side to do something in retaliation for the thievery. But nothing happened.

Caiman flew over to her now. "Think this is enough? Look at them, Tink. They are beauties, ain't they?" He looked at the blooms from all angles. "Sturdy little things." He flipped them over and examined the stems. Two of them had started to ooze.

"Careful," Tink warned. "Isn't that the part we need?"

"I think so," Caiman said, swiping some of the sap. The goo was phosphorus in color; bright white and almost waxy. He rubbed some between his fingers. "Blimey, it's cold!" He gave a laugh, his whole body moving for a moment before it went completely rigid.

"Caiman? Caiman, what's wrong?" Tink cried out.

"I don't know, I—" Caiman's eyes widened, and he started to scream. A gray, mist-like substance seemed to ooze out of his body. Then it started to eek out faster, shaking him violently, as if it were ripping away from him.

Tink shrieked in horror. What was happening? Was the penumbra ripping his body apart? *It severs the dark parts*, the book had said. But Caiman didn't have darkness in him. The other pirates did. "No! Stop! Please!" she begged the Forbidden Side.

Caiman was wailing now. "Tink, help! Help me!" he cried as his body continued to convulse, the mist flowing from him till it formed a shape.

What was that? Not a cloud or fog, it appeared to be almost human. The dark spot widened and grew, shifting shapes and moving fast. Was that . . . a ghost? The gray creature started to move toward her, and Tink tried to get away, frightened. That's when she noticed the shadow had eyes—sunken holes of nothingness. Voids to a disturbing unknown.

"Get away from us!" Tink cried out, and the shadow did as it was told, zipping through the mist. Caiman fell to the ground, landing at an odd angle. Tink zipped toward him. "Caiman? Caiman, are you all right?" She tried shaking him as best as her small hands could, but he was much bigger than her, and completely dazed. He tried sitting up and collapsed again. "Caiman!" Tink cried.

His eyes opened for a moment, fluttering, then closing again. His voice was barely a whisper. "Help."

"I'm going to get you out of here. Hang on!" Tink sprinkled more dust over Caiman's body to make sure he had enough to make the journey back. "I'll get you back to Wanderers Cay."

"No, please . . ." His voice was drifting away. "Get me to the ship before—" He gave a shudder and a gasp and passed out.

EIGHT

"Hang in there, Caiman," Tink begged as she used the dust to guide Caiman's body back through the fog. They made their way past the shrieking Prism Falls, and then, mercifully, straight out over the quieter sea. The *Jolly Roger*'s skull flag waved like a stain against the blue sky. She felt her heart constrict when she saw it.

Tink looked over at Caiman again as he floated through the air. She could see his chest rising and falling, but he was still knocked out. The penumbra were in a sack, tied to his arm for the journey. She wasn't sure what else to do with the blooms. She refused to leave them behind after all Caiman had done to gather them. She could only hope they wouldn't lose all their sap during the flight.

Of course, the smart thing to do would be to drop the penumbra off at Wanderers Cay and tell the others what happened. But Tink didn't care about being smart. She cared about saving Caiman. If she went home first, the others would probably talk her out of taking him to the ship. (She could hear Ash already: *Are you mad?* Maybe she was.) But she knew nothing they had in the cave could help. He wouldn't have said he needed to get back to the ship, unless he thought there was something on board that could save him.

Tinker Bell always paid attention when Caiman spoke of Mainlander traditions and lost things. He talked a lot while he gardened, and she usually sat on a bloom while he waxed on about tonics they had on the ship that cured all sorts of ailments. (They even used leeches, which she thought sounded dreadful.)

Please let them have an antidote, Tink begged the island as they got closer to the *Jolly Roger*.

She wouldn't forgive herself if something happened to Caiman. He wasn't from Never Land. He was an outsider. Maybe that's why the Forbidden Side had tried to tear his body in two. *This is all my fault*, she thought, her fear mounting, angry tears springing to her eyes. *Why did I drag him there? Why did I let him cut it?* She looked over at his motionless form drifting through the air and felt another pang. *He's been through so much already. He has to pull through.*

Clouds were moving fast again, dark and ominous in the distance, bringing an impossible change in weather. Below, Tink spied movement on the ship. Small figures were rushing back and forth across the deck. When they looked up and saw the strange sight of a glowing young man and fairy floating toward them, they stopped short and gathered on deck. Tink could hear the commotion as they got closer. A pirate with a spy glass started pointing and shouting. Tink tried to calm her nerves as she guided her friend's body down, holding her breath as she thought about coming in for a landing among the men. They made a clearing as she approached, and that's when she heard their panic.

"Caiman is flying!"

"He ain't moving. He's a ghost, I tell ya!"

"Captain! He's bewitched! A mermaid got him, Captain!"

"Why's the fairy here? What's happened to Caiman?"

Tink ignored the fuss and used the dust to lay Caiman's body down on the deck. The pirates fanned out around him. They were too afraid to get close to his body, which was still sparkling at the edges. Seeing the pirates up close, Tink realized Caiman looked nothing like any of them. He was younger, for one, and maintained good hygiene for all the earth on his clothes and under his nails. These men, on the other hand, reeked. Their stench made it almost impossible to stay put, the smudges on their faces, and the sweat stains on their clothes making one man hard to distinguish from the other. Their clothes looked rather patched up and haggard, much like Caiman's did. Still, Tinker Bell tried to get their attention. Time was of the essence. She flew from one man to the next jingling irately.

"Help him!" she cried. "Why are you all just standing there?"

"What's she saying?" asked one. "Any you lot understand her?"

"She sounds like bells," said another. "What you want, fairy?"

"You hurt our friend, fairy?" said a third, who reached up with a meaty fist and tried to grab her. "We hurt you, little bug!"

"I'm not a bug!" She dove at one of their heads and stepped on it.

The pirate shrieked.

"Catch her!"

Tink flew higher, her face burning now, her anger growing at their naivete. And then suddenly, she heard a voice from below that was deep and surly.

"Quiet, you scurvy dogs! Can't you see we've got a guest?"

"So-sorry, Captain," stuttered a small, squat man in spectacles. He had a white beard and was wearing a knit hat and a blue-and-white shirt that seemed to be struggling to cover his midsection. His pants were ripped at the bottom, giving her a good view of his sandals.

Captain?

The man who had just commanded the deck was Captain Bartholomew, the legendary pirate Caiman spoke of with equal parts awe and fear. He wore a large burgundy cavalier hat with an ostrich plume sticking out of the top. Despite her annoyance, Tinker Bell couldn't help being fascinated by the captain's dress. His wine-colored suit had a fuzzy look to it, which was fancier than anything the other pirates had on. Sensing her staring, the man looked up at her now, his hat tipping back to the cloudy sky. He had milky-white skin, black hair, dark eyebrows, and a wispy black mustache. "Miss Bell, it's so nice to finally make your acquaintance. Won't you come down and join us?"

Tink froze. *How does Captain Bartholomew know my name?* She hovered just out of reach contemplating her next move. Did she trust the captain enough to fly down and speak with him? These men were pirates. Lying was in their nature. If Tiger Lily was right, they weren't allowed on Never Land because of nefarious deeds they'd done elsewhere. She stayed in the air and folded her arms over her chest.

"Our dear Caiman has told us much about you," Captain Bartholomew said, flashing her a crooked smile. "How you and your fellow Wanderers have helped him navigate Never Land."

She paused. Caiman had told the pirates about her?

"We've wanted to make your acquaintance for a long time now," he added. "But of course, we can't leave the *Jolly Roger*. As I'm sure you're aware."

Tink flew down like a shot and moved up and down in front of Caiman, pixie dust trailing behind her. "He's hurt. Please help him," she jingled, trying to use her hands to get her point across. "He was researching flora on Never Land and I think one of the species he was collecting did something to him."

"A pl-plant hurt him? Don't you worry, Miss Bell," stuttered the one in the red hat. "We can see he's in bad shape. We'll—we'll help him."

Tinker Bell paused. "You can understand me?"

The man nodded his head as Captain Bartholomew spoke for both of them. "Mr. Smee and I can, dear girl. Why, Caiman himself taught us how to understand fairies and the inhabitants of this great land of yours." He paused. "Well, best we can from here." His mustache curled downward in a frown.

She inched closer, curiosity about these Mainlanders getting the best of her. The captain couldn't be more different than the gruff men she'd met on the deck—but not the way Caiman was different. No, it was his composure, his poise, his thoughtful gaze. This was not who she'd pictured when her friend had spoken about the feared Bartholomew. As she looked all around the ship at the men watching them, she realized there was so much she didn't know about Mainlanders.

"I must admit, you're the first fairy who has been kind enough to visit. I guess the idea of pirates can be quite frightening, as you say?" He scratched his pointy chin.

Tink's mind jumped to the bruises on Caiman's arms.

"Now, I can see by your expression, the boy has told you some things about us, too. But you must understand, Miss Bell!" Captain Bartholomew begged. "I would never do anything to harm our dear Caiman. Finding him on my ship was the best thing that could have happened to me. Those plants, that marvelous collection of greenery. It's ingenious! Why, it is I who stopped the very fight he had with that pirate . . . errr, what was his name, Smee?"

"Errr . . . Killian, sir?" the man called Smee responded.

"Yes, Killian!" The captain slammed his hand down on a crate on the deck. "Some of the other fellows haven't been quite so welcoming. They're a close bunch, you see; and they don't take kindly to stowaways. I'm guessing it's more the principle of the matter than anything, you understand. But when I heard he was hurting our dear boy, I dispatched him at once." He smiled somewhat eerily and Smee placed his hat over his heart.

So, the captain wasn't the one who hurt Caiman? She had just assumed . . . Of course, Caiman hadn't said . . . At that moment, Caiman started to cough. All three of them looked over at him, lying on the deck.

"What's that, lad? Are you coming to?" Bartholomew asked, cupping his ear. "Men, fetch me some lanterns so we can get a closer look. And smelling salts! Let's get the boy in my quarters at once!" he purred. Then he smiled at Tink again.

She flew upward, watching the pirates scurry around the ship, running this way and that, as two carried Caiman into a small room on the ship. Inside, the quarters were softly lit. She saw lots of well-made wood furniture, the table covered with all sorts of delicacies that smelled wonderful. What were they? How did they have so much food? Had they been storing up the supplies Caiman had been bringing?

She flew forward to look at their Mainlander things and stopped when she realized the captain was watching her. These humans had been nothing but hospitable so far—if a little stiff and grimy. Slowly, she nodded and followed them inside.

The men laid Caiman down on a plush bed with pillows that looked soft like clouds. One took a fuzzy blanket that looked like the captain's suit and placed it over Caiman's body. Others returned with lanterns that glowed as brightly as her pixie dust. They used some sort of splint, rubbed it with another piece of wood and touching it to the oil, fire roared up behind the glass.

How did they do that? Was that water in the glass?

"I've got the smelling salts, Captain!"

A pungent scent filled the air and Tinker Bell came closer to get a better look.

Mr. Smee held a small glass bottle that looked like water. He put it under Caiman's nose. Suddenly, Caiman started sputtering and turned onto his side.

Tink beamed in surprise. Medicine that worked like magic!

"Caiman!" She rushed to his side and landed on his chest. "You're all right!"

"Tinker Bell," he said, his eyes opening and closing. "Where am I? Where . . . is this the ship? I . . . I'm sorry for . . ." His eyes fluttered closed again for a moment.

"Caiman?" Tink nudged him with her feet.

"I'm all right," he said, though his eyes were still fluttering as if they were too heavy to open. "I just need to rest."

The other pirates started to gather round.

"Men," the captain called. "That will be all. We will look after him from here." They filed out of the room, grumbling to one another.

"Tink?" Caiman said again, his voice hoarse.

"What is it?" she asked. "I'm here."

"I don't feel right," he said, trying to sit up and then falling back down again. "I'm dizzy and it feels like I might lose my breakfast at any moment."

"Maybe it was from the flying?" She didn't like how pale he looked.

"It's as if . . ." He felt around his back. "Did something happen to me on the Forbidden Side? I heard myself scream and then it felt like my body was on fire and—" He gasped, his face wincing in pain. "Oh no. It's happening again. Make it stop, Tink! Stop! It's like I'm burning up from the inside."

"Oh dear. Oh dear, oh dear!" Smee rushed over and gave him a goblet filled with drink.

"He's in bad shape. What plant could do this?"

Tink felt like she had no choice but to share what she knew. "There was a flower he discovered in a book I gave him. He thought it could—um, help Never Land. He cut a few blooms and then his body seemed to react. Something broke in him. It was almost as if . . ." Tink shuddered, thinking of the gray apparition, its cavity eyes. "Almost as if he lost part of himself."

"Lost part of himself, you say?" Smee repeated, his eyes widening. "That's not possible, is it?"

"Anything can happen on Never Land, Smee." The captain sat up straighter. "By the looks of it, he seems to be in a good amount of pain, there. Perhaps the plant was poisonous. Oh, this is a dastardly predicament."

Tink tried to stay calm. “There must be a tonic you can give him to help.”

Mr. Smee removed his cap and wiped his forehead again anxiously. “I’m afraid we don’t have anything stronger than the smelling salts here.” Caiman moaned. “Oh dear. That boy. Always trying to do too much.” Caiman cried out in pain again and held his side.

Bartholomew placed a hand over his heart. “Aye, Smee. I don’t know what will become of the boy. He looks so ill.”

“Then do something!” Tink shouted angrily, feeling desperate now. “Find the solution. Make him an antidote. A Mainlander medicine. You’ve been holding on to the plants, haven’t you? Caiman said they’re used to make tonics all the time. You could try!”

The captain and Mr. Smee looked at each other. “I wish we could, Miss Bell, but that falls out of the expertise of a pirate, I’m afraid. Of course, we do know about certain remedies that could ease his pain. There are plenty of tonics that fight infection, and ones that help the body compensate for whatever’s missing. Why I’ve heard of folks surviving without vital organs—incredible advancements the modern field of medicine has made. Isn’t that right, Smee? But one would only be able to find those things . . . what did Caiman say you call it . . . on the *Mainland*.”

He leaned forward on the table, and a bushel of apples in a basket tumbled toward him. He held one up. “I only wish there was a way to get there now and find medicine for our boy.”

“There’s no way out of the Never Sea, I’m afraid,” Smee added. “We are marooned here, which means Caiman is, too.”

“NO,” Tink jingled, her desperation growing as she made a snap decision.

"You may be stuck, but I am not. I will go to the Mainland. I'll bring back whatever's needed."

"Oh, Miss Bell! Would you?" Mr. Smee clasped his hands together, a single tear falling down his round cheeks.

Caiman moaned again, his eyes closed.

"You would do that for all of us?" Captain Bartholomew asked, studying her.

"I would do it for him," she said, fire flowing through her veins. "Now tell me what to look for and I'll go at once."

It didn't take long to get a list of tonics that could help Caiman recover from the plant's poison. She tucked the small piece of parchment in her dress, checked the pouch of pixie dust tied to her waist to make sure it was full (it still was, thankfully). And then she was ready. She felt a twinge of guilt that she wasn't looping in the Wanderers first, but they'd understand when they learned what happened to Caiman. Looking at his ashen face, she knew this couldn't wait. She flew to her friend's side again and placed her hand on his cheek.

"I'm going to get help. That's my job. Yours is to fight this ailment until I get back. Remember, you're a survivor, Caiman. Fight this!" she whispered in his ear. She thought she saw something flicker across his face even though his eyes were closed.

"Good luck, Miss Bell," the captain said, placing his hat over his heart. "Please hurry."

Hurry. She felt the pressure mounting. With a polite nod to the captain and Smee, who opened the cabin door, Tink took flight.

Tink was sure of one thing as she took to the sky. She may not know how to rid Never Land of its perils, but she could make it so this penumbra business was just a blip in the island's journey, an impossible obstacle in their path. She would solve this problem, save her friend. Failing was not an option, now more than ever.

NINE

Even though it had been many moons since she'd visited the Mainland, the route was seared into Tink's brain. Her first trip there had been short. Of course, it would be this time as well, if she could help it, but she now was prepared. She thought about Smee's instructions for finding apothecaries and hospitals—places that would most likely keep the tonics they needed. She hoped the task would be as easy as he'd made it sound.

Tinker Bell's eyes searched the sky for an important landmark and found it. The brightest beacon there was in the sky. Now all that was left to do was reach it. She picked up speed, her dust trailing behind her.

Hang in there, Caiman, she thought.

And then something plowed into her right side.

Tink gasped in surprise, trying to get her bearings as a sharp pain radiated from her right arm. Her wing was now flapping at an odd angle, the throbbing blinding as she heard the squawking. Birds were diving for her.

The Never Fowl.

Fighting the burning pain, Tink tried to fly out of range. She could see more birds in the distance, flying through the darkening sky. Only one had caught up to her so far, but it seemed determined to knock her clear out of the air. Why? She tried to channel Tiger Lily's commanding voice.

"Get away, Never Fowl!" she jingled. "Leave me alone!"

The first bird came at her again, his squawks sounding like a hiss. "Dark forces. Be careful," she thought she heard it say again. Tink shuddered. What exactly were they trying to tell her? Did they know she was headed to the Mainland; breaking the rules of the island once more?

Tink tried to pick up speed to get away. Fighting the burning in her right arm and wing, her eyes found the second star again. The bird bumped at her again and the squawking of the other birds sounded louder. They were closing in. That's when Tink's anger grew. And so did her resolve.

When the Never Fowl came at her a third time, Tink dropped fast, flying under the bird's belly and weaving in and out of clouds, ignoring the agony of her wing and pressing onward, the bright light of the star growing closer and closer. The birds were closing in, but she didn't dare look back. One pecked at her wings, knocking her sideways again and she recalculated. *Almost there. A few feet more.* The Never Fowl tried to nip, but she dodged just in time. As the star started to waffle in front of her eyes and she felt the wind pick up, the bird finally backed away.

The star seemed to pull her through. But then . . .

"Ahhh!" Tink felt her injured wing snap back, and she cried out in pain.

She held the injured wing close to her chest and let herself get carried to the other side, feeling her body move faster and faster till . . .

BOOM!

She was on the other side. Tink tried to control her breathing as she looked down through the clouds, clutching her right arm. The Mainland. She'd made it. She winced, feeling her wing speed slow. What had that beastly bird done to her? She tried to focus. *Get to the ground. Find the tonic.* She needed to find a safe place to get her bearings. *Get to Kensington Gardens*, she commanded herself and dove downward.

But the closer she got to the ground, the quieter the world seemed. Where were the sounds of the children? The laughter? She stopped short and frowned. This wasn't the park. Had she gotten turned around amid the pain and confusion? What was all the smoke? Was there a fire? She smelt something burning. The air below was so thick and heavy with smoke, her eyes started to water. The smell was putrid.

She must have taken a wrong turn. This couldn't be the same Mainland she visited last time. Tinker Bell flew on, fighting the pain that alternated from dagger-sharp to a radiating ache. She ignored the potent fumes and followed the trail of lights below looking for something that was familiar. What were those tall stacks climbing into the sky from which the smoke billowed. And why was the fog so dark, so suffocating?

The pain threatened to overtake her as lights came into view, tightly packed together like fireflies. Were those tall structures houses? She seemed to recall seeing a few when she'd been here the first time, but there were so many more now. What had become of her park?

Tinker Bell hesitated as she flew closer and spotted a river. Boats moved along the murky water, blowing even more stacks of smoke. The smell alone was enough to make her dizzy. Tink pushed herself to keep going, flying closer, and finally a few Mainlanders came into view. She saw a man in a hat, a paper tucked under his coat, the words *War on the Horizon* just visible at his side. Then she spotted a pair of ladies clutching arms as they walked together. When Tinker Bell finally spotted a child, she felt a glimmer of hope.

But as she got closer, she realized something had changed here, too. These children looked nothing like the beautifully dressed ones she'd seen the first time she'd been on the Mainland. These little ones seemed to be suffering, their clothes ragged, their expressions vacant and numb. Now that she was close enough to see their faces, Tink realized the older Mainlanders looked equally miserable. They shuffled slowly through the streets, adults and children alike, begging for food. Was there a shortage here? And what was that honking sound? It seemed to be coming from the contraption on wheels that moved without a horse.

She heard a shout and startled. Two men were locked in what appeared to be a tug of war over a loaf of bread and a crowd was gathering. Peering at their faces, Tink felt a sense of alarm. Why did everyone look so sad? So dirty? So uncomfortable?

She heard crying and immediately thought of baby Peter. Was he nearby? How old would he be now? Time worked so differently here. She hovered in the sky, heartbroken, and spotted a woman carrying a child down a tightly packed street. For some reason, Tink felt the need to follow. She immediately wished she hadn't.

Children. Dozens of them, their faces dirty, their bodies shivering, were packed together, sitting among piles of furniture in a tight alley. Her heartbeat fluttered as she spied them lying in filth, many coughing or crying. Someone was burning something in a giant can and children stood around it trying to keep warm. Behind the group, several people were fighting over what looked like a blanket. She looked from one helpless child to another and tears began to stream down her face. What had happened to the beautiful Mainland she'd seen last time?

Something flew through the air and Tink saw it just in time to fly out of the way. It smashed against the wall behind her, glass fragments flying through the air. There was more shouting and then two men came at each other with fists. Tink couldn't take it anymore. She flew up and away, in horror, wondering where to go. It was as if everyone here was in need of help, not just Caiman.

Maybe I can fly somewhere else, she thought. Could there be more than one Mainland? She turned around too fast and felt a sharp stab of pain run down her right side. She wasn't sure how much longer she could fly. Her mission suddenly felt impossible. *Impossible is just a problem to solve,* Tink told herself, even as a deep desire to sleep washed over her.

The sound of thunder made her look up. Clouds had moved in quickly, blocking out the early morning sun. A storm was coming. Tink shivered. The pain on her right side was throbbing now. A raindrop fell to her right, then another to her left, and she moved to dodge both.

Find shelter, she told herself, looking around for somewhere to ride out the storm. She couldn't go back to that awful alleyway with all the crammed people, looking like fish caught in a net. She had to find the place that had tonic. "A medicine man" is what Smee called it. How exactly would she find one of those? The drops were coming faster now, and she knew she had to get out of the rain soon. She wouldn't be able to fly if it came down any harder.

The sound of more honking made her look over. Those strange moving vehicles not being pulled by horses rushed past her down the street, stopping in front of a tall building. Tink followed.

"This boy needs help!" she heard someone shout.

Tink paused, watching from the top of a gate post at the front of the building as two men in matching dark clothes and unusual hats carried a lifeless boy on a white board up to the gates. A third was banging on the gates, shouting. "He's hurt, come quickly!"

Men in white jackets must have heard him because suddenly they rushed out of the building and opened the gates.

"What happened to him?" asked one, examining the boy with a strange instrument.

"Hit by a carriage. Might have run over his foot. Can you help him?"

"Yes. Bring him inside. Quickly now."

Tink watched as they carried the boy inside and shut the doors behind them.

Help.

She glanced over at the large sign hanging on the gates she was standing atop of and tried to make sense of the letters she saw in front of her: GREATER LONDON HOSPITAL FOR BOYS.

A hospital. That was on Smee's list of tonic places!

At last, a spot of good luck. Hang on, Caiman!

Tink stepped off the gate post, fighting the feeling of her right wing moving against its will. Using the last of her strength, she flew toward the doors.

But halfway there, the pain became almost unbearable, her whole body on fire. She couldn't see or keep a path straight in front of her. The big doors went in and out of focus and for a moment, she almost dropped out of the sky.

"No!" she shouted to herself. She was so close now. She couldn't give up. The rain was starting to fall steadier now. *This is what you get, Tink, for being rash,* she berated herself. *The Wanderers would have told you not to do this on your own.*

Don't give up now, another voice cut in. *Find an opening. Get inside!* Tink felt her heart race, starting to panic, her body so weak and cold, all she wanted to do was collapse, but her brain was awake enough to know that was a bad idea. She flew upward, searching for a crack in the building to wait out the rain, her body drooping, her side burning, her head fuzzy, as she dodged raindrops.

And that's when she heard it—a child's laughter.

The most beautiful sound in the world.

Tink floated toward it, the happy sound a balm for her aching limbs. She found herself flying haphazardly toward a ledge attached to a window and felt a puff of warm air. There was an opening, there at the corner! With the last of her strength, Tinker Bell dove at it, sliding through the opening and touching down onto the ledge. Finally, she collapsed. Tink willed her heartbeat to slow, attempting to focus on the room in which she found herself.

Dozens of children were running around, talking loudly and giggling. Was she hallucinating? Tinker Bell tried to fight the pain in her head as she watched these young Mainlander boys. Their faces were clean, their clothes not tattered. The children here seemed to be in a better position than the ones in the alley. What was this helping place called the hospital? Where were their tonics? While her focus was hazy, she still spied many lost things that were somewhat familiar—the clock mounted on the wall among them. There were also a dozen identical beds that reminded her of the black iron hospital gates and tables with toys and plants. But best of all there were children and they seemed happy.

"Do it again!"

"Please?"

"Show us how!"

"All right," a deep, ringing voice said.

Tink tried to prop herself up to see where the new voice was coming from. She leaned on her left side, trying to ignore the pain on her right and spotted a new, intriguing figure among the boys.

He was taller than the rest by at least a foot. Definitely older, like Caiman. And he had dark hair and skin the color of the bone-colored cup that had washed up in Never Land recently. Even so, his cheeks appeared rosier than the children's. Tink found herself mesmerized as he brushed his hair away from his face, showing off surprisingly warm brown eyes.

"Let's try this again," she heard him say as he pushed up his white shirt sleeves. His broad shoulders seemed to make his dress shirt look a bit snug and his pants also looked a bit tight, though for all she knew, pants that only reached a boy's calf was the style on the Mainland.

"I'm going to have to take this down before Nurse Beth gets back," he added. But the twinkle in his eyes betrayed his warning. "Watch me one more time. And, Slightly? Get back in bed."

A boy with a bandage wrapped around his head climbed into bed.

"What do you want to eat?"

"An apple," said the child called Slightly.

"Apple coming right up."

The older boy pulled a bright red apple out of his pocket and placed it in the bucket. He tied a rope to one end of the bucket and threaded the rope through a small wheel on a bracket by the ceiling and held tight to the other end of the rope.

"Ready?" He pulled the other end of the rope, and the boys watched in amazement as the bucket started to rise off the floor. Slightly caught it when it reached his bed height and took out the apple.

The boys cheered.

Tink lit up when she realized what the young man with the ringing voice was doing. He was making a pulley! Just like the ones she'd added to the cay. Was he a tinkerer, too?

"Please, can I try?"

The voice came from a small, yellow-haired boy wrapped in a thin blanket.

The inventor stepped aside and let the little boy add an apple to the bucket and take a turn at the rope.

"It's not moving," the child groaned, his face red with exertion. "Ugh, this is impossible!" He let the rope go and the bucket came down with a crash.

"Nice one, Nibs!" one of the other kids said.

"You've broken it!" cried another.

"Now, now," the young inventor said. "Giving up already? Come, lad." Slowly, methodically, he helped the light-haired boy—*Nibs*, was it?—thread the rope through the system, then turned him around. The tinkerer held out the bottom of the rope, looping it into a ring, which the boy took tentatively. Then the older boy encouraged Nibs to walk a few paces, prompting the bucket to rise with ease. "Impossible is merely an invitation to problem-solve."

Tink's eyes widened, her heart speeding up. Had she heard the young man correctly? She leaned forward, trying to get a closer look. But she was having trouble focusing, the blur of activity and throbbing pain making her disoriented.

The others cheered as Slightly caught the bucket, then held up a second piece of fruit in victory.

"We can find somewhere to hide it," the older boy told them. "And maybe find a way to fasten the wheel so that Nurse Beth doesn't notice. That way when you're hungry at night, you can pass each other a snack."

"I'm always hungry!" said Slightly, taking another bite.

The boys all laughed and Tink attempted a smile, but the pain in her side seemed to be vibrating now, so strong she could barely stay upright. The pixie dust around her was on the fritz, glowing bright then fading. Tink wanted to sleep so badly but sensed that was not a good idea. A loud peal of thunder made her jump. The pain was crackling so hard now she couldn't move. *Help!* she cried as loud as she could.

The boys seemed to look up at the sound and she watched as one child locked eyes on her.

"Oy! What's that?" she heard him say.

The next thing she knew, she was falling. Tink hit the ledge hard, banging the crown of her head.

And then she was someplace else entirely.

PART TWO
LOST

TEN

TINKER BELL WAS FALLING AGAIN.

Down, down, down through a gray mist, till she landed on the beach with a soft thump. She was forgetting something—or someone? Yes, there he was—the figure of a pale young man, spread on the sand, next to the pirates' dingy.

Tink narrowed her eyes, trying to make sense of the familiar scene.

"Was it a wreck? Are you hurt?" Tiger Lily's voice cut through the fog. Tinker Bell noticed her friend and then a small figure hovering over the girl's shoulder. Oh. Right. It was Tink. On *that* day. But how was she back here?

Tiger Lily looked around. "Is there anyone else?"

The young man was covered in tears and sand, barely able to lift his head. "Just me. I'm the only one who can get off the ship. No one knows why."

Past Tinker Bell and Tiger Lily exchanged a look.

The scene blurred, and suddenly Tinker Bell was back at the Wanderers Cay.

"Is this wolf's violet? I didn't know it could grow into so many colors." The young pirate was now sitting on a hammock, a cup of mugwort tea in his hand, admiring the blooms dotting the cave wall. His shoulders seemed relaxed, the coloring on his cheeks returned.

Tink watched as each of her friends welcomed their visitor—Mimic's warm smile, Blair's flicking tail, Tiger Lily's encouraging gaze, pausing on her past self, perched on a ledge.

Ash whistled. "Wolf's violet indeed! You know your stuff, Caiman."

Caiman. Right. She tried to wave, but her arm and wing protested in pain.

Meanwhile, Caiman stared blankly at Ash's hovering form. Of course. This was before he'd learned to understand the fairy language. Sure enough, Tiger Lily jumped in to translate.

"My mum was a botanist," Caiman said softly, his eyes misting again.

Tinker Bell adjusted her position on the cave floor, mindful of her sore arm, her pounding head. But as Caiman described his mother's nomadic life on the Mainland, Tink got swept up. She glanced up to find her past self equally enraptured. She'd almost forgotten this story.

"What was her name?" Blair asked, resting her head on her hands in the pool's shallow end. "What was she like?"

Yeah, what was she like? Tink echoed, but the words wouldn't leave her lips. She appeared to be a phantom in the old scene.

Oblivious, Caiman smiled softly. "Mariana. And she was kind but firm. So many times, scientists and professors and farmers would try to shoo her away, not believing this single woman—with a child at that—would have anything to contribute to 'their world.' But she never took no for an answer. And when they saw her collection, her notes, more often than not, they changed their minds. Asked her questions. Hired her for special projects."

"Wow." Tink watched as her past self was noticeably impressed.

Mariana's life's work included a traveling atrium containing seeds and noting variations in species in every place they could get passage to. One day, she would write a book. Her ultimate goal was to share the science and magic of the natural world, the incredible things flora could do if one knew where to look.

Soon the botanist's reputation preceded her. Sometimes the work called mother and son to a university to help with some particular research, or a hospital to assist with new tonics. In fact, their trouble had started when they'd been asked to provide healing tinctures to a seaside hamlet where many of the denizens had been infected by a mysterious disease.

"That was the beginning of the end." Caiman shuddered. For by the time he and Mariana arrived, the rapidly spreading illness had overtaken the village. A plague—and a highly contagious one at that. To hear Caiman tell it, the place was a town of horrors, all death and overturned furniture from the looters who hadn't waited for the last of the bodies to turn cold.

"The Mainland sounds bloody awful," Blair put in.

"Well . . ." Past Tink chimed in.

Not all of it, Tink thought.

"How awful for you," Tiger Lily said, putting a hand on Caiman's arm.

Mimic refreshed Caiman's tea before gently prodding. "And how did you come to reside on the *Jolly Roger*?"

Caiman took a deep breath, then continued his tale. When it was clear there was nothing for them at the hamlet, mother and son had fled to the docks, searching for a way out. They'd be turned away again and again, until Caiman suggested they hide in the last rugged ship's stores.

"Biggest mistake of my life." Caiman's lip trembled. It was only a short time later that they'd realized the two of them had already been infected by the hamlet's plague. They grew violently ill on the high seas, giving away their hiding spot. The crew had come to take them straight to the captain's quarters. And that was when they'd realized the ship they'd snuck onto belonged to the infamous Captain Bartholomew.

"Strangely, he seemed fascinated by Mum's atrium," Caiman said. "He agreed not to throw us overboard, to allow us to be quarantined in the brig if we vowed to become part of his crew, to use my mother's work for his benefit. Somehow he knew there was a chance our condition would improve. Lo and behold, the minute we entered Never Land's waters, I could feel my body healing. . . ." He looked around at the captive audience. "The island saved me."

Tinker Bell nodded. This made sense. Never Land was so powerful. Its effect on Mainlanders clearly worked in mysterious ways.

But wait—what was the other part of the story? The missing piece. Caiman had been saved. She peered at the pirate's welling eyes.

Yes. It was Caiman's mother who had not fared so lucky.

It was his mother's life's work he refused to leave. Guilt tying him to that awful ship. Bruising him as much as the pirates' hands. Tink hadn't known Mariana, of course, but she couldn't imagine the woman would want this for her son.

Oh, Caiman, why couldn't you let—but the question vanished as Tink watched the cave walls waffle, then fall open.

A gull's shriek and sharp wind affronted her senses. She gripped onto the wet rag in her hand. Was she? Yes, it seemed Tinker Bell was now aboard the *Jolly Roger*, scrubbing the plank. Now this certainly wasn't a memory. How had she gotten here?

"A little more elbow grease if you please, Miss Bell." The pirate captain leered over her, spittle from his mustache dropping dangerously close to her wing.

"I wonder if we have more of those tomato poufs in the cabin," Mr. Smee chimed in. "I'll go find some."

"That won't be necessary, Smee," the captain replied. "Miss Bell is almost finished, and then she'll be on special assignment for me. She loves the Mainland, you see." He turned, then lowered himself to her level. "Don't you, Fairy? She's just going to lend me a bit of her dust, and then—"

"Noooo!" Tinker Bell yelled, finally able to get the word out, elongating her protest—until she was flung backward. She zoomed toward the Rock—the giant, freestanding cove not far from the ship. But she didn't slow.

Flashes of cave then blue sky and green foliage raced by. Tinker Bell felt herself thrown into a jangle of twigs. Was she . . . ? Yes, yes, she was. Tinker Bell was sitting in a giant nest.

Tink felt a flash of frustration. This was getting ridiculous.

"DARK FORCES! NEVER LAND IN DANGER! WHY ARE YOU SLEEPING, FAIRY?" a Never Fowl screeched, its giant beak jabbing at Tink's head painfully.

"I'm not—I wasn't—" Tink protested. She threw her hands over her head.

"DON'T TURN YOUR BACK!"

"That's not what I'm . . ." But the pain and confusion, it was all too much. She'd had enough of this nonsense. She wanted it to go away. She wanted to be back on the Mainland. But mostly, Tink wanted to sleep.

And then, as if in answer to her silent plea, everything went black.

ELEVEN

Ouch. Tink opened her eyes a smidge, then closed them. The light was so bright. Her head started to throb, which made the pain everywhere else in her body even worse. Why was it so unbearably hot? And cold? Tink couldn't find the energy to open her eyes again. She let out a sneeze and could feel the pixie dust being lost because of it.

"What is that thing?" she heard a small voice say. "And is it glowing?"

"Blimey, it is glowing! It's a lightning bug."

A Mainlander hand reached down and grabbed Tink, placing her in their palm. She was too weak to protest. She could barely lift her head.

At least she knew she was out of that nightmare. She'd reached the Mainland all right. This all felt too painfully real.

A finger prodded her middle. "That ain't a bug."

Do you mind? Tinker Bell shifted. If she'd felt even a teensy bit stronger, she would have bit the Mainlander's finger. Instead, her head felt like it was pounding as hard as her wing and injured arm.

"It is too a bug! What else could it be?"

How dare you, she tried to cry out.

"Can I see? Let me see!" another small voice said.

There were so many voices talking at once, she couldn't focus. Tink fought to open her eyes. She was being cradled by someone in the palm of their hand and a group of children surrounded her, breathing close like Ash always did. They were all boys of various shapes and sizes, but up close she could see their faces gaunt and sickly, like those she'd seen on the street. She felt a pang of distress at the sight of them, but none of them looked as unhappy as the children she'd seen outside. Even if they were dressed strangely. Tink squinted. *Very* strangely. Had she knocked herself unconscious? Or were these children wearing animal costumes?

"Why does it look like a girl?"

"Just squash it already," said another.

No! she yelled, trying to sit up, but the pain was too much. She fell back down again.

"You codfish!" said another voice, louder than the rest. "Don't you realize what you got there? Give her to me!" A new hand appeared, grabbing her and placing her in another Mainlander palm. "You're all right," said the figure softly, his face looming over hers as he peered at her. "I won't let them hurt you."

Tink blinked up at the face, curious in her haze. This boy had bright red hair. He wore a shirt that was clearly too small for him, and his hair stuck out at odd angles, his face angular, dark circles under his eyes, that were dark with tiny flecks of green.

"She ain't no bug," he told the others. "She's a fairy."

Finally! she thought with annoyance.

A few boys started to laugh.

"Pfft! No such thing as fairies." A few of the other voices sounded their agreement and Tink felt her spirits plummet. An overwhelming sadness seemed to permeate every inch of her. If anything, she suddenly felt sicker. What was wrong with this place?

"Fairies are real, I tell ya!" her defender shouted again. "She's wearing clothes! See her dress? She's a girl fairy."

"She *does* look like a girl," said one of the other voices.

"'Cause she is one," he boasted. "I know. I met a fairy once. When I was a baby."

"How could you remember if you was a baby?"

"I'm smart, that's why," said the boy.

She watched as he puffed out his scrawny chest, and Tink peered at his eyes again. Were they sort of familiar?

"Everyone knows fairies are real. They're magic."

"If she's magic, maybe she can grant us wishes like a genie!" said another voice. "Give her to me!"

"No! Give her to me!"

A commotion started again, each boy calling out what they wanted and Tink panicked as the boy's palm began to be jostled as other Mainlander children tried to reach her. She attempted to fight through the pain and stand, but she collapsed again, clinging to the palm for fear of being thrown off and trampled.

"I want a pony!"

"Make me rich!"

"I want a fat, juicy steak!"

"Let go!" said her defender, turning fast and almost knocking her off his palm. He tried to cup his hands together now to protect her, but all it did was bang her around, her wing firing in agony. "Stop it! You're going to hurt her!"

"BOYS!" came that familiar ringing voice, much louder to the rest. "What are you doing?"

It was the inventor!

"So-sorry. Sorry. Sorry" came a chorus of voices, everyone backing away now.

"I want you all back in bed or I'll tell Nurse Beth you need an extra helping of castor oil," the human tinkerer said.

There was a pounding of feet as children went scattering in all directions, hopping and jumping into their beds. All but the boy holding her.

The taller figure in the white shirt appeared and towered over them. Tink heard him clear his throat. "That's enough now, Peter."

Peter? Tink knew that name.

I met a fairy once when I was a baby.

She turned and looked up at the boy who'd protected her, the one with the familiar eyes and red hair. *It can't be the same child, from Kensington Gardens, can it? That's impossible! And yet . . .* Had fate brought her to this hospital? Magic? Tink wasn't sure, but there was something uncanny about the way Peter looked at her, the confident way he lifted his chin. He'd grown from wee babe to scrawny child, making Tinker Bell wonder once more how differently time passed here. No wonder the Mainlanders used those clock devices. How else would they keep track?

"I saved her," Peter was saying. "And I'm keeping her." Despite the fire in his voice and manner, he looked so pale and sickly. What had happened to him? Where was his mother? Was she the woman who had lost sight of his pram? How had he wound up here?

"Hey, why should he get all the wishes?" one of the boys started again.

Tink and the older boy standing in shadows sighed at the same time.

"No one is keeping anything," the older boy said, his deep voice sounding agitated. The others quieted. "Give this, erm . . . specimen . . . to me, Peter, so I can get a good look at what we have here."

Peter hesitated. "You aren't going to hurt her, are you?"

"No," said the other boy. "I promise. Now hand it over." Tink strained her neck to try to get a closer look at this kind tinkering Mainlander as Peter gently transferred her from his palm to the other boy's. His dark hair framed his face, perfectly complementing his distinctive nose and strong jaw. Tink inhaled sharply, breathing in the scent of honeysuckle. The smell reminded her of home.

Home. She startled. There was something important she was forgetting. Something about Never Land. Something she was meant to be doing.

She could feel the thought in the corner of her mind, just out of reach, beyond the pounding of her head. Was it in her dream? Tink grasped at the wisps of dancing images to no avail. The nightmare that had haunted her was slipping away and now she couldn't even remember what the dream was about. It had felt important and yet she couldn't remember what it was about. She slumped down once more in his palm, exhausted.

"What— How— Terribly sorry— Are you all righ—" the young man stuttered. He moved his palm, then quickly stiffened when he saw Tinker Bell wince. "Why, you look like a tiny human!" he said in a strained, high voice, losing all sense of his former composure. It would've been funny if Tink didn't feel so unwell.

"'Cause she is one. A fairy," Peter told him matter-of-factly.

"But no. You're a *fairy*?" he said. "How can this be real?" he whispered, almost to himself.

"Of course fairies are real," Peter said, offended. "Everyone knows that."

"There has to be an explanation—perhaps the cheese we had earlier went bad. And this is a reaction of some sort."

"And we're all having the *same* reaction?" The boy called Slightly had come closer.

The inventor reddened. "Right. Well maybe—" He shifted his hand, making Tinker Bell tumble on her bad wing. A dozen stars peppered her vision, and she swayed.

"Oh, I'm so sorry. Hey, are you all right? You're injured." He righted his hand, gently setting her on one of the boys' giant pillows. The soft landing made Tink want to cry.

"I could've told you that," Peter said. "That's why she hasn't been flying this whole time. See how her wing is bent? I think it's broken."

Broken! No! Tink needed her wing to work so she could . . . so she could . . . what exactly?

"You can help her, can't ya?" Nibs pleaded. "You have to help her. That's what you do."

Please? Tink tried to lift her head but was too dizzy.

"I'm going to try. Let me take a look at her, all right?" The tinkerer's face was so close to her now, she wanted to reach out and touch the dimple on the right side of his mouth.

Thank you, Tink murmured. A wave of exhaustion threatened to overcome her. She fought to stay awake.

Peter brought his head in closer. "You hear those tinkling sounds? I think she's trying to talk to us."

The older boy leaned in, too, and she breathed in his scent. "I do hear that." His expression was pure awe.

"See? Fairy," Peter said triumphantly.

"She certainly looks like no one I've ever seen before," the older boy said, his eyes so close to her now that she could count his thick lashes if she wanted to. They were beautiful.

There was a creaking sound and suddenly she heard heavy footsteps. "Boys? What are you doing out of bed?"

"Nurse Beth," Peter whispered.

Peter and the older boy glanced at each other. Without a word, Peter took off running. The older boy moved to block Tink. "Hello, Nurse Beth," he said pleasantly. "Just getting the boys some exercise before bed. For good health."

"I didn't see you there." Her voice brightened. "How are you, dear?"

Deer? Like the animal? Is that his name? Tink wondered. It was equally silly and charming. Somehow, it fit with the serious sort of tenderness he'd shown the boys. She tried the name on for size. *Deer*, she jingled.

"I suppose a stretch is fine. Just don't overexert them," Nurse Beth warned.

Tink tried to turn her head to see the woman around Deer's back. She was dressed in white, too, like Deer.

Ironically, given Deer's name, he was the only one not dressed like an animal. He didn't even seem to be in bed clothes. In addition to his smart white shirt, there seemed to be straps that attached his pants to his shirt, looping over his shoulders. His shoes were polished to a sheen, but showed their wear, and his dark hair was combed and shined, even if a few wayward curls were starting to spring up.

"I'll be back to take their temperatures in a bit."

There was a collective groan.

"Thank you, Nurse Beth," said Deer. "I'll make sure they don't get too riled up."

Tink heard the door to the room close again. The inventor let out a sigh of relief. "She's gone, boys."

Peter sat up fast. "Is the fairy all right? Did she fly off?"

"Take a breath, Peter," said Deer as he slowly pulled his hand from his back and held his palm out. He looked down at her. "She's still here. Why don't you all busy yourselves with some games in bed while we wait for Nurse Beth to return and I'll attend to our newest patient?"

"She's a bug!"

"She's not a bug!" Peter roared.

Not this again, Tink thought, aggravation competing with her pain.

"Boys! Please!" Deer shouted, sounding frustrated. "I can't concentrate. A little less noise, if you don't mind."

"Sorry," they all said, quieting once more.

Finally, Tink said with a sigh. She couldn't hear herself think.

The handsome tinkerer sighed and lifted his palm up to eye level to look at her.

Tink felt a flash of embarrassment. She wished they could be talking about the pulley system. About the hospital. About . . . what she had come there to do. Which was—? Tink couldn't remember. In any case, for some reason she hated that this particular Mainlander was seeing her at her worst.

"Could Peter be right?" he whispered to her, his expression curious. "Are you truly a fairy? But that's impossible. . . ."

Impossible, huh? she jingled, even though she knew he couldn't understand. She could tell he was examining the glowing dust surrounding her wings.

"Just a problem to be solved!" Peter sang out.

"Right," Deer said, letting out a small, awed chuckle. Tinker Bell's wings fluttered, and instantly regretting the movement, she clutched her right arm.

The young man frowned. "Oh no. Let me see. Do you mind if I . . ."

Tink followed his gaze to her injured wing. She nodded.

Gently, with his other hand, he touched the bent edge. She winced. "Terribly sorry," he apologized. "Are you all right? I didn't mean to hurt you."

I know, she jingled, trying to smile through the pain.

"Right," Deer said, his brow furrowed, and he seemed to be in work mode. "I bet I could fasten a small sling," he said, pursing his full lips. "Maybe with a toothpick and perhaps a small piece of cloth. I need some thread. Yes, I think that might help. A sling and some rest. We can make you a safe spot to heal and then maybe you can tell us who you are and what you're doing here." He stared at her perhaps a moment longer than he needed to. "Remarkable."

Tinker Bell felt like she was glowing. *You think I'm remarkable?* She thought of this young man, so eager to tend to the children. So eager to help her. *Well, so are you.* Without thinking, she reached up, her finger grazing his cheek.

He looked surprised. Quickly, she pulled her hand away. What was she doing?

"Don't worry. I'm going to make sure you're right as rain." He smiled back at her, and she felt a warmth spread from her fingers to her toes. "You're safe here."

And for some reason, Tink believed him. They stared at each other again, unable to look away, his brown eyes as lovely as his namesake. As gently as though he were holding a precious egg, he carried her over to a table near a strange metal-looking item. It had a large grate on the front that was burning bright inside like a fire. Using his free hand, she watched him grab what looked like dandelions and place a group of them on top of a small piece of cloth on the table. Was he making her a nest? As she started to drift off, she felt him gently lift her off his palm and place her on top. She rolled onto her injured wing and jingled in pain.

"I'm sorry." He gently turned her on her left side.

That's better, she jingled, happy to have the pressure off her wing. She felt him moving his hands and saw him picking up and putting down a few things. He had a silver piece in his hand with string attached to it and appeared to be sewing something.

You sew, too? she jingled, or maybe she just said it in her head. She tried to stay awake to watch him, but as the fire roared, the children chattered, and the rain continued to patter against the glass, Tinker Bell could only focus on Deer's face. She did that till she could no longer keep her eyes open. And then she fell fast asleep.

TWELVE

When Tinker Bell awoke, the world was dark.

For a moment, she thought she was next to the Never Sea, the sound of waves lulling her to sleep.

Her first indication that she wasn't home was that waves seemed to be emanating tiny clicking sounds, along with the whispers of someone talking to themself.

Tink sat up, her body aching at the movement, but fairy be, thankfully not throbbing with pain like it had earlier. She went to stretch her arms and stopped. Her right arm was bandaged in a small piece of cloth that went over her shoulder and wrapped around her right wing making it immobile. Panic rose inside her as she tried to move her wing and realized only her left one could flap. She attempted to take to the air, only to feel herself pulled back down to the ground again. Pixie dust sparkled in her wake. What had happened to her?

"You're up!" In the darkness, she saw a face reflecting in the moonlight and recognized Deer.

I can't move, she jingled, her emotions spinning as she tried in vain to get up off the ground. She'd fly with one wing for a moment, then crash down again.

"Don't. You'll hurt yourself," he whispered. "Relax and just breathe."

Just breathe.

Ash.

She needed to get back to Never Land! But first she needed to . . . Tinker Bell frowned, straining to remember why she came to the Mainland. Flashes came back to her in snippets. Flying to the Mainland, hitting her head. The boys, Peter. Deer's face was outlined in the shadows as he reached down and held his pointer finger out to her.

"Your wing will be all right," he said softly. "It appears you sprained it, which is why I made the sling. The less you try to move it, the quicker it will heal."

Tink tried to take a few deep breaths to calm down. Warily, she reached out her right hand and pressed it to his finger pad. His hand was warm. She felt her breathing slow. *Sorry,* she tried to signal. *Seeing the bandage on my wing frightened me.*

Deer smiled. "I'm sure the bandage frightened you," he said, reading her thoughts correctly. "Peter wanted to write you a note explaining what happened but got tired and drew you a picture instead."

Deer held up a small lantern with a flame that cast a glow over the surface she was standing on. With light, she realized she was standing on a soft material that reminded her of cotton with dandelion flowers acting as the bottom layer. The cotton had been made into a ball that resembled a bed, and beside it, someone had overturned a thimble for her to use as a tiny table. A small crust of bread had been placed on top. As the flame flickered on her surroundings, Tink saw a small structure made out of wood squares with letters on it.

"Those are blocks," Deer said as she stared at the walls. "Blocks are . . . uh, children's play things."

She spotted Peter's drawing and lit up inside and out. Sure, the wings were too large, and he didn't capture her dress right, but Peter had written something underneath: *You will fly again, fairy!* How sweet. She smiled up at Deer. *Thank you.* She still felt like she was missing something important, but her head retained its dull ache and it was hard to think straight. She tapped the lantern. It looked like one she'd seen recently . . . where was that again? Two hazy figures appeared in her mind, then disappeared just as quickly.

Deer nodded. "Sorry it's so dark. I do most of my work at night on the floors of the hospital. I'm an orderly," he explained.

She must have made a face to show her confusion because he went on.

"It means I clean the hospital." He looked around for something then held up a broom and a bucket. "That's my job . . . for now, but I've gotten so good at it, most of the time I spend in here with the boys." He looked out at the dark room. "Nurse Beth doesn't mind. This was the same room I was in when—" He trailed off. "When I'm done with work, my mind is too busy to sleep so I keep busy making things for the boys."

Aha! Tinker Bell felt a jolt of triumph. So he *was* a fellow tinkerer. When he wasn't minding the hospital or caring for the children.

"Truthfully, I don't mind working through the night. I like the silence. Some days those boys can be a little exhausting," he added with a wry grin.

Yes, I can see that, Tink said, nodding and chuckling. *They're a lot.*

"They can be a lot," Deer said simultaneously, looking over at the beds in the darkness, the sound of the children's snores and breathing suddenly coming into sharp focus now. Tink smiled, but Deer's face clouded. "They've been through so much between the war, losing their families. Being so ill." His voice petered out and she could feel the sadness in it. It made her long to want to press her hand to his cheek again.

Tink took a step toward Deer and banged her foot against something hard. *Blast!* The object spun for a moment, then clanged down on the surface. Thankfully, the noise wasn't loud enough to wake anyone.

"Sorry," Deer said, picking up what appeared to be a tiny wooden wheel. "When I told the boys you wouldn't be able to fly for a few days, they wanted to give you your own carriage to get around." He picked up what looked like a tiny toy wagon and showed it to her.

They both grinned at the same time.

"The only toy they could find for your size has a broken wheel. They couldn't figure out how to fix it before they went to bed so I've been working on it."

Fix. That was something she could do. In the relative darkness of the lantern, Tink looked around the table for something she could use. Undecided, she picked up the wheel Deer had just shown her and looked at it from all angles. They needed to find something that could act like a pulley, both holding the wheel in place on the wagon and allowing it to rotate.

Then she spotted a small piece of what she assumed was rope, already tied in a circle. She picked it up and felt the material. It stretched and pulled but didn't come apart. This might work nicely. *I wonder if it has a name.*

"That's a rubber band," James explained. "We use it to tie things together. I use it for all sorts of things myself."

Tink took the rubber band and held it next to the wheel, her aching mind searching for a solution. She saw a small round ball with pins sticking out of it. She pointed to them as well.

"Sewing pins," he said, understanding her with ease.

May I? she jingled, pulling a pin out of the ball.

"You want one? Be my guest," said Deer, watching her.

It took a few moments, but using the pin and the rubber band, Tink managed to reattach the wheel and hold the wagon together. Then she stepped inside, and Deer gave it a small push. It worked! She felt like a queen being rolled around.

"Hey, you fixed it," Deer said, marveling at her. "So quickly, too. Do you— I don't suppose you enjoy doing this sort of thing? Making things? Repairing them?"

Tinker Bell couldn't help but roll her eyes. *What an understatement.* To her surprise, Deer laughed. "Stupid question, I see. Well, I've got a bit of a makeshift workshop here. Want to see my latest project?"

Tink nodded, intrigued. She went to jump up and fly again, forgetting she couldn't. Tink landed hard on her side. Humiliation made her face warm.

"Oh dear." He frowned, his face flickering with shadows. "Are you all right?"

Why was he calling her *deer*? Now she was really confused. Not to mention mortified. Tink nodded and stepped out of the wagon with her chin held high, trying not to appear rattled. She walked over to the other side of the table where Deer had taken a seat. That's when she noticed the large black metal item sitting on the table in front of him.

"It's the hospital's property, but Nurse Beth lets me use it at night for all my sewing."

So he did make clothes! Tink frowned. Was she mistaken, or did Deer look embarrassed about this?

"Not that I'm ashamed to sew," he added hastily.

I make garments, too! she jingled, and motioned to her leaf dress. It was looking a little worse for wear and she knew she'd have to get ahold of some leaves soon to make a new one. Still, she spun around proudly, showing off her work.

"I think you're saying you made that dress, yes?" He leaned in closer to see it. "Great craftsmanship," he said. "Is that a leaf?" She nodded again. "Impressive. The dress-up clothes you saw the boys in are my latest bit of work. And they seem to be a hit; boys won't take them off." He chuckled. "They love running around like animals, so they were halfway there already."

That explained their strange dress! Tink pointed at the basket of thread on the table. *Do you make other clothes?*

"They're constantly tearing things so I'm always mending at night. I sew as a hobby, for the boys' costumes and such, but I think tailoring is a noble profession. My dad was a tailor. And sometimes I wonder if I would have taken after him had, well . . ." He looked away and she saw him swallow hard.

"Maybe in a different life, I suppose." Deer looked at her again. "I lost my parents when I was a boy. No bigger than Nibs."

Oh. If she could, Tink would have flown to his face and pressed a hand to the worry lines that had appeared next to those warm eyes.

"Both suffered scarlet fever. They didn't recover, but me . . . the nurses say I'm a survivor," he went on, tapping his fingers on the table. "Maybe that's why they kept me here."

Tink's heart gave a lurch. *I'm a survivor.* Why did that sound so familiar? Why did she feel like she'd said those very words herself not long ago? Deer spoke them with such determination, with such passion, as though willing it to be true. It was enrapturing.

"I was here so long they eventually turned the orderly's closet into a room for me," Deer went on. "Gave me a place to live, and a job, which is all well and good, but the thing is . . ."

He paused, as though this was the heart of the matter. Tinker Bell took another step toward him.

"Well, I just wonder. How long can I stay? There is a war going on, and more mouths to feed than food, more illness everywhere." He ran a hand through his dark head of hair. "I lie awake at night, the questions coming fast, wondering how I will earn my keep. What I'll be able to do out there, how I can rise above my station. And how I'll be able to help the lost boys here when I go." He motioned to the room.

Tink glanced back at the sleeping boys in the beds. So that's why they were here? They were sick? How sick? Was Peter ill? Would his body recover like her wing? She wanted so many answers the thoughts hurt her head. Deer sounded so much like her—the constant thoughts she couldn't silence, the many things she wanted to do, understand, see.

"I don't know why I'm burdening you with all this," Deer added, his eyes cast downward, allowing her to look at his lashes once more. "I guess it's because I don't have many people to confide in." His eyes found hers. "And you, being, well, you—this extraordinary visitor—I feel like you're someone I might be able to share my secrets with. If that's all right?"

I want to share my secrets with you, too, she jingled, feeling her own heart beating. *I just wish I remembered what they were.* She couldn't help but be frustrated at her head, which seemed to have locked some of her memories away.

"I'm rambling, aren't I?" Deer shook his head.

A beam of light crept along the table. Outside the big glass walls of the building, Tink could see dawn approaching, the sky starting to turn from blue to orange and yellow. It was one of her favorite moments of the day; it was the one time her brain quieted.

Deer turned to the window now too. "Sunrise. This is my favorite time of day, you know. Getting up before the boys, looking out at the world and seeing how beautifully calm it can be. It's the one time my thoughts are quiet."

She felt the hairs on her arms stand on end.

"My apologies. The boys will be awake before we know it and then I will have to put this table safely away. Would you like to see how it works?" He motioned to the machine on the table again and she nodded. The machine appeared to be on a metal base that was attached to the table. A piece of cloth was tucked under an arm that had a needle, much like the one she just used on the wagon. "I'm tinkering with an invention for this sewing machine. It'd be an addition that every manufacturer would want to use."

A plume of pixie dust sparkled out around her. *I'm a tinkerer, too!* She waved her one good arm and nodded. It was mad how much she and this Mainlander had in common.

"You fixed that wagon so easily; I wonder if maybe you'd be willing to help me with this?" He bit his lip, his quiet confidence seeming to wane for the first time. "I know I have a brilliant idea, but I don't know how to bring it all together. Yet!" He sounded excited now. "If I can make this work, I think it could be big in the world of clothing and tailoring. And then I could have it patented, and I'd be rich enough to leave this place, and find a home for me and the boys and actually make a better life for us. There are possibilities in this new age with the right idea, possibilities for change . . . but I'm getting ahead of myself." He shook his head and grinned a smile that made Tink's heart flutter. "Let me explain."

Tink sat down on the thimble nearby and watched him.

"The hospital doesn't own a sewing machine that is electrical. They do exist but are quite expensive so ours is the standard type, operated with the treadle." She pinched her nose and he smiled shyly. "A treadle is what you press your foot on—a lever under the table, that powers the machine. Like so."

He demonstrated and she heard that clicking noise again. She also noticed the thread on the needle was working its way across the fabric, stitching. Tink marveled. These Mainlanders really did make their own kind of magic.

"Now working at night, like I do, is hard with only the light of the lantern to see with. Sometimes I can't even see the needle to thread the machine!" His eyes were aglow now in the flicker of the lantern's flames. "So I thought, what if there was a way to make an attachment on the machine that provided the perfect amount of gas lighting right over the needle, so you could see to thread it. Even in the dark."

She clapped her hands. She wasn't sure she exactly understood, but it did sound like a practical solution.

"You like the idea?" He lit up. "Oh, I hoped you would! It's smart, right? I think the Singer company would buy it. Especially because it would be powered by the treadle itself. So, when you pump your foot on the pedal, you're also lighting up the machine. No unnecessary parts." He frowned. "If I can figure out how to make it work though. . . . I know I'm close. I just need to find a way to do it and get it to the patent office before someone else thinks of the idea first." His face fell again—so much like hers—highs and lows coming so quickly. "Of course, I've been working on this for so long, and everything I've tried is a disaster."

Tink stood again, walking around the machine, looking from the lantern on the table to the machine. She stepped under it where the needle dangled down dangerously like stalactites in a cave. How could they get a light in there? *Hmmm . . .*

The sound of coughing startled them both. Deer jumped up quickly and rushed over to the child in the middle of the attack. Tink longed to fly after him and help, but she remembered very quickly (trying to fly and failing again) that she couldn't yet. *Blasted wing!*

"It's all right, Peter," Deer said in hushed tones. "Have some water and just try to breathe. Just breathe."

There was that phrase again. She knew it. . . . Ash said it . . . and there was a reason. She'd come from Never Land because . . .

Peter sat up fast, gulping like a fish out of water. "Where is she? Is the fairy all right? Did she survive the night? Did you fix her?"

"Shhh . . ." Deer said, just a hint of annoyance in his voice that he quickly pushed away. "Don't wake the others yet or I'll have to—" He sighed. "Never mind. I suppose we're done for tonight. Get out of bed—slippers first, please—and follow me. She's over here and she loves the picture you drew."

"I knew she would," Peter said with a yawn. "I'm the best drawer in Room Fourteen." The minute he saw her, his whole face lit up. "Look at your sling! Are you all right? You have to be. Don't let your light go out."

I'm fine, Tink assured him, warming to his sweetness. Even still, she saw him frown.

"Something isn't right though, is it?" Peter asked, and it was almost as if she could see his mind working. "If you're going to be a patient in Room Fourteen like the rest of us—and not an enemy of the Lost Orphan Boys—then there's something we *must* know. Straight away. Before we go any further. Before we can welcome you into the fold."

Tink frowned. Did these boys have enemies?

But then Peter's expression broke into a sly smile. "We've got to learn your name."

THIRTEEN

TINK ROLLED HER EYES AT PETER'S THEATRICS, BUT SHE HAD TO ADMIT, HE had a point. It would be much easier if they knew what to call her besides *fairy*. Tink used her left hand—her only useful hand at the moment, she needed to keep reminding herself—to rub her chin. *How do I describe my name?*

Deer and Peter were watching her closely.

"That jingle. Did she just tell you something?" Deer asked Peter.

"She's thinking, all right? Trying to figure out how to tell us."

"How do you know that?" Deer looked at the boy incredulously.

"I just do somehow. I can't quite understand the jingles, but I still know what she's saying." Peter shrugged, his nightshirt hanging on his thin frame.

Was he always this thin? Or was this because he was ill? He seemed to have a lot of energy, at least.

"But how do we even know she has a name?" Deer asked.

Oh, come on. Tink put her good hand on her hip. Just when she'd thought he was so intuitive.

For his part, Deer looked properly chastised. "I'm terribly sorry. Of course you have a name. Everyone does."

Tink lowered her arm. *Thank you,* she sniffed.

"I wish I could understand you," Deer said almost in a whisper.

She looked at him longingly. *I wish you could, too.*

"I'll help," Peter told him. A ray of light through the glass shone on his face. With morning here, the whole room brightened, and she heard the boys stirring in their beds.

"Come on, fellas! We're figuring out her name."

"Whose name?" A boy in a bear suit climbed out of bed and lumbered over to the others, still yawning as children began climbing out of bed. Their heavy footsteps made the table Tink was on shake. She tried to keep her balance.

"Slowly, Cubby . . . Slowly . . . you don't want to knock her off the table," Deer reminded him.

"Sorry," said the little bear.

"Whatcha doing?" called one of the other boys.

"Is the fairy still here?" said another.

"She's here!" Cubby yelled. "We're giving her a name!"

Boys all around the room came running.

"We aren't giving her a name! She *has* a name," Peter said crossly. He folded his arms over his chest and huffed, staring up at Deer to correct the others.

Tink put a hand on Peter's arm since he was next to the table. *It's all right,* she jingled. *No harm done.*

"I'd know your name by now if they'd all go away!"

Peter! Tink scolded. *Be kind.*

"Now, Peter, practice some patience, would you?" Deer said, sounding exasperated as the boys all crowded around the table talking a mile a minute. Deer looked apologetically at Tink as the boys kept yammering. "Will you excuse me while I put away the sewing machine? I don't want it getting damaged."

Tink felt her left wing droop. Her right wing felt like a phantom limb. She nodded. She'd been looking forward to taking a look at the inner workings of the machine. She already had a million ideas on how to attach that light Deer had dreamed up. She couldn't wait to try them out.

And if she were being honest, she liked talking to Deer in the quiet of the night when it was just the two of them. Even though they didn't speak the same language, she'd felt like they could understand each other.

"Maybe we can continue to work on it this evening? When the boys are asleep?" Deer suggested over all the shouting.

Tink's body tingled. She nodded effusively. *Yes, I'd like that. Tonight.*

"Everybody, quiet!" Peter whistled loudly to get the boys' attention and when that didn't work, she watched him pick up a small instrument and ring it.

Tink gasped. *That's it!* she said excitedly, pointing to the small golden bell. A vaguely gruff voice interrupted her thoughts: *She sounds like bells. What you want, fairy?*

She shivered. Who had said those words to her? Why did she remember them? Again, that sense that she was missing something terribly important nagged at her.

"Peter." Deer crossed the room in two long strides and took the instrument from him. "This is Nurse Beth's bell. Did you take it?"

"Maybe." Peter wouldn't look at him. "It's a good way to get people's attention when you need things."

Tink and Deer sighed at the same time. They exchanged a look. Tink tried not to laugh. *He's got a point.*

"Nevertheless, it's not yours. We will have to give it back," Deer told him.

Well, don't give it back yet. Tink pointed at the bell again. *That's my name.*

The boy in the fox costume nudged the boy next to him. "I think she's saying something," he squeaked. "Look!"

But everyone was talking over one another again.

"What did you say, Slightly?" asked Deer, his voice being drowned out by a child in a skunk costume tooting a tiny horn.

Peter, Cubby, Slightly, and this tiny skunk gathered closer.

"Tootles, don't blow that horn in my ear," Deer tried again.

Tink gestured to the bell in Deer's hand. *My name is Tinker Bell!*

"Look! I think she's saying something!" Slightly tried again.

"Quiet!" Peter yelled. "I can only understand her if I hear her jingles."

"You're mad," said two identical boys dressed as raccoons.

Ignoring them, Peter leaned down to the table again. "What's your name?"

Tinker Bell, she tried.

Peter wrinkled his nose. "Total bell?"

No, no, no. She shook her head. *Tinker Bell!* She pointed to the bell in Deer's hand again.

"I got the bell part, am I right?" Peter asked. She nodded. "But the first part—it's a T word?"

Yes, she jingled.

"Towerbell?" tried the one dressed like a rabbit who was nibbling on a pencil. *(Nibs*, Tinker Bell recalled.)

"Who would be named Towerbell?" Peter asked wryly.

"It was worth a shot!"

"Tapbell?" guessed Slightly.

"Clarabelle?" said one of the raccoons.

Tink shook her head again and again and kept pointing, unsure how to explain herself. Then she had an idea. She rushed over to the small driverless wagon she'd fixed for Deer and pointed to it again.

"Someone fixed the automobile!" Cubby exclaimed.

Deer nodded to Tink. "She did. She likes to tinker, like I do."

Tinker! Tinker! Tink jumped up and down now. Her injured wing twinged with the sudden movement.

"Tinker . . ." Deer started.

Tink collapsed on the thimble nearby. *Yes! Yes!* This was exhausting.

"Your name is Bell. Tinker . . . Bell?" Peter tried again. She nodded some more. "Tinker Bell!"

"Tinker Bell." The other boys tried the name on for size.

Finally! she thought, relieved. It was so much nicer to be introduced properly.

"Boys, line up, introduce yourselves properly, too," Deer prodded, and they did as they were told. She already knew Peter, Cubby, Nibs, Slightly, the one who she would refer to as "Tootles" because of that blasted horn, and the raccoons who apparently were named Marmaduke and Binky. Well, she'd never remember those names. She'd just refer to them as "the twins."

"Did you tell her your name?" Peter asked Deer.

I know it already, Tink jingled. *It's Deer*.

Peter burst out laughing and Tink felt her cheeks flame. "She thinks your name is Deer! Like the animal!" The other boys started laughing, too.

Heat pooled through Tinker Bell. Why was this so amusing? Children really were a different breed. She looked away, clenching her fist as they snickered. The young inventor, however, came around the table, concern etched on his face.

"Boys, you've offended our guest. Apologize at once."

"Sorry," they all said contritely.

Well, at least they sometimes had manners.

"Go get washed up. Nurse Beth will be in soon to take your temperatures," he told them.

There was more groaning as all but Peter floated away to do as they were told.

The young man turned to her. "And *I'm* sorry for not making my own introduction sooner. I'm James. Very pleased to make your acquaintance, Tinker Bell." He bowed slightly, and Tink felt herself blush again. "I can see how you got confused," the young man—James—continued, his voice kind. "Nurse Beth calls me dear quite a bit. Also love. Sometimes darling."

Now it was Tink's turn to laugh. *Darling?*

"What, is that funny?" he asked, a twitch on his lips. "Darling?"

Tinker Bell couldn't help it. She burst into more chortles, laughing so hard her eyes teared. Maybe it was the exhaustion and her injuries. Maybe she was delirious. But suddenly, this whole situation seemed utterly ridiculous and she could understand why the children were so easily amused by this name business.

Peter crowed from the back of the room. "Darling!" The other boys followed suit, calling one another darling and exchanging low bows and curtsies.

"Well now, look what you've started," James said. But his warm eyes were twinkling.

I don't know what you mean, Tink said, trying to compose herself. Then giggled. *Darling.*

FOURTEEN

Now Tink understood why James couldn't tinker with the invention he was working on during the day.

Between his work as an orderly, the time he spent watching over the boys, and the time he stole away to fix and mend things around the hospital, he didn't have a moment to sit down, let alone concentrate on something new.

"Boys," James yelled wearily from his place on a ladder at the window. He'd been cleaning the glass when there was a loud crash.

"Sorry, James!" Peter called over to him. "We're playing war and another building was bombed." Peter took a wooden sword and used it to thwack the twins' tower they were still building.

"Hey!" shouted one.

"We weren't finished with that yet," said the other raccoon.

"Too bad. It's war!" he crowed, holding his sword high before swiping it downward to knock down a third creation—was that a bridge?—that Nibs and Cubby were working on.

"Peter!" they both shouted.

Tootles, the little one dressed as a skunk, started blowing his horn over and over again, huffing as he did so, his small face filled with terror.

"Hey," said Cubby, stuttering slightly as he stood and faced Peter. He was as tall as Peter, if not taller, but Tink could see Peter was the one all the boys deferred to in the room. "You're scaring him." He pointed to Tootles.

"He should be scared. War is scary." Peter swung the sword around, coming dangerously close to hitting Cubby in the head.

Tink's hands flew up. That was enough! First scaring the skunk and now all this needless destruction? She tried zipping off the table, but a searing pain quickly reminded her about her blasted wing. Instead, she started jingling wildly. *Peter, you put down that sword at once!*

Peter looked up in surprise, sword mid-swing. "Aww, I was just playing."

Tink stomped her foot. *I mean it, Peter. Give the sword to James. And let's stop playing this ridiculous game.*

Peter hung his head. "War isn't a game, Tinker Bell. It's real and it's coming," he said ominously, and then he dragged his sword across the room to present to James.

Tink frowned, a memory unlodging itself from the back of her mind. *War on the Horizon.* It had been written on that paper the first day she'd arrived on the Mainland. Tinker Bell touched her head again and willed more memories to present themselves. A flash of her falling. Of James taking care of her. Those made her smile.

Then she saw the boys' frightened faces and remembered to focus on the task at hand. Tinker Bell ran at her small carriage and jumped in, making it zoom across the table. Tootles saw it moving and ran over to grab it, bringing Tink closer to the other boys.

She looked up at them as they stared at her amid the wreckage of their towers and bridges. *All is fine. We're all safe and fine here in the hospital,* she assured them as the twins started coughing. Tink rushed over to a glass of water on the floor (which was not a good place for a glass) and pointed to it. The twins took it and shared it gratefully.

"Thanks, Tinker Bell," they said in unison.

"Tinker Bell, how come Peter can understand you?" Nibs asked as James quietly gave Peter a talking-to.

Tink shrugged. *I don't know.* It was something she was curious about as well.

Cubby pushed up the sleeves on his bear costume, which was showing wear. "Can we learn to understand fairy, too? I want to talk to you."

"So do I," said the twins in unison, the hoods on their dress-up clothes flopping forward and covering their eyes.

Tootles blew his horn in agreement.

Peter clearly heard the commotion and looked over, his mood still foul. "Well, you can't. I'm the only one who can. Tinker Bell likes me best, right?"

She sighed. Any Mainlander boy who can spot a fairy and converse with one was someone she was immediately sweet on. Despite the boy's clear arrogance, she liked his fire. Still, she gave him another hard look. *I am not playing favorites.* Even if she was.

"What did she say?" asked one of the raccoons.

"Tinker Bell said she is not playing favorites," James cut in, as if he'd understood her.

Peter grinned slyly. "No, she said she wants to play a new game. Pirates!"

Pirates? Tink stood up straighter. *You know pirates?*

The other boys groaned. Tootles gave a half-hearted toot.

"You always want to play pirates," said Nibs. "I'm tired of that game."

"Who could ever be tired of fighting pirates?" Peter asked, pretending to swing the sword he no longer had. He ran and jumped on the edge of a bed. "What say you, pirate?" He used a voice way deeper than his own. "Will you surrender? Or do you want to walk the plank?"

Tink laughed despite herself. He sounded just like the rogues on the *Jolly Roger*! The *Jolly Roger* . . . Why did she know that ship? Had she been on a pirate ship before? Tink put a hand to her head, willing the knowledge to come through the fog, to remember whatever lost thought was needling her.

Slightly yawned and then started to cough again. "I'm too tired to play. I want to hear a story."

"Well, you're in luck, because I'm not only the best pirate-fighter. I'm the best storyteller in London," said Peter. "Want one with soldiers? Fairies? I love fairy tales." He balanced on the edge of the bed and Tink worried he might fall.

"We want to read a real . . ." said one twin.

"Book," said the other, finishing his thought. "Like *The Blue Fairy*."

Tinker Bell looked at the twins. *There's a real book about fairies?*

Cubby, Slightly, and Nibs had already moved on and were playing with tiny figures that looked like small Mainlanders. It sounded like they were under attack. A tiny toy soldier flew into the air and sailed over her head.

"We don't need a book. We've got Tinker Bell," Peter said, still waving his hand like a sword, balanced precariously on the bed frame.

You're going to fall, Tink jingled.

"Peter, get down before you fall!" James warned.

She groaned in frustration. What Tink would give to fly right now. Instead, she marched closer to the bed and prepared to toss pixie dust so he'd look down. Instead, a piece of paper waved in front of her face, distracting her.

Nibs had left his tiny figures and was showing her a drawing.

"This . . . this is for you," he said softly. His ashy-brown rabbit costume and floppy ears had seen better days, and his pale blond hair was in deep need of a haircut, but the boy's dark eyes were full of tentative hope and wonder. "I know Peter drew something for you already, but I've been working on my own. Don't tell him."

Tinker Bell walked in front of the illustration and gasped. It was anything but rudimentary, like the childlike drawing Peter had made (not that she'd say that, of course, but the difference was startling). This was done in pencil and was detailed down to the uneven hem of her leaf dress and her tiny slippers. Nibs had captured the way her bangs just brushed her blue eyes and how her blond hair stayed knotted on top of her head thanks to a piece of twine. Somehow he'd caught the delicate wave to her wings, making them appear luminescent even without color on the paper. Her right wing even had a perfect rendition of her makeshift sling. She wished she could find a way to take this drawing back with her to Never Land.

Tinker Bell studied Nibs, new questions leaping through her mind. *You are so talented. What you could do if given the chance.*

Nibs dark eyes seemed to peer into her very soul. He smiled so big and wide, she felt her heart explode. "I knew you'd like it. I'll put it up on the wall by your house so you can look at it every day till your wing gets better."

Peter was still talking a mile a minute. Somehow his story about a pirate had turned into one about a fairy and now a pirate fairy.

"And then the pirate fairy became co-captain of the ship, with me, of course, and she used her magic dust to make the ship fly into the sky where it sailed high over London and—"

"I'm tired of this one," said Slightly, sounding sniffly. "Can *you* tell us a story, James?"

"Don't bother James. He doesn't have time for such larks, boys," said Nurse Beth, bustling into the room. Tink dove for her carriage to hide. Tootles picked it up and placed it on his bedside table, for which she was grateful as the other boys all ran back to bed.

"James has a job here," Nurse Beth said crossly. Then she cast the young man a look, as if her words held more meaning. "In fact, we'll be needing someone to clean the operating theater for Dr. Collins, dear. There was some issue last night. Surgery went far longer than expected. Such a mess. I'll walk you out."

Tinker Bell felt a surge of fire in her belly. Suddenly, Nurse Beth's pet names for James did not seem so funny.

The other boys pretended to look busy, but Tink leaned out of her wagon to eavesdrop as the two Mainlanders headed for the door.

"I've noticed you spend a lot of time in this room with these boys, love," she said quietly, her brown eyes trying to convey meaning Tink didn't understand. Her pale face was expressionless. Most of her hair was tucked under her white cap, but a few wayward brown and gray curls peeked out as she held James's gaze.

Love. Tinker Bell glared.

"Well, my bed is in their closet," he reminded her.

The nurse sighed wearily. "When you're not working, you should be taking care of yourself—not making outfits for the boys, not entertaining them. Look, I know you feel for them. Lord knows they must remind you so much of your own situation. But please don't get too attached. Their future is not tied to yours."

James looked as if he'd been slapped.

"I feel for you, love. It's why you have a job here and a place to stay, but money is tight everywhere, what with the war coming and all," she whispered. "More folks will be needing the hospital, and we're short-staffed as it is. I want you to make sure you're being useful, so you don't lose your job. There aren't a lot of options for those like us." She placed a hand on his shoulder. "Folks with no name or family to speak of. We've got to watch out for each other."

Tink felt her face burn with anger. How dare this woman act like these boys were something she would flick off the bottom of her shoe. How dare she tell James to stop caring. To stop trying. She shot a glance at him, wondering how he'd respond.

James seemed calm, his eyes pensive. "I understand. Thank you, Nurse Beth. I've just realized I'll be needing my mop. I'll go collect it and be at the theater soon." Peering closer, Tink could see his neck was throbbing, but he kept his composure until Nurse Beth sighed again and then took her leave.

Then Tink saw him throw down his rag and kick the bucket of water, startling the boys, before marching into the broom closet that doubled as his bedroom and slamming the door behind him.

FIFTEEN

THE NEXT DAY, JAMES KEPT HIS DISTANCE, DOING MORE CLEANING OUTSIDE Room Fourteen. The boys seemed to sense he needed his space and entertained themselves, chattering and wandering around the room. Tinker Bell kept watch the best she could from her perch. At one point she had to raise her voice to reprimand Peter as he led the boys in a game of follow-the-leader and leapt bed to bed, particularly after Tootles fell off and started crying. Peter reluctantly translated to all the boys they were to play in their beds till Nurse Beth came back.

"I hope Nurse Beth forgets," Slightly muttered.

"Me too," one of the twins responded. "My stomach's already in knots. Do you think she'd let us skip tonight's tonic?"

"Fat chance," the other twin replied.

Tonic. For what felt like the thousandth time, Tink chewed the familiar word over in her head.

Whatever the Mainlander concoction was, she knew it must taste awful. The boys groaned and made faces as they swallowed whatever was in the tiny bottles Nurse Beth poured onto small utensils and forced down their mouths.

"Nooooo. My mouth already feels dreadful," moaned Cubby.

Drink some water. She waved her pixie dust to get the boy's attention, then motioned to the glass. He took a sip.

"Think of something else," Peter said. "Just the other night I dreamed I'd finally left the hospital and swam with mermaids."

Nibs pulled at his rabbit pajama tail as he looked at Peter with wide eyes. "You dreamed you left the hospital?"

Peter preened like a peacock. "'Course I did. I do it all the time."

"I heard someone say none of us are ever leaving," said one of the twins.

The room got very quiet.

The boy made eye contact with Tink and suddenly she felt her own gut twist. She'd noticed the twins' faces were paler today. Were they, too, worried about their future? Or just missing James?

"Tink says you're going to be fine," Peter invented. "And then you can come swim in the enchanted sea with me."

"Enchanted sea, Peter?" asked Cubby, the hood of his bear costume half covering his head. "What's that?"

"Where the mermaids live, of course. You don't think they swim in the Thames, you do? There's no pirates there."

The boys quieted to listen to his story as they always did. Even Tinker

Bell sat down. *Here we go.* But she was smiling and happy to not talk about illness.

"What's she jingling?" Slightly asked.

"She says I'd win in a pirate battle," Peter boasted, and the boys rolled their eyes.

"I'd beat them at their own game and—" He sneezed three times in quick succession.

Uh-oh, Tink thought. Was Peter getting worse?

Suddenly, one of the windows in the room started to clang and a panel flew open in the wind. Slightly and Nibs rushed over to pull it closed and latch it again, getting drenched in the process.

"It's really coming down," said Slightly, looking out the window.

"The streets are flooded," added Nibs.

"I feel like it's been raining for days," Slightly said.

"Because it has," said Nibs.

A rumble of thunder rolled overhead.

"Well, good." Peter looked up from the little figures he had gathered on his bed—the little soldiers that were the same size as Tink. "I hope it rains forever."

"Why do you say that?" Cubby asked.

"Because if it keeps raining, Tinker Bell will stay." He glanced shyly her way. "Fairies can't fly in the rain. Everybody knows that. So she can be one of us now, join our Lost crew. We'd be James's Lost Orphan Boys. Plus Tinker Bell."

Tink rolled her eyes but couldn't help but feel the tiniest bit touched at the sentiment. The boys were exhausting but she loved their energy, excitement, the way they were always bouncing from one idea to the next. It felt good to be useful and look out for them even if it was tiring. It turned out moments spent with children were equal parts delight and problem-solving. Besides, it was clear these kids needed someone to look out for them when James wasn't around. She wasn't sure James was as amused with their antics as she was, though he clearly adored the children.

Tinker Bell thought of when he'd returned late last night, the boys already fast asleep. He'd retained the sour expression from earlier. But then the two of them had worked a little on the sewing machine light in companionable silence, and she'd noticed his breathing slow, his broad shoulders relax. This morning, though, he was back to looking grim as ever, and she wished she could think of something to cheer him up. *I'll be here . . . for a little while longer at least,* Tink jingled to Peter.

"What did she say, Peter?" Cubby asked.

"She said she doesn't mind sticking around," Peter told them.

"Better than my parents," Slightly said under his breath. Tink felt a pull toward the boy, watching as he rearranged the blanket on his bed to cover his legs. He'd been shivering most of the day even though the room was rather warm.

"I really like having a fairy here," said Cubby, sniffling and blowing his nose in his handkerchief. He stared at her with big, round teary eyes and she wished she could fly over to sit on his shoulder.

When James didn't return after dark, worry knotted in Tink's stomach. The boys seemed to think this was fine. But when Nurse Beth came by to announce lights out and the young man still hadn't come into the room, she started to pace. As Tootles carried her carriage over to her tiny abode, she jingled to Peter. *Where is he?*

"James?" Peter asked, his voice catching mid-yawn. "Probably still doing his rounds." He grinned. "Why? You miss him?"

Who said anything about missing? Tink jingled, now both annoyed and slightly embarrassed. *I was just wondering why you all didn't seem concerned.*

Peter yawned again. "He always comes back. Night, Tinker Bell."

Night, she jingled, glad they couldn't see her face burning in the darkness. She waited till the boys were quiet and some were snoring till she removed her sling. It felt stiff to move and she struggled for a second to remember how it worked. She tried moving it slowly and gave a small gasp of pain. It wasn't as bad as it had been, but still, it hurt. She quickly put the sling back on and sat down on the thimble to stare at the door, waiting. When it felt like ages had passed, she turned toward his bedroom door again, anxious to do something. And that's when she had an idea. She removed her sling.

Tink stood at the edge of the table and looked down. She could fly with one wing if she really had to, right? She took a deep breath and without thinking, jumped.

For a moment, her body dropped. She could feel her balance was off, her one good wing flapping and trying hard to get her across the room. She struggled to keep going, finally coming in for a hard landing near James's door, which was ajar. She brushed herself off and slipped into the closet. Inside, she saw the sewing table. With another deep breath, she forced herself to try to fly up to the machine. All this movement made her damaged wing hurt, but she managed to pull off the second flight. She collapsed on the table, sitting for a few moments and catching her breath. She really wished she'd managed to carry her sling with her, but no matter. She'd hold her arm tight. Finally she stood and walked around the table for a bit, thankful there was a small lamp still on that allowed her to see. She examined the machine up close, stared down at the pedal, then back at the machine again.

So James wanted a light near the needle, did he?

Tink tapped her foot, thinking. Then inspiration hit. She dragged the large pencil over and began to draw the best she could on a piece of paper next to the machine.

James came through the door just as she was finishing the drawing.

"Tinker Bell!" he said, surprised, his voice barely more than a whisper. "Is everything all right? How did you manage to get in here?" His eyes widened. "Did you fly? Where is your sling?"

I don't have time to answer those questions! This is more important! I think I know how to make your invention work, she jingled impatiently, pointing from the drawing to the sewing machine.

"Did you . . ." He looked from the paper to the machine then back at her. "Solve my problem?"

She nodded triumphantly.

James picked up the paper, chewing his bottom lip as he studied the diagram. "Yes. I see. So, the lamp would be attached to a hook on the side of the machine, providing light to the area where I thread the needle?" She nodded. He scratched his head. "That could work. Especially if it's connected to the foot pedal so that the switch on the lamp came on when you pressed the pedal. No extra steps for the mender, just a few extra parts. Tinker Bell, you're a genius!" He gently picked her up and brought her close to his face.

I know, Tink jingled, feeling like she might explode with pride. They stared at each other a moment, and Tink breathed in the clean scent of pine that reminded her of the Never Woods.

The Never Woods. Never Land. Home. A problem to be solved . . .

"I don't know how to thank you," he said softly. "If this works—it could change all our lives. We should test it."

We? She nodded emphatically. *I would love to.* Tink hesitated half a second then reached out her hand. James knew what she was doing. In turn, he held out his pointer finger, pressing it to her small hand. She could hear her own heart beating. They held each other's gaze for what felt like forever.

Then a boy coughing from the other side of the door broke the moment. James hastily put her down, his cheeks flushed like hers.

"Well, yes, if you're not too tired, maybe we can try working on it now," he suggested. Tinker Bell nodded again, the desire to keep going overwhelming her. What was happening? Why did she care so much?

"Good. Good," James said. "I need something to take my mind off today." He cast his eyes downward. "I'm sorry I just left like that. Were the boys okay?"

They were fine, she promised.

James ran a hand through his hair and she stared at the motion. "After what Nurse Beth said, I had to get away and think. I'm worried, Tinker Bell." He looked at her again, his face grave. "Both for my own future and theirs. What is going to happen to us?"

Tink sat on the pencil, head perched her in hands as she listened.

"They have no one but me looking out for them. Some of the nurses try, but they have a lot of patients. Many children come and go, but my boys have been here a long, long time. Like me." He smiled softly. "They need help being kept in line, of course. Peter tries to be a leader, but he's still young himself and very rash. Always voting boys out and such. Like he's king." He chuckled. "But he has a good heart."

Where is his family? she jingled.

It was if he could understand her. "I don't even know what happened to his family," James said. "Someone found him too ill to walk and lying in an alleyway. They brought him to the hospital."

Tink held her hands over her chest. *Poor Peter.* Again, Tink wondered what had become of the woman who wheeled his pram.

"He won't talk about his past. I don't know if he's blocked it out. He was so sick those first few days, but he has the strongest spirit." He took a moment to go on. "I hate to play favorites but . . ."

I like Peter, too. Tink knew exactly what James meant. Peter had that infuriating yet loveable spark about him. She couldn't bear the thought of him being put out on the street. She couldn't handle that image for any of them. *I like all the boys.*

"Not that I don't adore all the boys," James went on, echoing her thoughts once more. "Nibs has a good heart. He's probably the most sensitive, not that I could blame him. He's been through a lot, too." A darkness fell over James's face again. "He lost his whole family from scarlet fever last fall. Been here ever since."

Oh, that's awful. Tinker Bell's wing drooped.

"And Cubby, he's the oldest. He'll outgrow the children's hospital ward soon and then where will he go? He'd lived in a tenement, but his family is long gone. I don't know if they're alive or dead. No one has ever come to visit him. I'd get the hospital to hire the boy, but you heard Nurse Beth. I'm not sure if they'll even keep me for much longer." He sat down, as if the weight of his story was too much for his legs to bear. "I don't care what she says, of course. I can't just abandon them."

You shouldn't! Tink stood up, her expression pinched. *Don't listen to her. The boys need you. You're all they have.*

"I really don't want their whole lives to be about being sick or abandoned in equal turns. I want them to remember they are still children, meant to play and have dreams and laugh. Before it's time to grow up. That feels important, too. Don't you think?"

Tink nodded, sitting down again and placing her head in her hands again to stare at him as he talked. *I do.*

James grinned, showing off that dimple again as he looked at her. "You agree with me. I thought you might. Peter said you being here is good luck."

Luck? Tinker Bell wondered. *To me it feels like fate.*

"Personally, I think it's fate," James said softly, watching her again. "I feel like you arrived just when we needed you most. We needed a change. I know I did. A hope to cling to. A chance that could change all our futures. People like Nurse Beth say it's impossible for me and the boys to do that, but I . . ."

But you think impossible's just a problem to be solved, Tink finished. *Like me.* She paused, wishing he could understand her, then continued anyway. *My job was tinker in Pixie Hollow, but I wanted more. I came here because . . . I came here because . . .* She could feel the truth just below the surface, trying to bubble up.

"I have a feeling you're looking for something, too," he said, and picked up the paper with her drawing again. "I wish I could help you, the way you've helped me," he said. His sigh had heft to it. "Sorry. I'm babbling again."

Tink shook her head no, then slowly changed her answer to yes. *Babble away. I love listening to you talk. I babble, too.*

He laughed quietly. "I can't help myself. I know I can't speak your jingles, but it doesn't matter. You're easy to talk to, Tinker Bell."

So are you, James. She felt a sensation like a jolt and wondered if it was what getting struck by lightning felt like. Her whole body was warm. She couldn't remember ever being so in sync with someone before.

The door to his closet creaked open and Tink saw the silhouette of a small bear.

"Cubby, what are you doing up?"

"I can't sleep. I'm thinking too much." His eyes looked watery. "And I don't want to think about them anymore."

Tinker Bell's heart sank. *Them.* The family he lost? She and James shared a look.

"Why don't I read you a story to help you fall off again?" James asked kindly.

Cubby hesitated. "Can Tinker Bell come, too?"

Of course, she jingled, and the boy smiled.

"Get back in bed and we'll be right over," he told Cubby, who did as he was told.

James put out his hand again to pick her up. "Thanks, Tinker Bell. He'll be out in minutes and then we can come back and get to work. If that's all right, that is?" She nodded and he smiled, showing off that dimple again. "I have a feeling we could solve a lot of problems together, you and I. We could . . . we could change the world."

Change the world. Tinker Bell flickered. She wasn't sure why, but something about those words made her uneasy.

SIXTEEN

For the next few days, Tinker Bell met James every night to work on the invention after his rounds were done and the boys were asleep.

Without realizing it, a few days turned into a week. Tink was so busy she lost track of time. When she wasn't with the boys, her mind was crackling with ways to make James's sewing machine light invention a reality. They were so close now. Tink could feel it.

"I think you're right," James was saying, his eyes peering under the sewing machine again at the needle. "Two wires aren't working. We need to try to use one to power the lamp and the machine. Not everyone has electricity, and with the war, resources are becoming even more scarce."

Exactly. Tink nodded. Holding the pencil she'd become accustomed to, she pointed again to her drawing of the wheel. All this would be a whole lot easier if they could just power every machine with pixie dust. But, of course,

Tink liked thinking up new possibilities, new solutions. *What if—if we thread the wire together? So, it would work at the same time.* She walked over to his hand, feeling her heart flutter as she neared him. She stepped over his pointer finger and motioned to the crank wheel where the foot pedal was attached.

"Yes, the wheel. What about it?" he asked, looking at her with such intensity, she felt a little dizzy. "You think we should wind the wires together?"

She loved how he really listened, how he *wanted* to understand her. Sometimes it seemed to be instinct. Other times, it took concentration, effort. The thing was, he never stopped trying.

No, she jingled. *What we need is a wider wheel crank so that we can have both wires running side by side.* She drew the image again and he watched her with keen interest.

"Adjust the crank so both wires fit!" James exclaimed. "Tinker Bell, you are brilliant."

Brilliant. Her heart sighed. *I know. So are you.* She pointed to him. *Darling*, she teased.

"Me? No." He laughed as he rummaged around a box in his room. "This is a wheel I kept from a broken machine. Wasn't sure if it would come in handy. Let's try it out."

She watched him get to work, switching out the crank on the sewing machine and rewiring to accommodate both the lamp and the foot pedal. At one point, he looped the wire in the wrong spot, and Tink moved to intervene, gesturing until he realized his mistake. It took him a while to get it right, but oddly, she didn't mind. Was it wrong that she liked looking at him? From his broad shoulders to the curls at the top of his head, and the way he scrunched up his nose when he was trying to think of a solution—she loved everything about him—inside and out. Her heart thrummed. She'd never felt like this before.

Just then James looked up, as if he could sense her thoughts. "What is it?"

Nothing, she jingled, shaking her head.

He smiled coyly. "I caught you staring again."

Me? she pretended to be outraged. *You were the one staring.*

"It's all right. I do it, too," he admitted, his cheeks coloring again. "What I wouldn't give to have the magic you have. Working with you on this is my favorite part of the day."

Tink felt her heart lurch once more. *Mine too.*

They looked at each other for a beat too long before they each pretended to look at something else.

"There we go," he finally said when he was done threading the wiring. "Let's try this out." Tink stepped back and watched as James began to press the foot pedal and the crank on the side of the machine started whirring. It felt like they were both holding their breath as they waited to see what would happen to the small lamp. It flickered before finally lighting up.

It's working! Tink jumped up and down. *We did it!*

"We did it!" James started to laugh and then his dark eyes welled with tears. "The invention works! It works! Do you know what this means? I can get this to the patent office in the morning before my shift! Write to Singer. Maybe they'll want to buy it! This could be our way up and out of here." He was standing now, pacing the room with excitement.

But all Tink heard was *our. Our. Our. Our.*

"We could save enough money to buy a home for the boys. Have proper rooms. A space to create more inventions."

We. We. We. Her heart was beating faster now.

"None of this would have happened if you hadn't come here, Tink!"

Tink. He'd never called her by her nickname before.

"I just can't believe this is real." He ran a hand through that thick hair of his. "Though of course it is. If you're here then the impossible is possible. We did it together!" he shouted, and she motioned frantically for him to lower his voice. "I can't help it! I'm so happy I could kiss you!"

They both froze.

James's face turned a dark shade of violet.

Tink practically tripped over the thimble on the table. She felt like she might burst into flames. She wondered if he could hear her heart thrumming.

"It's an expression," James said hastily, his voice now a whisper. "I meant . . . I . . . I'm just really glad you're here."

And for once, Tink was glad he couldn't understand her jingles. Because she had no idea what to say.

The next morning, Nurse Beth barged into Room Fourteen first thing as James was checking on each of the boys still tucked into their beds. "My dear, Dr. Collins is looking for you. Best for you not to dawdle."

Tink bristled at the nurse's impertinence. But when she glanced back at James, she found him looking at her. He winked, then mouthed, "Back soon," before following Nurse Beth out into the hall.

Alas, James was gone for most of the day again, much to Tinker Bell's chagrin. She watched over the boys, jumping in to help adjust a cold compress or assist them with the snack pulley. Most of them were even quieter than the day before, some even taking long naps while Peter regaled them with his stories. He only paused to take a sip of water, and that was after Tink insisted. (Really, that silly pirate voice of his was going to do in the child's vocal chords.) Every time the door opened, she'd look hopefully from her perch, only to find Nurse Beth or another hospital worker making their rounds.

By the evening, Tinker Bell's disappointment started to simmer into something like ire. This was ridiculous! How could James keep leaving them like this? The boys needed him. And she'd had a new idea for the light—a funnel that would make it easier to refill the gas. Though if he took any longer, maybe she'd just keep it to herself.

"Tinker Bell?" came a small voice. "I'm too hot." It was Tootles calling for her from his small bed.

Okay, I'm coming.

Flying wasn't easy—she still had to strain to make it on one good wing, and James insisted she keep her sling on most of the time, but she could feel herself getting stronger. Today, anger propelled her. Tinker Bell glanced out the window on her flight over. It was pouring again, certainly not ideal for letting in some fresh air, but the boys needed it. They all seemed sicker by the day. She made her way over to the little boy, helping him pull off the thin blanket, sprinkling water on his face.

"Thank you," he whispered, closing his eyes.

Tink looked across the way to the hall, which she could see through the open door of Room Fourteen. The giant clock on the wall ticked, and for some reason this irritated her all the more. How obsessed Mainlanders were with time. Bedtimes, pills being taken on time, meals eaten at certain times.

And now look at her, staring at the clock, wondering what time James would return. What did *soon* mean to him? How much longer would he be? The hot fury returned full force. Now she was mad at herself. Look at the ridiculous things stealing her attention—and all for a silly Mainlander boy.

It wasn't until all the children had long been asleep, a mingling of snoring and wheezing filling the air, that James strode into his small room. Tinker Bell had her back to the door as she worked on filing the front of the tiny wooden carriage to improve its speed. She knew seeing the fast-moving wagon would cheer Tootles right up. Therefore, this automobile was all she was going to focus on. Not the boy she'd been waiting for.

"Tinker Bell, the most extraordinary thing happened." James's voice rang out. "You'll never guess—" He stopped short. Tinker Bell could feel him pause and take her in. "Tinker Bell?"

She wouldn't look at him. She had important work to do, too! Really, what did he expect? Drop everything now that he'd decided to grace them with his presence? Tink filed harder, shaking the table.

"You're angry, aren't you?" It wasn't a question.

Well at least his powers of observation were still intact.

"Is it one of the boys? They can be so naughty sometimes. Did they do some—"

Tink snorted. One of the boys. *Honestly.*

"Oh." James's voice softened. "You're angry with me."

He came closer now, sinking into the chair next to the table. Tinker Bell put the file down but still didn't turn to face him. She knew what was coming.

Here was the moment he'd say she was getting too worked up, too emotional. She braced herself for the pointed barb, the joke, the change of subject meant to shake her out of it.

But James was silent. Waiting. Which was almost more infuriating. When Tink couldn't take it any longer, she whirled around, sucking in a breath, prepared to jingle irately . . . until she saw the contrite expression on his face.

"I left you here for far too long," he said. "After I told you I'd be back soon."

Yes, you did. Tink nodded, but the fight had already started to eke out of her.

"I was so wrapped up in— Well, that doesn't matter. What matters is that it was unfair of me to disappear on you like that. And on the boys. I'm sorry."

Crossing her arms, Tink moved a few paces closer, calming down a bit now that he'd apologized. *What were you going to say before? About the extraordinary thing?*

"I . . . never mind my news. I want to talk about you." James leaned closer. "Where did you come from?" he asked, his face lingering. "It occurs to me that I never even asked."

She liked his gaze on her and it hurt to turn away from him. It was like a cloud blocking out the sun. Tink glanced toward the window on the far wall. The faint pitter-patter that had provided their background noise all week was gone. The rain had stopped. Now the air was silent. Tinker Bell picked up a pencil from the table, and glanced at the paper before her, wondering how to explain home. She tried to write the letters in a neat scroll.

"Never Land," James read aloud. "Where is that?"

Hearing him say the name of her home out loud made her injured wing flutter without her even realizing it. James reached out and touched it gently.

"I know you're wearing your sling less and less. We should really see how your wing is working. It should be about healed by now, I expect."

Tinker Bell paused, a new thought intruding on the moment. It had stopped raining. And if she was healed . . . well, then that meant it was time to go home. To Never Land. Without James and the boys.

The idea made Tink feel like she couldn't breathe.

Still, James was watching, so she tried flapping her wing without pain. It felt odd.

"Move slowly," James said as he watched her. "It's going to seem strange at first. You're out of practice. Don't do anything foolish and don't exert yourself too much right away. Just small distances at first—not flights across the room or anything, unless absolutely necessary." He paused. "It would . . . it would pain me very much if you got hurt again."

Tinker Bell raised her eyebrows.

This time, it was his turn to blush. "I mean, who else would make sure I didn't get a big head? The *darling* business and all that. Actually, that reminds me. I got you something."

You got me a present? Tink's heart fluttered once more.

James walked over to a table by the doorway. "Dr. Collins and I had a bit of a stroll in the garden today. And when I saw these, I knew you'd like them." He picked up a bundle of vibrant violets and brought them over to her. She reached out her hand to touch one of the blooms.

The sweet fragrance reminded her of Pixie Hollow, then of something else she couldn't quite place. Those purple blooms. Why were they so familiar?

A plume of pixie dust burst around her and Tink gasped, her wings fluttering faster now. Images shot through her mind like cannon balls.

Caiman was hurt.

He needed tonic.

He could be dying.

The Wanderers didn't know where she was.

How long had she been here? What if she was too late to save him?

She had to get back to Never Land!

But that also meant she really would have to leave this place. James. And the boys. Straight away.

Her competing thoughts flew fast and she found her panic rising, the jingles in her throat coming out all scrambled.

"Tinker Bell, what's wrong? Tell me," James begged.

Tink tried flying around, but she was still so out of practice, she fell back down on the table, unable to worry and fly at the same time. She jumped up again and tried motioning frantically.

"There's an emergency?" James tried. "Something—or *someone*—needs help?"

Yes, yes. In Never Land. She had to try to make him understand what she needed to do. She—

"James? Tinker Bell?" a voice called, sounding frightened.

The two of them spun around.

Peter stood in his nightshirt, the front of it drenched from sweat. He looked unsteady. He held the bed frame and swayed as he started to cough. "I don't feel right," he said. The next thing they knew, he collapsed at their feet.

SEVENTEEN

Peter was very ill. That's what Nurse Beth told James.

"All we can do is wait and see if he pulls through," she said, trying to push tonics down his throat. Tonics that might help Caiman.

That is, if he were even still alive to take them. Tink wrung her hands with guilt and worry.

Stay. Go. Stay. Go.

Caiman had waited long enough. He needed her. But so did the boys. And James. How could she leave them when Peter might die?

She couldn't.

Instead, Tink kept vigil over Peter while he lay feverish in bed, drifting in and out of consciousness. James slept in a chair that he dragged from bed to bed in the evening to sit near each boy as they attempted to fall asleep, crying for mothers who were long gone or dead and wouldn't be coming.

Almost overnight, the twins could not get out of bed. A day after that, Nibs, Slightly, Cubby, and Tootles started running high fevers as well. Their coughs sounded like the seals that sometimes sunned themselves on rocks near Mermaid Cove.

How quickly the joyful, mischievous air in Room Fourteen changed.

According to the renowned Dr. Collins, who rushed in around lunch, Room Fourteen wasn't the only one in trouble. The whole hospital had been plagued with the same illness. They used words like *outbreak* and *fatal*.

"People don't recover from this," Nurse Beth whispered.

"These boys will," James said with bluster.

The Lost Orphan Boys. *Their* boys. Looking at them lying so listless in bed, Tinker Bell felt the same way. They had to make it. They just had to.

"If you don't want to be sick as well, you should try to keep your distance," the older woman warned. "It looks like tuberculosis. There have been outbreaks before, but never one in the Greater Hospital like this one. People are sick on every floor and getting worse by the day. I've been told to leave as well. You need to think of your own health, James."

"I'm all they have." He winced. "They're all *I* have. We're family."

Family. It was a word Tinker Bell understood well. She thought of her own found family—Blair, Mimic, Tiger Lily, and Caiman—and felt another pang of guilt. Were her friends worried? Were there more disturbances on the island? How was Caiman?

She had so many questions and few answers. Plus, the guilt was killing her as she took stock of her pixie dust. Her pouch was less than half full now. She couldn't stay on the Mainland much longer . . . unless she decided to stay permanently. And that wasn't an option either.

"Do your rounds, dear," Nurse Beth's voice cut into Tink's warring thoughts. "Then I suggest you take your leave."

Tinker Bell glared at the form of the retreating woman. She thought about flying over and pinching her on her way out the door, but who would that help? The idea disappeared quickly when Slightly coughed so violently, he threw up. James moved quickly to clean him up and refill the pitcher with clean water, but his shaking hands knocked it over and made Tink jump.

She felt her wings kick in this time, and for a moment she fluttered in the air without giving it a thought. In any other circumstance, she would've been relieved to be able to fly painlessly again. Now it felt like a cruel trick. She was getting better while the children only seemed to get worse by the hour.

She waved to James, motioning to the door. *Go. I'll watch over them.*

"Are you sure?" he asked, looking as if he'd aged ten years. He had dark circles under his eyes from not sleeping. "I will try not to be long."

I've got them, she promised with a small smile, but inwardly she was afraid, too. Taking short flights, she flew from bed to bed and found the boys' symptoms were many—fevers, body aches, rashes. The coughing was the one that worried her the most. She heard the sound even in her sleep. Each cough was different, but equally terrifying. Some of the boys sounded like they were wheezing, others had a ferocious bark.

Tinker Bell's head was spinning.

How had this progressed so quickly?

"Tinker Bell?"

Peter.

Tink heard the faint whisper and flew slowly toward the sound of his voice. She spun around, her eyes adjusting to the darkness. James had turned off the light in the room since so many boys complained their heads hurt. He said the darkness was soothing. Tinker Bell found it depressing. The darkness seemed to want to swallow them up whole.

She was surprised to find Peter wide awake, looking out the window at the Mainland. At first this made her spirits rise, but then she saw him in the low light of the outside streetlamp flickering nearby. He was shivering, his pale brow perspiring with sweat. His coloring had gotten worse in just a few short days. He was clutching his stomach.

"You're flying. Your wing is all better," Peter said, his relief short-lived as he winced. "And you're still here. I dreamed you left us for the pirates."

I'd never leave you, but especially not for pirates, she said, smiling wanly. All around her, she heard boys shift and turn, their coughs getting the better of them. *And I would never leave without saying goodbye.*

Peter closed his eyes for a moment and rested his head back against the pillow. "That's nice . . . but I . . ." He started to cough again. She motioned to the water jug. "I can't reach it," he said. "I don't think I'm going to make it, Tinker Bell."

Don't say that! Tinker Bell started to jingle madly, and he put up his sweaty hand to stop her.

"Don't be cross with me. Please? I'm just so tired. I want to go to sleep and fight pirates and crocodiles forever."

Tinker Bell's face twitched. This boy and his childlike wonder, even in the face of death.

His expression was pained. "This fight . . . I don't know if I'm going to win this time." He started to cough violently again and all she could do was helplessly flutter in front of him and wait for the coughing to subside.

"That was a bad one," he said finally, removing the handkerchief from his mouth.

Tinker Bell froze. There were specks of blood on the handkerchief.

Peter looked up at her in alarm, then his mask quickly hardened again. "It's fine. That's happened before. You don't have to tell James. I don't want him getting sick, too." He hesitated, as if it hurt to talk. "It's too late for the rest of us, but not him."

Stop saying that! Tink jingled, her face getting hot.

"I'm not trying to make you mad, Tinker Bell, I'm just being honest." There was a wheeze to his voice. "We both know I'm very ill. I've heard Nurse Beth talking. We've got the same thing that killed some of our families. People don't get better when they have this cough." A slight breeze rustled through the open window. "Fresh air isn't a cure. Neither is shipping us off to some quiet place they keep talking about. The hospital just doesn't want to see us die."

You aren't going to die, Tinker Bell insisted, but she could hear her own heart beating. Peter looked worse off than any of the boys at this point, though Cubby wasn't that far behind. He was delirious, talking in his sleep. Peter's mind was right, but he didn't look well.

For a moment, Caiman's face appeared where Peter's should be, and Tinker Bell remembered how frightening it had been when he'd collapsed. She was supposed to be finding him a cure and instead she was watching others she loved succumb to illness, too. She refused to lose any of them. She needed to do something.

"I'm trying to rest and get better, but I'm getting worse. You and I both know it." Peter's eyes held hers. "I know I keep saying I'm not frightened.

That's what I tell the other boys, but the truth is, Tink, I am scared. Just a little." He tried to inhale, and she heard the crinkle to his breath, the wheeze deepening. "I feel like I can be honest with you."

You can, she jingled softer now.

"You know what I want?" Peter asked, his wheeze overtaking his words. "I don't care about growing up—who wants to be an adult anyway? They don't have fun. All they do is worry about everything and they have to be responsible like James. And what does it get him? He lives in a tiny room in the hospital and cleans all day and still doesn't make enough money to go somewhere better. London's a mess. I don't want to go back to some tenement." He shuddered. "No, what I want is to go someplace far away from here where there is no sickness and no responsibility." His face took on an ethereal look. "I want to live in a place where I can be king and rule the land and sea. I'll be a good king, too. There won't be rules about what children can do and what they can't. Me and the other boys will just live there and be free."

The skin at the back of her neck prickled. What Peter was describing felt like Never Land.

He started to cough again, this time, his whole body moving with him, his face filled with pain.

"This hurts so bad," Peter said softly. "I want the pain to stop."

I know, she jingled, the lump in her throat threatening to choke her. *I wish I could help you.*

"You're a good friend, Tinker Bell. Staying here with us," he said as he started to drift off again. "Especially since you can fly away now and be free yourself."

Outside, Tink could see darkness slowly taking over the city. The rolling clouds had moved out and for the first time in a while she could see stars in the sky. She looked up, searching for the one star she needed: the second star to the right. It flickered as if in greeting.

She could fly to Never Land. Leave right now.

She looked back at Peter and then to the door where James had gone through hours before. Her eyes looked then at the tonic on the table, and she thought of Caiman again.

Tinker Bell had never been more unsure of what to do. Tears streamed down her face.

"Might see some sun tomorrow Nurse Beth said, so it would be good flying weather," Peter continued as he began to drift away. "Don't feel bad—we knew you couldn't stay forever. Not really." He opened his eyes and looked out the window again for a moment. "I hope Nurse Beth is right. I want to see the sun rise in case . . . well, you know."

Tinker Bell shook her head as her tears fell faster now. *Don't say such things, Peter.*

"Don't be mad," he begged. "I'd hate if you were mad at me, Tinker Bell. When I fall asleep, I'm going to dream of you, and the day we met." He glanced at her again. "That's my favorite story."

His words were killing her. She felt so hopeless.

Peter's eyes closed. "I know if you had any magic that you could spare, you'd use it to save us."

Tinker Bell's heart was thudding hard now as Peter's breath hitched. She landed on his chest to make sure she could feel it moving up and down. It was slow, and the wheeze was even louder up close, but she could still hear it. She could hear the other boys coughing, too. She looked at each boy with a mixture of affection and fear and finally anger. No. This was not how life was going to end for any of them.

A plan was hatching. One that was probably against all the rules she'd ever known.

But damn if she cared.

Tinker Bell stared at Peter's pained face again and decided right then and there. Reaching into her pocket, she grabbed a fistful of pixie dust and sprinkled it over his body.

She held her breath and watched as he started to glow, then rise up, the sheets slipping off his body. As he floated up, Tinker Bell cried with relief. Then she heard him gasp as he awoke and found himself hovering in the air over his bed.

Peter looked around in amazement at his hands, now glowing with the pixie dust that gave him flight and he didn't question it. Instead, his eyes were rimmed with tears as he glanced at Tink and whispered quietly, "I knew you could do it."

EIGHTEEN

When James returned to Room Fourteen, his lost boys were floating in the air.

"What in the . . ." James's pale face grew even paler as he shut the door quickly behind him.

"We're flying!" Nibs coughed violently between words. Though he managed a crooked smile Tink hadn't seen in days.

"Fl-flying?" James sputtered as if he couldn't believe what he was seeing. "Knock me down with a feather . . . am I dreaming?" He looked around, his face equal parts alarm and wonder.

The room had taken on an ethereal feel. The pixie dust from Tinker Bell's pouch had lit up the ceiling like the sun, washing over the dreary quarters where so much sickness lived. Now the space glowed with a warmth it had been missing. As ill as the boys were—and Tinker Bell was not a fool to think the pixie dust alone made the boys well—the chance to fly seemed to help.

Tootles's little skunk tail flew straight up in the air as he left formation and fluttered upside down past James, unable to control his body. He tried to right himself but needed Nibs's help to do so. Nibs gave the smaller child a push, and he flipped over twice before finding his balance. Once he was right side up, he gave a half-hearted blow of his horn and then started to cough again.

"This is no dream, James," said Peter. "Look at us go!" Peter sailed through the air. As sick as he was, he had picked up the new skill the quickest. It was as if the pixie dust itself had given the boy a new lease on life.

"But how . . . Why . . . When did this happen?" James sputtered. Tinker Bell watched as he rubbed his eyes. "Tinker Bell, you did this?"

Tink nodded, zooming across the room to him. She couldn't help but be pleased with herself.

"She found a way to save us," Peter told James as he floated by on his back, his hands resting behind his head. "She's taking us back to her land. There, we won't be sick. And we can fly! Well, with help, of course."

James gasped and looked back at her. "You're taking them to Never Land?"

She held out her hand and tried not to be scared. *I'm taking all of you back with me.* If they were with her, she had all she needed from the Mainland. Peter had already put the tonic in his pocket to carry for her. She would get it to Caiman as soon as they landed.

James just kept staring at her, and she could see his chest rising and falling fast as if trying to work out a particularly tricky tinkering problem.

"She's taking all of us," said Peter, and Cubby somersaulted through the air around the room.

"Are you coming, James?" one of the twins asked as they tried to circle above him.

James didn't answer him.

Soon all the boys were in formation flying around the room, coming dangerously close to the ceiling fan.

"Wait, I'm first," said Peter, paddling forward as if he were swimming through the Never Sea. "I'm the leader." He pushed himself in front of the others.

James's face flickered with a host of emotions. "But you're sick. You can't just fly off to Never Land. Tinker Bell, they can't."

"Can too," Peter said gruffly. "We're leaving with her. You can't stop us."

"But . . ." James hesitated again, and Tink felt her heart start to crack.

Come with us, James. Don't you see? This is how we can help the boys. And how we can help Never Land. It's in trouble, too. It felt like such a natural solution. If James came back with her, maybe they could get to the bottom of Never Land's disturbances, find a solution together, like they had with the invention. Maybe he would be able to see their troubles from a different angle . . . just as she had done with his. The two worlds were linked. They'd both said it—this was fate. And now more than ever, Tink could see how they could work together, how both the magic and innovation provided the balance, the push-pull needed to do extraordinary things. To make the impossible possible.

She reached out her hand again.

James did not move closer.

"I don't think this is a good idea," James said. His voice shook. "What if you get worse where Tinker Bell lives? How will we get you help without medicine? How do we get back?"

His face was once again etched with worry lines that made him look far older than his years. He absentmindedly pulled at his curls as if trying to rip his hair off his head and his voice seemed rather grave.

Is he starting to get ill, too? Tink wondered. *Or is he afraid?*

Please, she jingled. *I know the island will help them. It's cured another Mainlander of disease before. But we have to go quickly, before it progresses too much further. They need Never Land. And Never Land needs us.* I *need you.*

"Tinker Bell also said Never Land needs your help," Peter said, translating. "And she said she does, too."

James looked at her now. "You do?"

Tink nodded and stared at him hopefully. *The island's magic is in trouble, and I haven't been able to figure out what's wrong. You and I make a good team,* she jingled, and Peter translated once more. *I was hoping maybe together we could figure out how to fix it, like we did your invention.*

"James finished his invention?" interrupted Cubby. "I want to see it."

"Me too!" said Nibs.

"Can we bring it with us?" asked one twin.

"No, silly. A sewing machine can't fly . . . can it?"

"Of course it can! If she has magic, it can." The twins started arguing.

James ignored them. His eyes were on her, and she could feel her heart beating faster. She knew how his mind worked now. He was slowly coming to a decision. She wished she could stroke his cheek, but he was so far away.

James pursed his lips as if he wanted to say something, but his expression softened. "We do make a good team." He looked at the boys, then back at the fairy. "And I would do anything to help you boys."

The twins stopped arguing and started to cough and James's face filled with anguish as he watched their small bodies convulse. Peter sailed down and hovered in front of James.

"We're dying here, James," Peter said, his voice gravelly.

Tinker Bell had never heard the boy sound so serious.

"Peter—" James started to say.

"It's all right. We know what's happening to us," Cubby added, his eyes starting to well.

"No one is going to fix it," Slightly said, wheezing. "We don't have mothers and fathers."

"Or if we do," said one of the twins.

"They aren't coming for us," finished the other. "This is our last chance."

"We're going, James," Peter said decidedly. He looked back at Tink. "If Tinker Bell says she can take us somewhere magical and beautiful, where we might get well and be free, why would we ever want to stay here?"

James's face fell. "No, I can see why you wouldn't."

Peter held out his hand now, too. "Come with us."

I know you're scared, Tinker Bell jingled, her heart pounding now as she waited for him to decide. James had to come. The boys would fare much better with him there. And the Wanderers would love them. She held her breath.

Suddenly voices came from the hallway. Rounds were starting. Nurse Beth and Dr. Collins would be coming in any moment. James looked back at the doorknob as if he knew this, then back at Peter. He sighed deeply. "What do I have to do?"

Tinker Bell almost cried.

The other boys cheered, but their voices were faint, sneezes and coughs interrupting the merriment. Peter coughed so hard, he drew blood, but he wiped it on his sleeve. He looked up, smiling softly as if it took a lot to even do so. "Tinker Bell told us all it takes is faith and trust and a little bit of pixie dust."

Tinker Bell's fingers rested on the pixie dust she had left in her pouch and then she flew above James's head.

James closed his eyes and swallowed hard. "Faith and trust and pixie dust?"

Yes. Tinker Bell sprinkled the air around him with dust and the boys watched as it clung to every inch of James, sparkling around him as it did them, too.

James looked at his own hands in surprise and then she heard him gasp as he started to float above the ground. "Oh my . . . oh my . . . oh my word . . ." James whispered to himself, trying to stay steady. He took a nosedive straight away. He threw his hands out fast, looking terrified.

"It's okay. Just relax," Peter said as the other boys crowded around him.

James took a deep breath. "All right." Slowly he held his arms out wide and closed his eyes. When he opened his eyes again, he was floating higher.

You're doing it! Tinker Bell cheered. *James, you're flying!*

The doorknob starting rattling again. Voices outside the door grew louder. "Boys, can you hear us? Open the door."

"Where's the blasted key?"

Tinker Bell and Peter looked at one another.

"To the window, everybody! Quickly!" Peter led the way, his arm out in front of him, like he was holding a sword. "We need to fly!"

"We *are* flying," said Cubby.

"We need to fly to Never Land . . . right?" Peter asked Tink.

Tinker Bell could feel the boy's fear. This was a child used to being forgotten like he was that day in his pram. He'd lived a life of disappointment. Peter may have believed in her, but he was also well aware the world was cruel.

Well, no more of that.

Yes, Tinker Bell told him. *Focus on happy thoughts.*

Peter nodded. "If we want to stay in the air, Tinker Bell says we have to think happy thoughts."

"Happy thoughts? That's how we stay afloat?" James sounded skeptical.

The door to the room started to creak open.

Peter took a deep breath. Then he stepped off the ledge.

All the boys gasped at the same time. Tinker Bell held her breath, but when she peered out the window, Peter was hovering in the air, looking like a fairy himself, backlit by the sun in the early morning light.

"Come on, now! You do it, too!" he told the others.

The other boys closed their eyes, whispering words of encouragement to themselves she couldn't hear. Maybe they were memories. Maybe they were wishes. But one by one they each took flight. The twins. Nibs. Slightly. Cubby. Tootles. Till all that was left was James.

He was halfway out the window as he looked out at the others in the air high over the Mainland. While not sick, suddenly he sounded like he was wheezing.

"Go, James!" shouted Cubby.

The other boys shouted their encouragement, too.

"Don't be a baby!" came Peter's voice, louder than the rest.

Tinker Bell flew to James's side. *You can do this. I know you can.* She landed on his shoulder, squeezing it encouragingly.

James leapt off the window ledge into the air, his eyes closed tight.

PART THREE
FOUND

NINETEEN

THE BOYS CHEERED AS JAMES TOOK TO THE AIR, EACH ONE ENCOURAGING HIM to open his eyes.

Tink watched him take in the sights around him, his broad body trembling; the world from this high up without a net to catch him.

It was quite a view.

The Mainland looked different than it had a couple weeks ago. From this height, most of the world was tranquil. Tink inhaled deep gulps of fresh air, only now realizing just how stifling Room Fourteen had been. Then she looked at the others. Peter was right behind her.

"Lead the way, Tinker Bell," he said. "The others will follow me."

Tinker Bell nodded. It felt good to fly again and her wing was ready to be put to good use. She shot out in front, pixie dust behind her. She'd never had anyone trail her on a flight before. Well, other than Ash.

Tink smiled wryly, wondering what the garden fairy would think about all these new additions to their group. He'd embraced Caiman. And saving Never Land would more than make up for the disruption. He would be all right.

Tink increased her speed, looking behind to make sure the others were keeping up.

As they sailed out over the city and up toward the night sky, Tink's thoughts traveled to the other Wanderers. How was Tiger Lily faring? Blair and Mimic? Had they returned to the falls? Tried anything else to remedy the song?

Questions tumbled over one another and for a moment she was so overwhelmed, Tinker Bell worried that she'd forgotten which way to go. *Breathe, Tink. Just breathe,* Ash's familiar voice echoed in her mind. She found she'd missed it.

Flying was instinct. The air was cool, the sky was clear, and within seconds her eyes found what she was looking for—the second star to the right.

"This is incredible!" came Peter's voice as he sailed up beside her, keeping his promise on that "leader" business. "Look at London!" He pointed to the city below. "Big Ben is so tiny from up here! Imagine landing on one of the hands and looking out at the city. That would be something."

Tinker Bell noted the hands and numbers on the round face near the top of the giant clock tower, the whole building gleaming. A laugh bubbled in her throat. She certainly wouldn't worry about time in Never Land. Despite her fears, there was something about returning with the boys that felt very right.

She fought the wind shear and kept going. They were all lined up behind

Peter, while James pulled up the rear, his furtive glance moving from the boys to the ground below. He needn't have worried. The children's hoots and hollers of joy echoed in the night sky. After so many days of sadness, their laughter was infectious.

Peter crowed, then started to cough and Tinker Bell felt her stomach tighten. When the boy regained his composure, he turned to her. "You know what we should do next time we're here?"

Next time? Tinker Bell's stomach swayed. She wasn't sure there would be a next time. She had no plans to return to the Mainland anytime soon. Now that the boys were safely with her, and Peter had Caiman's tonic, why would she ever come back to this sad, strange place?

"Fly by the nice homes in Mayfair," Peter continued, looking at the world so small below. "See what they're eating, what they're talking about." He puffed out his chest. "Maybe someday they'll tell stories about me—the boy who could fly." He grinned wickedly. "I could swear Nurse Beth saw us jump out the window."

She did? Tinker Bell gave pause.

"How much longer?" came Cubby's whine from behind, and Tinker Bell realized she had to focus.

The second star to the right was nearing and Tinker Bell knew the next parts of the journey would happen in quick succession.

She shot forward to show the boys what to do. A few seconds later, they arrived at the star and it began to brighten. Before any of them knew what was happening, there was a flash, and suddenly it felt as if time seemed to speed up and slow down all at once. The sensation reminded Tinker Bell of taking a deep breath and waiting for the rest of the world to catch up. She glanced back and saw the boys and James suspended in midair as if frozen in time. Then there was another flash and . . .

Boom!

They were on the other side. The island of Never Land welcomed them on the bright horizon.

I'm home, Tinker Bell thought, not realizing till this very second how terribly she missed it. It was morning here, the sky was clear and bright, taking on the orange and purple colors she'd missed on the Mainland. In the distance, she saw the flag of the *Jolly Roger* and her wings tensed. Getting Caiman the tonic was her top priority. She'd have to get the boys safely on land first though.

Tink waved to Peter to follow her and sped up again, headed straight for the island. She could hear the other boys chattering behind her.

"Is that it?"

"Is this Never Land?"

"It's an island!"

"What continent are we on?"

Tink smiled to herself. She couldn't wait to show them everything on Never Land once she knew Caiman was all right. She was almost at the shoreline when she realized something was terribly wrong.

The beach had blackened, the sand as dark as coal. The mountains, once so lush green and bright, had turned a sickly brown, the land completely dried out. What had happened while she was gone?

Tink's eyes landed on Wanderers Cay in worry, and she looked for movement below. There was none. Instead, much of the island was eerily quiet—no birds or animals in sight. Even Tiger Lily's village appeared silent. Pixie Hollow was too far away to see much more than its grand tree, but it was missing its usual shimmer of pixie dust, appearing dull and lifeless. Mermaid Cove, too, had no preening mermaids soaking up the sun. Not that there was much sun, now that she got closer to shore. It was as if the low clouds were clinging onto the island. A flash of lightning in the distance made her pause. Her panic started to rise. Almost forgetting she was being followed, Tink sailed over the mountains, then gasped, stopping short in the air.

"The falls . . ." she cried. Absently, she noticed her voice sounded different now that she was back home—fuller, louder. But her attention was quickly diverted. "Oh no. No, no, no . . ."

If she didn't see the familiar mountain shape and the craggy rock formation, she wouldn't have believed it was Prism Falls at all. The majestic landmark had been reduced to a mere trickle; the pools below the water looking like nothing more than a puddle. The water was drying up. Never Land's magic source was disappearing. Even from this distance, she could hear a faint ting-y sound, whatever water left still out of tune.

"*That's* a waterfall?" Peter asked, understanding her easily. He pursed his lips. "I've only seen pictures, but shouldn't there be *more* of it?"

"We need to land right away," Tink told him. "The island is in trouble." Her heart was in her throat. She'd been gone too long.

"Boys! Tink says we're landing!" she heard Peter say as she started to descend quickly.

And that's when she noticed something strange out of the corner of her eye. It wasn't a bird, but it moved like one, so fast she thought she'd imagined it. It couldn't be a Never Fowl. What was it? Her eyes darted around until they finally landed on the creature. When they did, Tinker Bell gasped.

A *shadow* creature.

Just like what she'd seen with Caiman on the Forbidden Side.

It wasn't so much gray as a shape absent of color, wispy as a deep fog, zooming across the dying plains.

Whoosh.

Cold air blew around them, and for a moment, Tinker Bell worried it was the start of a cyclone. But no. It was a pack of *more* shadow creatures—more than a dozen of them. They were moving fast, swooping over the dying trees in the forest in a pack, and Tink couldn't get sense of what she was looking at. Just then one turned as if sensing it was being watched. Tinker Bell locked in on its empty eyes and her stomach dropped. "How—how is this possible?"

"What are those things?" Peter whispered loud enough to be heard. "Tinker Bell, do you know?"

She felt dazed as she looked at the pack of shadows taking over her island.

There was a rush of air, and Tink felt her right wing get clipped by something that had flown up out of nowhere.

Never Fowl.

Tink tensed, prepared for a face-off, but this time, she realized the giant blue bird wasn't trying to hurt her. Instead, now, she watched, her stomach pooling with dread as it fluttered in front of her.

"FAIRY, YOU HAVE ABANDONED NEVER LAND—" came the bird's chant.

"Abandoned? No," Tink cut in, her stomach tightening. "I'm here—*we're* here—to help. We—"

The Fowl interrupted her. *"YOU HAVE ABANDONED NEVER LAND IN ITS HOUR OF NEED,"* the bird repeated in a clear, low voice, glancing down at the shadows below. *"THE FALLOUT WILL CHANGE THE ISLAND FOREVER."*

TWENTY

THE NEVER FOWL'S WARNING RATTLED HER SO MUCH, SHE COULD FEEL HERself plummet, her mind firing with thoughts as she descended.

The boys followed behind her, oblivious to the chaos they were flying into.

Chaos she'd probably started by visiting the Mainland the first time.

Chaos she might have evoked by going back again, even if her reasons the second time had been vastly different.

You thought about staying there forever to be with James, a small voice in her head reminded her.

Tink pushed it away and snuck a glance at James, who was holding Tootles's onesie as they dropped out of the sky. Her heart skipped, betraying her with just one glance at him. As if he knew she was watching, James looked over and gave her a shaky wave, before returning his hand to his side, as though afraid he'd fall if he held it out a moment too long.

Tink waved him forward, hoping her face looked encouraging. She tried to push her worrisome thoughts away, but she felt the tightness in her chest return, the guilt eating away at her.

What had she done? Where were the Wanderers? Was Caiman all right? Would the *boys* be safe here? Had she taken them straight from one plague into another?

"Was that bird talking to you, Tink? What was it saying? Tinker Bell? Can you hear me?" Peter asked, waving a hand in front of her face.

The other boys were catching up now, flying alongside Peter, still talking excitedly.

"Did you see that blue bird? It was massive! I've never seen anything like it," said Slightly.

"What about that pirate ship out over the sea? A real pirate ship!" said Nibs with excitement.

"I never want . . ." said one of the twins, his costume's tail blowing in the breeze.

"Today to end!" said the other as Tootles blew his horn.

Tink couldn't think straight. She hovered near the ground, coming in close to the beach by Wanderers Cay and immediately started heading toward it. She stopped short suddenly and felt her stomach constrict. Seaweed and red tide had washed up onto the shore, a small dead fish a casualty among the algae. It was very quiet. Blair couldn't be anywhere near this place or she would have been throwing a fit. Tink looked around at the dark sand and tried not to panic.

The boys landed around her. They were all still chattering, several taking off to run along the beach and look around. None of them seemed to realize something was wrong. None but James.

"Tinker Bell?" He was breathing heavily as if the flight not only had taken a lot out of him physically, but mentally, too. "What is it? What's the matter? How can any of this be—" He glanced down at the seaweed stinking up the shore and wrinkled his nose. He lowered his voice. "Is this the problem you spoke of?"

"Yes and no," she jingled, shaking her head for emphasis. "Something is very wrong here. I need to find my friends right away."

For a moment, she wondered if James could understand her now that they were in Never Land. She stared at him hopefully, her wings fluttering slower.

James pursed his lips and looked at a tree near the shore that was clearly rotting from the inside out. "It's . . . very . . . nice."

Clearly not. Tink blew out a sigh.

"James!" Cubby cried. Tink and James snapped to attention and looked over at the boy who was running as fast as his legs could carry him, the hood on his bear costume off and flopping behind him.

"Are you all right, Cubby? What's wrong?" James grabbed the boy by the shoulders.

"Nothing!" Cubby was grinning ear to ear. "That's the thing! I feel fine! Better than I have in forever."

James looked him over, placing a hand on the boy's arm to as if to steady him. "I'm sure it's the adrenaline, Cub. Or the fact you're outside. Remember I was telling you how fresh air is good for your condition? But we don't want to overexert ourselves. You're still sick and need to take it easy. The—erm—well, that *journey* must have taken a lot out of you."

"Wow! Sea stars?"

"Look at the color of this rock!"

"James! James!"

Tink turned and saw all the children were frolicking. Slightly did a cartwheel on the sand. Nibs was mid-somersault. The twins were playing leapfrog. Tootles ran along behind them, blowing his horn as hard as he could. For the first time in days, Tink didn't hear him gasp for air between each exhale. And if she wasn't mistaken, color had returned to all their faces. She felt tears spring to her eyes.

At least she'd been right about *something*. They hadn't been too late. For all its troubles, the island had healed the children.

Peter flew in front of James and somersaulted through the air before sticking the landing perfectly. It was as though he'd been flying his whole life. Peter crowed, then spotted Tinker Bell. "You did it, Tink. You saved us."

"Now, Peter," James admonished. "I'm sure there is something we need to do now that we're here to alleviate your illness." He glanced at the fairy, his eyes full of questions. "Something to give you, perhaps? How does the healing work, exactly?"

"No, James. Look at all of us! It's already done," Peter insisted. "We're not coughing. We're not tired. I'm not shivering. I *feel* better. The second we crossed over to Never Land I knew something changed. Look at me now." He spun around. "Tink saved us," he repeated, grinning wide, the tiny point to his ears red. The glassiness in his eyes was gone, the dark circles on his pale skin seemingly evaporating before her eyes.

"It wasn't me, Peter," she jingled. A flurry of emotions was threatening to overtake her—pride and fear about her home intermingling. "It was Never Land. I knew the island would help you."

"The island, too, then." Peter grinned. He crowed again.

James pulled Peter toward him and put his hands on his face, examining him closer. "Well, your color *is* better. Your head is cool." He put his head close to Peter's chest. "I don't hear your wheezing." He looked around, confused. "All of you do look remarkably well. But I—" He turned back to Tink again. "How could an island do this?"

Tink looked around at the trampled beach around her. "I told you. This place is magic." *But for how much longer* . . . she added to herself with a sinking feeling.

"Magic," Peter repeated reverently, looking around, his hands on his hips, surveying the land. "Never Land is a dream come true. I never want to leave." He whistled. "Come on, boys. Let's explore the beach and look for pirate ships!"

Pirate ships. The *Jolly Roger*. Caiman. They needed to get to the ship.

"It's just not possible!" James said. She looked over to see him now sitting on a rock, holding his head. "It just isn't! Humans being able to fly through the sky, through stars and, and, and . . . wind up here. Wherever here is." He looked around now, his eyes slightly wild. "This isn't real. That's what it is," he said to himself. "I'm dreaming. This whole thing is a dream and any second I'm going to wake up." He smacked his own face. "Wake up!"

Tink knew he was having some sort of crisis, but there just wasn't time for her to help him with this. Frustrated, she darted over and pinched his arm.

"Owww!" James said, affronted. "What did you do that for?"

"To show you this isn't a dream." Tink gestured around her, then at herself.

He ran a hand through his hair. "More impossible things, huh?"

She nodded.

He calmed for a moment, then wound up again. "So those terrifying shadows flying over the island and all the torched earth and dead trees . . . this strange red sand beach? This isn't a dream or a nightmare—you're telling me it's all real?" She nodded emphatically. "If that's true, then now that the boys are healed, we should head back to London at once. This place isn't safe, Tinker Bell."

Tink flew back a few feet. "This *place* is my home," she jingled angrily.

"You sure about that?" a sharp new voice cut in.

TWENTY-ONE

TINK JUMPED, THEN BREATHED A SIGH OF RELIEF AT THE FAMILIAR FIGURE fluttering nearby. "Ash!" The fairy had snuck up behind her and for a split second she had the instinct to hug him. "I've missed you!"

"Have you?" His face was practically purple as he flew closer. "Where have you been?"

"Another fairy," James whispered.

Ash narrowed his eyes at him. "And you brought a Mainlander here? How? Who is this?"

"Well, well, well, look who finally came back."

Tink turned again to see two figures break through the waves beside their stretch of sand. Blair emerged from the water and pulled herself onto a rock in the cove, her long, emerald-green tail flapping hard against the rock, making a smacking sound. Blair's hair was now a lovely shade of blue, and on her upper torso, she'd fastened a top made from sea kelp in a cream color, the accent tying to what looked like a starfish clip in her hair.

A dolphin crested in the water next to the rock, then quickly morphed into Mimic's human form. He stood, striding toward the shore. "Tinker Bell! You're alive," he said flatly. "When you disappeared . . . well, we feared the worst." As he came nearer, James stumbled back in shock.

"Did he just . . . Is she . . . Are they . . ." the young man stuttered as the other boys came running.

"Oh my stars, it's a mermaid!" yelled Cubby, running to the shore and getting the feet on his bear costume wet. "An actual mermaid! Boys, look! Like in Peter's stories." He stared, his eyes wide. The rest of the boys crowded round, mumbling to each other and coming closer to ogle Blair as well. Tootles squeezed between the legs of Slightly to get a closer look. "You're beautiful," Cubby gushed, his cheeks reddening.

"Well, aren't you a sweet little Mainlander," she cooed, preening under their collective gaze. Then she turned stonily back to Tink. "So, what happened to you? We thought the pirates dispatched you! Or you were kidnapped! Or dead!"

"I thought you were alive," Ash cut in.

"Well," Blair crossed her arms. "The big takeaway is we all assumed we would never see you again."

"I'm sorry," Tink said. "I have so much to tell you, I know. I didn't mean to be away as long as I was. You see, I hit my head on the Mainland and injured my wing, but I'm all right now. And I need to get to Caiman—"

"What are Mainlander children doing here?" Mimic demanded. "Did you bring them here, Tink?"

"How?" Ash asked, and gasped. "Tell me you didn't use pixie dust. Tell me, Tink. The dust is for fairies only!"

Tink pushed a strand of her blond hair behind her ear and looked away. "Says who?"

James coughed, clearly uncomfortable with the commotion, even if he couldn't understand all of it. "Tink . . ."

"Tink!" Ash flew at James, hovering in front of his face. "Who is he? What exactly is going on here?"

James tried dodging and weaving out of the way. "What is he doing? Why is this fairy so close to me?" he asked, panicked.

"Ash, if you'll give me two seconds to explain, maybe you'll be a little less judgmental and a little more helpful," Tinker Bell cried. "Caiman needs me—"

"Caiman is missing!" Mimic interjected, his voice loud.

Tinker Bell's fire felt like it'd been snuffed out. "What? Missing? No. He's on the *Jolly Roger*. He's sick. He—"

"We're happy you're home, Tink, but you have to understand," Mimic cut her off, his voice deadly serious. "You up and disappeared on us. Poof. No note. No contact. No warning. We checked the falls. The Forbidden Side. Nothing."

"Then my friend Delene from the lagoon said she'd seen you and Caiman flying to the *Jolly Roger*," Blair said with a superior air.

Tinker Bell's eyes widened, cursing herself for not going back to the cove, for not telling anyone her plan before she took off. "Well, yes, I was with Caiman, but . . ."

"We worried the pirates did away with you," Mimic continued. "Blair and I spied by sea, Ash by air. But we didn't see either of you on any part of that dreadful ship. So we searched the island. Tiger Lily has practically run herself ragged trying to find you two!"

"And then the island started to fall apart," Ash added worriedly. "It seemed nowhere was safe from those god-awful creatures. The gray specters. You must have seen them on the way in? The island is crawling with them. We have no idea where they came from."

"We've been in hiding for weeks," Blair added. "This is the first we've come back to the cove since the shadows tried to snatch Ash."

Tink whipped around, looking back at the other fairy. "The shadows tried to take you? Are you all right?"

"I'm fine." Ash sniffed. "I've been in Pixie Hollow."

"Oh. Well, good." Tinker Bell wasn't sure what else to say about that.

"So far it's safe there," he added, adjusting one of the buttons on his tunic. "Unlike Shifters Beach."

Tink's blood turned to ice. "What do you mean? Mimic . . . Your herd?"

Mimic looked away.

Ash flew to his shoulder, patting the shape-shifter before continuing. "Shifters Beach is no more."

"No," Tink whispered.

"Some got out before the shadows' fire," Blair put in. "They warned the mermaids to leave the lagoon. Before those terrible beasts commandeered that, too."

Tink's jaw dropped. "How is any of this possible?"

"The shadows are taking over the island," Ash said grimly. "The more of them there are, the sicker Never Land gets."

"Never Land is sick, too?" Peter interrupted. Tink jumped. She hadn't realized he'd snuck over.

Ash looked at the boy in surprise. "Did he just understand me?"

"Of course I did," Peter said. "Clearly I belong here. Perhaps I'm part fairy myself."

"I'm sorry, *what*?" Ash stuttered.

At that moment Cubby wandered in, peppering Blair with questions a mile a minute. Mimic's pained expression waffled and transformed into various animals in quick succession—wolf, bear, falcon—making the twins gasp and add more screeching commentary to the mix.

In desperation, Tink motioned for Tootles to honk his horn, which he did. Loudly. Everyone looked at her. James grabbed Tootles.

"Boys, let's give Tinker Bell and her friends a moment," James said.

The boys turned reluctantly back toward the water's edge. The twins pointed to the *Jolly Roger* offshore, and a few of the boys ran over to see. Peter was the only one who couldn't seem to tear himself away.

"I'm sorry I disappeared," Tink apologized. "I went to the Mainland to find a tonic to cure Caiman."

"Why would the Mainland have a cure?" Ash asked. "And how would you even know where to look? It's not like you've ever been before."

Tink felt her face warm, and Ash couldn't hide his surprise. "Oh. You have. When?"

"Wait—you've been to the Mainland before this and never told us?" Blair exclaimed, sounding more intrigued than angry. "What's it like?"

"Who cares? She's not supposed to be there! She's a tinker fairy, not a nature fairy!" Ash shouted.

"I don't need your permission, Ash," Tink glowered. She looked at Mimic. She felt like she had to explain, even knowing how trivial it all sounded now. "I just—I needed to know what it was like. But that was a long time ago, and I only stayed briefly! All I knew was that they had remedies the island doesn't have. And when the pirates suggested that Caiman might need a different type of help, *Mainland* help—"

"The pirates? So you *did* go to the *Jolly Roger*," Ash cut her off. "And you're trusting pirates now?"

"No. I mean, yes. I mean, you weren't there!" Tink cried. "You didn't see how sick Caiman was after we found the penumbra. I had to save him and if the Mainland had something that could—a tonic that could cure him—I knew I had to go at once. So I did."

"Alone?" Blair asked softly.

"Yes." Tink flew straighter. "But then before I could leave Never Land, the Never Fowl attacked me. I hurt my wing, and the Mainland was different from what I'd remembered. I flew around looking for a healing place and when I found one, that's when I fell and hit my head. I was, well, a bit disoriented for a while . . . I forgot why I was there in the first place, and my wing took time to heal. I couldn't go anywhere for weeks. *That's* why I've been gone so long." She gestured back at James on the beach. "If he hadn't helped me get well, I wouldn't be here now."

"That doesn't explain why *they're* here now," Ash cut in, pointing at the boys splashing in the waves as James hurried them back to shore.

Tink sniffed. "Well, as *I* got better, these boys got sicker. They were dying." She looked at each of them. "And the Mainland couldn't cure them. So, I thought we could solve all the problems at once. Mainlander tonic for Caiman, and Never Land's healing powers for them."

"That wasn't your decision to make," Blair told her sharply. "Never Land is not meant for outsiders. Look at the havoc the pirates have caused. Look at what happened to poor Caiman!"

"These Mainlanders are different," Tink tried to explain. "Look at them! They're pure of heart. The island wouldn't have let any of them walk its shores otherwise." She had them there. "On the Mainland, they were abandoned. With only me and James to take care of them."

"*James.*" Ash said the name mockingly. "Is that what the older Mainlander is called?"

"Yes. He's alone, too," Tink said, bristling. Then she looked at all her friends, trying to appeal to each one of them. She knew full well she wasn't in their good graces. That it was already asking a lot of them to forgive her for disappearing on them and leaving them to deal with Never Land's mounting perils. But she couldn't just write them off now that they were here. "Or he was before he started taking care of these boys. Look, they have no one left. They're like us. Wanderers. I couldn't just leave them behind. Not when I knew the island could heal them."

"Look, I'm sorry if we sound angry, but you have to understand, it's a lot to process," said Mimic. "We thought the Forbidden Side did something to you and Caiman. We were worried sick! We've searched everywhere for you. Now we learn you just abandoned us for these lost boys."

Tink's stomach turned at the familiar word. Had the Never Fowl been talking to the Wanderers about her? "You have it all wrong. They needed me—"

"The *Wanderers* needed you, Tink," Blair said. "Forget Shifters Beach and the lagoon. Forget the shadow creatures. There isn't a spot on the island left untouched by disturbances. You should see the map. The Xs have taken over. Even the Never Fowl seem to have disappeared."

Tink paused, her face flushing as she was reminded by her earlier cattiness. Right. So maybe the Never Fowl hadn't been bad-mouthing her. She wondered if she should tell the Wanderers about the Fowl she'd seen on their flight in, about its foreboding message.

"It was awful," Blair cut in. "When you and Caiman didn't come back, the shadows appeared, and Prism Falls' pools started to drain. Tiger Lily has been sick with worry about all of it. Her village is doing everything they can to figure out why the magic is fading, but so far, we don't have a clue. We don't know if Caiman is alive or dead. And frankly, we might be in the same position soon."

Tinker Bell felt her heart constrict. In the distance, she could see the children happily playing, lost no more. She may have saved them, but for what? She'd failed her friends and her home. Caiman could be dead. She wasn't sure if she should scream or cry. *Neither*, she thought as the fire filled her belly once more. "I'll fix this," she vowed. "I brought reinforcements." She motioned to James and the others. "They'll help us."

Ash snorted. "Oh, the human children will save us?"

"*James* can help; he'll see things we missed. He'll work as hard as anyone here."

The others just looked at her.

"Sorry, Tink," Ash said. "But I think you're too late."

TWENTY-TWO

"No. I refuse to believe that." Tink rose up, her wings fluttering so fast, it made Ash's hair blow back. "This is all just a problem to be solved. We can figure it out." She motioned to James to join them.

He jogged back over to the group, his hands in his pockets as he looked at each of them somewhat uncomfortably. "Hello."

"This is James," Tink said, unable to hide the affection in her voice.

Ash muttered something under his breath.

"Hello, James," Blair purred as she braided her hair. "And what part of the Mainland are you from?"

He cleared his throat. "Um, London, miss."

Blair touched her shell necklace. "London! That sounds lovely."

"Can we focus here?" Tink snapped. She didn't like the way Blair was looking at James or how he was looking back (though, in James's defense, he looked as nervous as he did mesmerized). "James and I worked well together on the Mainland so we thought he could offer his assistance with what's happening to Never Land."

"Did you now?" Ash jingled, staring James down. "On what, may I ask, were you so helpful?" James blinked in confusion, unable to understand him.

"We worked on inventions together." Tink blushed furiously, hating how foolish this sounded. But before she could explain further, shouts suddenly rang out from behind them.

Tink whirled around to find the boys playing tug-of-war with a piece of driftwood. Peter yanked too hard, and Tootles fell and started crying. She sighed, wondering if maybe Ash had a point about the boys. "Excuse me a moment," James said, and ran over to the others. "Look, we just need somewhere safe for the children to stay while James goes with us to find Caiman and get to the bottom of things with one of you." She glanced toward the cave behind Mimic and bit her lip. "Maybe they could stay here?"

Blair scoffed. "I don't watch children! And besides, you want to keep them at Wanderers Cay?" she asked, as Tootles cried harder and Tink heard Slightly and Nibs yelling. "Yeah, they won't attract any bad guys."

"What are those Mainlander children wearing anyway?" Mimic sniffed. "I don't know what animals they think they're fooling."

"They're not trying to fool anyone," Tink insisted. "They're wearing pajamas."

"What are pajamas?" Mimic shook his head. "You know what? It doesn't matter. The shadow creatures could return at any time and we can't be responsible for these . . . children."

"Besides, Mimic and I aren't even staying here," Blair said. "We've found the least affected area of the island is actually the water."

"Fine. Ash?" Tink tried. "Could you watch them for a spell?"

"I don't think I can show up with a group of children at the hollow." Ash looked away. "Sorry, Tink."

Tinker Bell could feel her blood beginning to boil. Where was she going to house the boys while they worked? She tried to turn off the whirling concoction of anger and guilt bubbling in her stomach. This was a dilemma she hadn't thought of. She crossed her arms and fluttered in front of the Wanderers. "Fine. I'll find somewhere safe to put them, then I'll come back and the rest of us can go together to check on the falls and Caiman."

"*We* already have things to do," Mimic said almost apologetically, a haze seeming to make his body flicker. Tink knew at any moment, he'd transform. "If you want to help, come find *us* once you've gotten the children settled."

James stumbled back as Mimic transformed again, this time as a centaur, and took off down the beach, to the delight of the boys.

You versus Us. Mimic's words were clear. Tink tried not to bristle. She'd done this to herself.

"I'm headed to Mermaid Cove," Blair said before diving off the rock again. "One of the stingrays told me he'd seen the shadows siphoning water from the falls and I want to talk to him."

"Why would the shadows be siphoning water?" Tink asked.

"That's what I'm going to find out. I'm sure I'll connect with you later." Blair flashed James a grin. "See you soon, London Boy." Then she dove under the waves once more.

"F-f-farewell," James stuttered, running his hands through his hair.

"Your boy is cracking. Good luck having him help you with anything," Ash said, popping up next to her, placing a hand on her arm.

"He'll adjust," Tink insisted, even as James began mumbling to himself about transformations and the laws of physics.

Ash grimaced. "He's not one of us, Tink. And he doesn't look like he wants to be."

Tink's stomach swayed as she watched James floundering around the beach, his expression pinched, his nerves on edge as he yelled at Tootles not to enter the water. She whirled around. "You're just jealous I've met someone who finally understands me."

Ash darted back, looking as though he'd been stung. Tink immediately wished she could take the words back.

"I'm sorry," she started to say. "I—"

"I see the way you look at him, Tink," Ash spoke over her. "But don't forget: He's a Mainlander and you're a fairy. You can love this James all you want, but he's not going to love you back. All the magic of Never Land can't change a heart's desire." His voice sounded strange. "I know that better than anyone."

All the magic of Never Land. A heart's desire. Tinker Bell's pulse started racing. "You're wrong," she whispered.

"I hope so for your sake," Ash said quietly. "But if I'm not, don't expect me to be here to help you pick up the pieces. Goodbye, Tink."

Tink tried to hold back the tears that were threatening again. Since when was she such a crier? She had to get it together. *Breathe. Just breathe*, she thought, and pushed Ash out of her mind. Tink thought fast, a plan forming. She needed another ally. "Peter?" she jingled.

He came running over and did a double take when he saw James muttering to himself. "What's wrong with him?"

A crack of thunder made all the boys jump. The clouds were moving fast again and finding shelter for the boys was priority number one. "James will be fine. Tell him we're going to find somewhere safe for you to go while I look for a friend of mine who might be able to help us."

Peter lit up. "Can I go with you instead?"

"No," Tink said, though she admired his bravery. "I need you to watch out for the other boys in your new . . . hideout," she said, thinking fast. "After all, you're their leader."

Peter stood up straighter. "I am, aren't I?" He called to the others. "Boys! Tink says we're going to our new hideout. Come along!"

"Tink said what?" James asked, his left eye twitching. He looked worse for wear. Tink noticed he'd even unbuttoned his collar.

"She's taking us somewhere safe while she goes to get help," Peter said as the others came running.

"Help. Help is good." James looked at Tink. "I can still help you, too. With your Never Land problem. If you need it."

There was a hitch to his voice that made her think he was hoping she'd say no. From above, she felt a single raindrop fall. They needed to go. She reached into her pouch and began sprinkling pixie dust on each of them. ("Blast it all, more flying," she thought she heard James exclaim.) "Follow me. Quickly now!"

The boys cheered as they lifted into the air again.

"Where is this hideout?" Peter asked, gliding alongside her.

"There is a dead tree near my friend Tiger Lily's village."

Peter frowned. "A dead tree."

"This is no ordinary tree," she said quickly. "It's the perfect hideout because the trunk is hollowed out and has several entrances and exits, and even caves underneath it. You'll all be safe there while Tiger Lily and I see what's going on."

"A hideout," Peter repeated, sounding entranced. "I'm the leader and we're going to a hideout with caves." He crowed, his voice loud like the thunder that was rumbling again. "I love Never Land!"

They arrived at the tree as the rain began to come down harder. The lone tree stood out against the rocky terrain surrounding it. Something had happened to it since the last time she and Tiger Lily passed it. The tree looked scorched, a husk of what it had once been, like it'd been hit by several bolts of lightning. Vines hung from the tree's dead limbs; the only sign of life left in the carcass that was an old massive stump.

Don't panic, Tinker Bell told herself. She darted inside one of the entrances, using her pixie dust to peer inside. Thankfully, the underground tunnels looked untouched. She'd only explored a portion of it back when she and Ash had been scoping out places to stay, but she knew the tangle of roots and cavernous rock formed a secret entrance into an underground area bigger than the cave the Wanderers used. Sure, the space was much more rustic than the hospital, but it had possibility. Relieved, she flew back out, then gestured for the boys to land.

"Wow! Is this it?" Peter asked, landing hard and sending up a plume of dirt.

Tink nodded. She glanced at the boys, waiting for their reaction. "I know it needs some homey touches but it's safe."

"It's a tree house!" one of the twins marveled, grabbing a vine and swinging into a large hole in the side of the tree without a second thought. The other twin did the same and then all the boys started cheering and racing toward the trunk as James stood watch, his clothes getting soaked in the rain while Tink stayed dry under a nearby tree's limbs. Inside, she could already hear sounds of the boys' playing echoing faintly. They stared at one another.

"See you all later!" Peter crowed once more, then took off at a run, prepared to dive into the hole after his friends.

"Peter!" James said, startling him into pausing. "You won't leave the others, will you? If I—if I go with Tinker Bell?"

She felt her heart flutter. So, Ash was mistaken. James was coming around. He was no longer muttering to himself so that was an improvement already.

"Of course not," Peter told him. "Don't worry about us. I'm strong enough to handle any of those pesky shadow things while you're away. I can scare them. Watch this." He cupped his hands and cleared his throat and then mimicked James exactly. "You're just a child, Peter. You don't know how to take care of yourself, let alone others."

Tinker Bell clapped her hands. Peter's mimic was uncanny! "Brilliant!"

Peter bowed.

James actually chuckled, too. "Very good." He looked at her then and for a moment, she saw her James, the one with so much spirit. "You should hear his impression of Nurse Beth at the hospital. It's . . . well, it's . . . never mind." James faltered, his face falling again.

Tink felt her wings stop for a moment. *He's unhappy.*

She watched as James turned back to Peter, his face serious. "Be careful. This place is different from London. Don't do anything brazen."

"When have I ever been brazen?" Peter said slyly as the chitchat from the cave below grew louder. Tootles stuck his head out of the tree and blew his horn for Peter to come join them.

"See you when you get back!" Peter took off running again, his arms outstretched. Tink smiled to herself, knowing exactly what the boy was about to do. He caught hold of a vine, and before James could stop him, Peter swung onto it and catapulted himself into the nearest hole in the tree.

James sighed. "That boy is too daring for his own good."

"It's like he's meant for Never Land," Tink said. She could picture him climbing down the vines and roots to reach the bottom of the cave that lurked beneath the tree. Tink could hear the other kids' voices echoing below, the group chattering like chipmunks.

She missed the sound of so many voices talking at once and her heart longed for the Wanderers again. Would Blair, Ash, and Mimic ever forgive her and warm to the children?

"So. Where is this friend of yours?" James asked as Tootles tried climbing out of the hole.

Tink tilted her head, frowning, but Tootles paid her no attention. Perhaps the little guy just wanted to see them off? She noticed James looking at her, waiting for her to answer his question, and she pointed toward the center of the island.

James gazed in that direction and his frown deepened. "And you're sure it's safe to leave them when those shadows are flying about?"

She nodded again. How many times would she have to convey this? Of course she couldn't be certain, but no one knew of this hideout. It seemed safer than most places on the island now.

"All right then. Let's forge ahead. I was hoping to have some time alone with you anyway so we could talk about . . . all this." James looked around, his expression pained.

Tink suddenly felt shy. She flushed. There was so much to do . . . and yet, this was the first time she would be alone with James in Never Land. She heard the sound of her heart beating so loudly she thought James would hear it, too. The glow of her pixie dust grew seemingly brighter as she flew over to James. He put his hand out, palm facing up, just as he'd done back on the Mainland and she landed softly on his callused palm.

"I'd like to talk," she jingled. "I want you to like it here, and I think if we can work together to save the island, you would see how magical it can— Oh!"

Something fast zipped past James and he jumped in surprise, almost knocking Tinker Bell off his hand. The air around them seemed suddenly cold and for a split second, Tinker Bell thought it was a random gust of wind. Tinker Bell took to the air to avoid falling and quickly realized what had caused the disruption.

A shadow.

It swept quickly around James, circling them as they both cried out in confusion, and before Tinker Bell could even give a warning, the gray monster picked up Tootles and started to carry him away.

TWENTY-THREE

"Tootles!" Tink cried at the same time she heard James shouting at the shadow lifting the boy into the air.

Tootles started screaming and dropped his toy horn just as the other boys came scrambling out of the tree.

"Stop!" Tink shouted at the shadow, rushing after it. "Put him down!"

The thing was fast, and she had to push herself to keep up with it. The shadow kept going, turning back to look at her, almost as if it was goading her on.

Up close, she could see the gray creature was whisper-thin and held the shape of a human. It stared at her with its eerie eyes as it rose higher into the air, carting the tiny boy dressed as a skunk along with it.

Tink reached out and grabbed hold of one of its feet. Her hands went right through it like she was moving through fog. *What?* How was the shadow holding Tootles?

"Tootles!" Peter shouted, rising into the air, the pixie dust she'd given him for the flight over still working. He chased the shadow down, swatting at it wildly. "Let him go!"

"No! Not this high up!" Tink panicked. The shadow had Tootles by the onesie's bottom, and the child's arms and legs flailed out around him as he tried to get out of his grasp. James and the other boys still on the ground had started throwing things and a rock came whizzing by her, narrowly avoiding knocking her out of the sky. "Careful!" she jingled, but they didn't hear her. She sped up, chasing the shadow as it headed toward the water.

"I've got you now, demon!" Peter cried, reaching out to grab it now, too, and finding his hands slipping right through it.

"Put him down!" Tink pleaded. "He's just a boy!"

WHIZ!

Tink felt a shot of air as something whizzed past her once more. This time it wasn't a rock, it was an arrow. Tink looked down in surprise. Tiger Lily! Her friend was high atop Pony, her eyes on the sky as she aimed another arrow at the shadow. Even more impressive, neither of Tiger Lily's hands were on the horse. She let go of a second arrow, her long dark hair billowing behind her as the horse picked up speed.

WHIZ!

This time the arrow hit the shadow's back leg and the creature hissed in surprise, looking back and letting go of Tootles. It flew off, disappearing over the mountain ridge.

"Yes!" Tink jingled, then realized a bigger problem.

Tootles was now tumbling out of the sky, headed straight for the sea. Below, James and the children started to scream.

Tink flew faster, catching up with Tootles mid-tumble and dusting him midair. The glittery substance enveloped him, and Tootles's body lost speed till he was hovering a few feet off the ground.

Tink stopped short, breathing hard. *Thank the fairies.*

"Tootles is saved!" Peter crowed as he grabbed Tootles's arm and slowly helped him to the ground. The other boys and James came rushing over as he landed, Cubby quickly handing Tootles his lost horn.

Tiger Lily rode up to the group, her bow and arrow strapped to her back.

"Who are you?" Slightly asked as she dismounted Pony and waited for Tinker Bell to drop down onto her outstretched hand.

"You're here!" Tink exclaimed.

"Tink!" Tiger Lily's voice was joyous and light in greeting—the opposite of the other Wanderers—and Tinker Bell felt a rush of warmth at seeing her friend. There was so much she had to catch her up on, so many questions she had, too. "I cannot tell you how happy I am to see you're all right."

"You found us just in the nick of time," Tink exclaimed.

Tiger Lily looked over at Tootles and the other boys and smiled. "When I saw the trail of pixie dust and all those Mainlanders in the sky, I knew it had to be you. I'm glad I found you when I did."

Tink turned toward Peter so he could translate to the others. "This is my friend, Tiger Lily."

The boys murmured a collective hello.

"Thank you for saving his life," James said, hugging Tootles by his side.

Tiger Lily nodded. "Of course," she said. "Any friend of Tinker Bell's is a friend of mine." She scanned the sky. "But we should move quickly. The shadows are growing bolder and there are so many of them now. It isn't safe to be out in the open."

"Come along, boys," Tink jingled to Peter and the others. She put a hand on her pouch to give them more dust. "Let's get you back inside the hideout."

James looked at Tink. "Er . . . I'll take them by foot, if you don't mind. I think they've had enough flying for one day."

The boys groaned and Tink tried not to feel the twinge of hurt in her chest. She nodded. "All right."

She let James and the others walk ahead, Peter trailing along begrudgingly.

"We'll follow them together and you can tell me everything," Tiger Lily said, sensing Tink's need to talk. Tink flew to Tiger Lily's shoulder, thankful for the respite. Whether she wanted to admit it or not, she felt drained from the day already and the sun hadn't even reached its midpoint in the sky yet.

"So Mainlanders," Tiger Lily murmured and looked over at the fairy. "The others were certain the pirates had you, but I knew the Mainland is where you'd go to seek answers." She pursed her lips. "I just didn't think you'd be gone so long."

"I'm sorry, friend. The trip wasn't how I planned it." Tink filled Tiger Lily in on everything—from her injuries to her work with James; the mad dash they made out of London when Tink realized she couldn't leave the others behind; and Mimic's, Ash's, and Blair's reactions when she'd arrived. Tiger Lily listened patiently without interrupting.

"And your wing, your head? They're both healed?" Tiger Lily asked once Tink had finished her tale.

Tinker Bell sighed. "I'm fine, but . . . so much has happened. It's all so much worse than I feared. And I know it looks like I've abandoned you all and Never Land when all I want to do is save it." Tinker Bell swallowed, waiting for Tiger Lily's response. Her friend never judged, but her words were always truthful.

"They'll come around," Tiger Lily told her. "They're frightened. We all are, including everyone in my village. Never Land *is* in jeopardy, Tink. I'm just so glad you came back when you did because we're all needed now."

Tinker Bell felt her resolve strengthen. "I will fight these shadows to the end with you. You know that. And I do have a tonic I think can cure Caiman." She felt her shoulders tighten. "If he's not . . . That is, if he still needs it. The others said you'd been looking for him. You don't think the pirates did away with him, do you? If that's the case, I will never forgive myself."

"Tink . . ." Tiger Lily shifted uncomfortably. Wisps of her hair blew slightly in the breeze. "There is something you need to know. Something I haven't told the others yet."

"What is it?"

Tiger Lily stroked Pony's mane. "Two days ago, I was at the tallest bluff—you know the one that has that direct view over the Rock and the *Jolly Roger*?" Tink nodded. "Well, over there, I could have sworn I saw Caiman on the deck and he seemed . . . fine. Better than fine. He was tending to his mother's atrium."

Tink shot up into the air. "So he's healed?" Her stomach eased with relief and she wanted to cry out. Then a new thought butted in. "But if he's better, why wouldn't he return to the Wanderers and tell you all where I went? And let you know he's okay?"

"That's what I've been wondering." Tiger Lily's expression was grave. "I planned on telling the others today. I was headed to the cay when I spotted you all here."

Tink's heart thudded in her chest. "I'm glad you did. But I don't understand Caiman. Maybe Captain Bartholomew wouldn't let him on land."

"If he were to tell anyone why he hasn't returned to the island, it would be you," Tiger Lily said, and eyed the boys skipping up ahead with James. "You have a way with Mainlanders. Maybe because you've always been tied to that world."

Tinker Bell frowned. "Apparently to the island's detriment."

"No." Tiger Lily reached out a finger to tap the fairy gently on the shoulder. "I love you, Tink, but some things are not about you. Including Never Land's decline. Other forces are at work here."

Dark forces. Just like the Never Fowl warned.

"Thank you for your honesty," Tink told her best friend again. "It's just what I needed to drop my pity party." They both laughed.

"Always. And don't worry. I'll tell Grandma and the others about the boys," Tiger Lily said. "I'm sure she'll be accepting considering their circumstances. And like you said, they must be pure of heart if they're here."

Finally someone who understood! "Thank you."

"Of course." Tiger Lily glanced at the boys again and frowned slightly. "I have to ask: Does *James* understand what staying in Never Land truly means? What he's giving up?"

"Think of all he's gaining," Tink tried.

Tiger Lily smiled softly. "The children are gaining a great deal, and we can talk to them about everything the island entails. But you said yourself, James wasn't ill. He's a young man with dreams of his own—inventions you were helping him with. James is a Mainlander, you need to be sure he understands that on Never Land he will never grow older. He will stay as he is—always and forevermore." Tiger Lily touched a pinkie to Tink's hand. "You have to be truthful with him about this."

Tink felt an uneasy pang as she looked at the Mainlander who had stolen her heart. Her doubts and fears about what James was thinking crashed over her once more. He certainly looked unhappy, but that was just the shock of it all, wasn't it? Could she make him see the joys of being here? He wouldn't want to leave the boys. And who would want to leave Never Land?

You did, a needling voice reminded her. Tink's heart beat louder. *I came back. We belong here together with the lost boys.*

But then she heard Ash's voice in her head, too. *You can love this James all you want, but he's not going to love you back.*

Was that true? It couldn't be. She saw how he looked at her when they worked through the night. That said, Ash did have a point. What exactly did their future look like if they spent their days together as fairy and human?

Someone has to change, she realized. *Him or me.*

And now she could hear her heart beating for a different reason. A new plan was forming.

If they saved Never Land, if they replenished the falls . . . maybe the island could spare some magic to grant their hearts' desire. One that would allow them to be together. Tink imagined a world with James as a fairy and her heart nearly burst with hope.

Her reply to Tiger Lily was no more than a whisper. "I'll make sure James understands everything."

TWENTY-FOUR

Back at the hideout, Tink and James made sure all the boys were settled and knew not to leave the tree before they set off again. It had been agreed Tiger Lily would return to the village to tell the others about the new Mainlanders and then she'd meet James and Tink at Mermaid Cove, where she knew Blair was headed.

"But I want to come," Peter begged. "You need me. Look how I helped with Tootles."

"Peter," James said, his voice tight. "Never Land is not safe for young boys. We asked you to stay here. Do as you're told." He shook his head, clearly losing his patience. Peter lowered his head, clearly crushed.

Tiger Lily and Tink shared a look. James didn't have to be so hard on the boy.

Tiger Lily put a hand on Peter's shoulder. "You were very brave back there with the shadows."

"I was, wasn't I?" Peter boasted, perking up.

Tiger Lily kept her face neutral. "I can see that. That's why you must stay behind, to protect the others and to talk to the boys about what living on Never Land means for all of you. Tink told me you plan on staying and that is a big decision."

"That hasn't really been discussed yet," James cut in, looking uncomfortable.

"Of course I am staying," Peter said gruffly, crossing his arms.

"Yes, yes, yes" came a chorus of cries from the others who had overheard Tiger Lily. Peter added a rooster crow for good measure, and then all the boys were dancing around in a circle, clearly delighted.

"We can play all day," Slightly cried.

"No one to make us take a bath, or eat food we hate, or go to bed," added Nibs with a gleam in his eye.

"No bedtime," said the twins in unison.

"This is all true, but there is something important you must know about what living on Never Land means: No aging. You'd never grow up," Tiger Lily told them gently. "Who you are now is who you would stay forever, exactly as you are. It's something you'll have to really think about."

There was a beat of silence. Then Peter crowed again. "That sounds perfect!"

The boys cheered some more.

James, however, looked bewildered as he turned to Tinker Bell. "You didn't tell the boys this before we left. Is this truly how the island works? It cannot only make a sick person well, it can keep them from aging?"

Tink cast a sideways glance at Tiger Lily. This wasn't how she wanted to start this conversation. She thought they'd be alone, like their nights at the sewing table. But Never Land, it was turning out, was harder for them to find time to carve out than the Mainland was. "We should speak privately."

"She says she thinks you should talk alone," Peter repeated.

Tink gave Peter a look. "Sorry. Just trying to help." He turned to Tiger Lily. "James doesn't understand Tink the way I do. She and I first met when I was a baby."

"You what?" James asked incredulously.

"I think we should go." Tink motioned for James to follow. She nodded to Tiger Lily. "You will see to it that they get inside before you go?"

"Yes," she promised. "I'll see you soon, friend. Be careful!"

Tink and James walked along in silence for a while, neither sure what to say. Tink wanted to offer him pixie dust again so they could fly, but something told her James preferred to keep his feet safely on the ground. (*What a shame*, a small voice in her head said.)

Why is conversation between us so strained? Tink wondered. She'd been alone with James dozens of times before, and while language wasn't something they could use to communicate, they'd always understood each other. But here, on the island, she could feel things were different. She wasn't sure if it was the island's troubles, or what had just happened with Tootles, but the air felt charged, as if they both wanted to say something but were hesitating. She kept glancing his way and noticed James doing the same.

Say something, she thought. *Anything.* She looked around at the dying wildflowers wilting in the burnt grass and the tree nearby that looked like lightning. Was there anything she could use to try to get her message across?

James cleared his throat. "I can see why you like it here," he said suddenly. "You can see for miles; land and sea. Sometimes with all the high buildings in London, it feels like night comes early, even in the middle of the day. Here, the boys are not only well, they can run and play, with no rules, no worries. Never Land would be a paradise for them."

A point in Never Land's favor! Tink flew up higher and smiled.

"But . . ."

Aaaaand here came the *but*.

James looked away. She saw him use his sleeve to wipe his eyes as he stared out at the Never Sea. "I'm grateful to you for all you've done for us. With my invention and more importantly, with the boys. You've changed our futures forever, Tinker Bell."

Our. Our. Our. That had to be another good sign. Ash was wrong. She knew it. She glowed from the inside. "I think we can all be happy here together."

"I'll admit, I've fantasized about us being together—all of us like a little family, something I always wanted, losing mine so young."

Tinker Bell's skin burned to the touch, her heart ticking wildly.

"For the longest time, it was just me looking after the little tornados." He chuckled to himself. "They are lost causes when it comes to washing their hands, cleaning their clothes—those animal pajamas may run away on them. And they certainly don't know how to make their own food."

Tink paused. She hadn't thought about any of those things.

"They're children and that's the way it should be. But the thought of them *never* growing out of this phase . . . that's hard to comprehend," James continued.

The back of her neck tingled.

"I worked so hard on that invention for so long because I thought I could find a way to change our fates. To shift our place in a society that might have forgotten about them. About me." James paused, seeming to consider something. "And the day we left, when I was gone from Room Fourteen for so many hours, it looked like maybe I'd done it. Well, *we'd* done it."

Tinker Bell tilted her head, the memory of James bounding through the door flickering through her mind. "Something happened with the invention."

James blushing slightly. "I was going to tell you, but then everything happened with Peter and . . . Oh, Tink. Dr. Collins wants to help me file the patent for the sewing machine light! Not only that—he wants to buy one for the operating theater." He started to speak fast. "He thinks they could use it in other machines, that it could help when surgeries go later than expected, and they need to see up close. I'd mentioned it off-handedly cleaning the theater one day, and the idea stuck. Tinker Bell, I could stand to earn enough to take care of the boys forever."

He seemed so excited by this prospect, so energized. And truly it was what he'd wanted all along. He'd used his tinkering to carve a new path. But this path did not include her. Not when she belonged here. Her shoulders tightened.

James turned his gaze back to her. "Of course, *you're* the one who made the light work and it might be all moot now anyway now that I've up and disappeared with all of Room Fourteen. The hospital must be furious. I don't even know if I'll have a job if I return." He cleared his throat again. "Look, clearly the boys could be happy here, if this is where they choose to be, but I'm not sure *I* quite fit in, at least not as I am. I'm rambling again, I know. I just have so many thoughts."

She understood that feeling well.

"What I should be saying is thank you. You've saved the boys' lives. How can I ever repay you?"

The clouds behind him were moving faster now and Tink longed to stretch her wings and fly, but she was rooted to this spot. James seemed both happy and sad. Something wasn't working. But what did that mean for master problem-solvers like the two of them? Wasn't this, too, something they could figure out?

Tears pooled in his eyes, and Tink flew over and used a gentle hand to brush them away.

"You don't let anything stand in your way," James continued softly, looking down, giving her a glimpse of those long lashes again. "You barrel through life, find the answers. No matter how difficult. I don't think I've ever met anyone as stubborn—or incredible—as you. I don't think I've ever *cared* for anyone as much as I do you."

What was he saying? Tinker Bell sucked in a breath. "I feel the same way."

James lightly touched her hand, then turned back to the roiling Never Sea and Tinker Bell's heart raced.

He cared about her! Yes, this was complicated, but not impossible.

Together they could make the impossible possible. His admission was all she'd hoped for. No wonder James had been acting so strangely. He'd found out his whole life had changed because of the invention, only to find it wrenched in another direction. Could it change again? Would he want it to?

I'm not sure I *quite fit in, at least as I am.* Was he saying he'd feel differently if he *did* fit into Never Land? If they could fix Prism Falls, and James and the boys stayed . . . maybe . . . would he . . . could he . . . use some of its magic to change? Did he love her enough to do that?

Tink felt the flutter of her wings, of the one she had missed more than she ever thought possible in its sling on the Mainland. She knew she was born to be a fairy, and a fairy she wanted to be all her days. Could James be happy as one too? Could it be his heart's desire? She longed to know for sure. *I need to ask him.*

James spoke first. "Tinker Bell, I—"

The sound of squawking stopped him. A flock of massive blue birds descended on them all at once, surrounding the pair. Up close, the birds looked even more menacing. With their curved bills and large, brightly colored crests, they were quite the sight.

"DANGER! DANGER!"

Now? Really? Tink thought wearily, her eyes narrowing at the Never Fowl. "I know! Why do you think I'm here? I'm trying to save Never Land," she ranted. "If you can't tell me anything useful, then please just go away." She paused, her anger turning to fear as she realized the birds weren't there for her. They were surrounding James, who was starting to back up nervously.

"DANGER! DANGER! NEVER LAND IN DANGER!"

"Nice giant, prehistoric-looking birds," he tried, throwing his hands out in front of him to keep them at bay. "Why don't you go look for some worms?" He glanced at Tinker Bell. "Is that what they eat? Worms?"

"Never Crickets are more their taste, but worms will do in a pinch," she replied even though he couldn't understand her.

The Never Fowl seemed to confer with one another, squawking among themselves, then they started toward him again.

"Whoa! Whoa! Whoa!" James cried. "What do they want with me?"

Tinker Bell wasn't sure. Could it be because he was a Mainlander? She flew in front of him to stop them. It was almost comical how much smaller she was than the birds, and yet she'd have to be the one to protect him. "Stop! He's here to help us. He's not the enemy."

The Never Fowl squawked louder than before. "*DANGER! DANGER!*"

A blast rang out and the birds flew into the air, dispersing at once.

"Was that a gunshot?" James cried, his eyes widening. "We have to get back to the boys!"

"Help."

A figure staggered out of the woods in front of them and collapsed, the lantern they were holding falling to the ground. Tink took one look at the figure's sandy blond hair, tattered dress shirt and vest, and the mud-stained boots and recognized him immediately. "Caiman!"

He was back on the island. He looked terrible, but he was here and Tiger Lily was right—he was alive.

Lightning cracked in the distance as she flew to his side and James slid onto the ground beside her. Caiman was breathing, but she could see the gash on his cheek and the blood on his forehead. What had happened? Did the pirates hurt him again? Had he been trying to get away from them all this time?

"You know him?" James asked.

Caiman groaned. "Tinker Bell? You're back. . . . You shouldn't be here. Go. Get back to the Mainland. Please," he whispered.

"Go? No, I came back for you. And for Never Land," she said, tears filling her eyes. "Are you all right?"

He shook his head and stared at the ground. A small glass bottle fell out of his pants, and he picked it up and pushed it back into his pocket. "No. Not at all." He looked at her again, his eyes red. "Please get out of here before—"

A strange screeching sound chilled her bones, followed by a clicking noise that forced her to look up. Dozens of the gray wispy shadow creatures were streaking across the scorched earth, headed straight for them.

"They've found you," Caiman said. "Get out of here, Tink!" His eyes were slightly crazed. "Go! I'll hold them off."

"What? Caiman, no!" she cried angrily. "I'm not leaving you again. We're getting out of here together."

This time, Tink didn't give anyone a choice. Reaching into her pouch, she threw pixie dust at both young men and they started to rise into the air.

"What are you doing?" Caiman panicked. "I told you to go!"

"We *are* going," Tink said, taking to the air. "We need to get to Mermaid Cove. That's where Blair is waiting. Tiger Lily will find us."

"No! We can't! You don't understand!" Caiman argued as he and James floated up and started to follow her through the trees, trying to bob and weave away from the shadows. He dragged his hands across his haggard face. "Fine! Head to the falls. We'll lose them in the chasm."

"Now you're thinking," Tink replied, zooming around a large redwood tree as the clicking sound grew closer. "Think happy thoughts, fellas, and follow me."

TWENTY-FIVE

TINKER BELL FLEW AS FAST AS HER WINGS WOULD CARRY HER. SHE JUST HOPED James and Caiman—both such new and nervous fliers—could keep up. The shrieking and clicking sounds of so many shadows pierced her eardrums, but she tuned them out, zipping over the beaches, zigging and zagging around Mermaid Cove and heading toward the mountains. Finally, she looked back at James and Caiman and beyond them to the sky. The shadows were gone.

"I think we've lost them," Tink told Caiman.

Caiman sighed with relief. "Good. Drop me at the falls and take your friend back to the Mainland as quickly as you can."

"Wait, you're not some mythical being, too?" James did a double take. "You know the Mainland?"

"I'm from the Mainland, chap," Caiman said. "And . . . and if you know what's best for you, you'll go straight back there."

"We aren't going back," Tink told Caiman stonily, annoyed he was trying to sway James's decision. Of course *this* was when he finally chose to grow a backbone. "I won't leave Never Land when it's being overrun by shadows and the magic is fading. I'm staying here to fight."

Caiman closed his eyes for a moment, then looked anxiously around him. "Just get me to the falls then. Please."

Tink couldn't understand what his issue was. Unlike the others, who felt abandoned by her trip to the Mainland, Caiman knew that she'd left to save him. Now he seemed to want nothing more than to make her disappear. She glared at him for a moment and noticed something.

Her time away from him had not been kind to the pirate. He may have healed from the penumbra's poison, but Caiman's bruised face looked even worse up close, his right cheek puffy and red where he might have been hit by something hard. Whatever had been happening to him on the *Jolly Roger* had continued. The captain had said they dispatched the pirate who had hurt Caiman, but clearly he'd been lying. Tinker Bell imagined Captain Bartholomew's fist connecting with Caiman's face and she wanted to rip that hand right off him.

"It's going to be okay, Caiman," Tink tried to reassure him, falling back to fly by his side. "This is my friend James. He's here to help us."

Caiman wouldn't even look at him. Tink cleared her throat and went on.

"I found a tonic on the Mainland to cure you from the penumbra, but I'm glad to see you don't even need it. I've been so worried. I didn't mean to be gone as long as I was. . . ."

"It was good you weren't here to see all this," Caiman said, not making eye contact.

"No, but maybe if I had returned sooner, the island wouldn't be as bad off as it is," she said. "Anyway, I'm glad you're well. . . ." There was something about him she couldn't put her finger on. It wasn't just the bruises. Something else had changed. "Are you sure you're all right? That day in the Forbidden Side . . ." She shuddered at the memory. "I thought the flower's sap tore you in two."

"You thought wrong, Tinker Bell. I'm *fine*," he said, somewhat bitterly. "I'm a survivor, remember?"

Tink frowned at the familiar words. *You aren't acting fine.* As they came out of the narrow canyon, she could see the ridge that hid Prism Falls. Her heart broke at the sight up close. The majestic waterfall had been reduced to a dribble, the shimmering puddles beneath it muddy and gray. If this went on much longer, all the magic of the island would be gone.

Tinker Bell pointed to an area near where the pool of water should be. "Let's land there and wait for a bit before leaving to get to the other Wanderers. They're going to want to see you, Caiman," she added.

Caiman didn't reply. Instead, he landed and curled up in a ball, rocking almost manically.

James dropped down beside her. "I don't think I'll ever get used to that feeling," he said to Tink, moving in closer. "Is your friend all right? He seems like a bit of an odd fellow."

Tink nodded. "He's been through a lot," she jingled, then shrugged, figuring that would convey her thoughts the best right about now. Looking at the lack of water in the falls, she thought guiltily back to her previous idea. How would James feel about being a fairy? Would he enjoy tinkering here as much as she did? If there was a chance they could be together, would he take it?

"You shouldn't be here," Caiman suddenly shouted. Tink whirled around as he advanced on her. "You were supposed to stay on the Mainland! You like it there! All those lost things."

"Calm down, mate," James cried. "Tinker Bell is trying to help."

Caiman shook his head, his expression pinched, and she noticed the bruise below his jaw was purple. "She can't. No one can help me now."

Tink felt a strange prickling sensation on the back of her neck. Her heart was thudding as she looked from the pirate to the muddy waters where the falls water once flowed deep. *Danger. Danger*, the Never Fowl had squawked when they found her coming back to the island, with James.

Did they mean the forces overtaking Never Land? Or were they warning her about *someone*? "Caiman, do you know something about what's happening to Never Land? You can tell me. I will help you."

"It's too late for that." Caiman unhooked the small lantern on his belt and held it up, examining it.

Tink felt her panic rising. "It's not! You know what's wrong, don't you?"

The pirate just kept shaking his head over and over again.

Tink zoomed over to him, prepared to get in his face and demand answers. "Caiman, tell me!" she shouted, but just as she got close, Caiman lifted his lantern and trapped her inside it, closing the latch and locking her inside.

"Caiman!" Tinker Bell railed, her small fists pounding on the glass, her feet kicking at it as pixie dust filtered through the air in the tiny space. It was stuffy and the air holes were small. She felt claustrophobic. "What are you doing?"

"I'm sorry," he whispered, his eyes red and rimmed with tears. "I tried everything I could. But you've given me no choice."

She felt dizzy already, the heat getting to her.

"Tinker Bell!" James's muffled voice reached her through the air holes in the top of the lantern, which were annoyingly too tiny for her to climb out of. She reached out for James, wanting to shout, but already she was feeling woozy. She saw James running toward Caiman, trying to wrestle the lantern out of the pirate's hands. Tink felt the prison sway left and right as they fought, knocking her back and forth against its walls. The heat was taking over now and as the lantern swayed, she collapsed inside it.

The last thing she saw before she passed out was Caiman hitting James—her James—in the jaw with a right hook.

TWENTY-SIX

When Tink opened her eyes, she once again found herself staring into the darkness. A light flickered nearby, and she realized quickly it was a lantern, much like the one she'd been trapped in. Now it seemed she'd been moved to a small bird cage sitting on a jagged ledge in a cave that was unfamiliar.

Lying next to her on the ground was James. And he was out cold.

Tink felt a flash of anger. "Caiman! What have you done to him?" She pulled at the bars on the cage. "Let me out now!"

"I'm sorry, Tink." Caiman's voice came out of the darkness. His voice sounded defeated. "I didn't want it to come to this. Really, I didn't. You know I'm not like them. But the captain gave me no choice. He said if you showed up back in Never Land, I had to take you to the Rock."

"You're taking orders from the captain now? You hate the pirates," she reminded him.

"I know that! Don't you think I know that? But they own me," he said, lashing out. "They know I'll do anything to protect my mum's work. Bartholomew won't let me have them or leave the *Jolly Roger* for good till the deed is done. And it almost is now." He held up the glass bottle she'd seen him drop earlier. "This is just about the last of it. Then Mum and I will finally be free."

Her heart was beating faster. "What did you do?"

Caiman knelt down next to the cage. "I didn't have a choice. You've got to understand, Tink. But I'm not going to let them hurt you. I swear it."

He looked uncertain about this fact, however, and his eyes were wild. She needed to get help. Tink had to think fast. Blair was headed to Mermaid Cove. Tiger Lily to her village. Who knew where Mimic and Ash were. How long before they suspected something was wrong? Or would they think she'd pulled another disappearing act?

Tink approached the familiar slide of self-pity before pulling herself back. Tink gripped the bars again and realized one was rusted and loose. If she could find something to break a few, she might be able to fly out, use her dust to get her and James away.

Tink looked around wildly. Her eyes landed on a pebble, the perfect size for her hand. "You're not a Wanderer. You're a traitor."

Caiman's face was pained. "I know." He turned away from her, looking out the entrance of the cave.

She used that moment to reach down and grab the pebble. *Keep Caiman talking*, she told herself. *Till you can get this loose.* "I don't understand. Why hurt Never Land? I thought you loved this place." She rubbed at the bars over and over with the pebble, jingling loudly so that he wouldn't hear.

He turned back to her and she stopped.

"Don't you see? The crew was never going to let me leave till I found them a way onto the island. They wouldn't let up." He closed his eyes. "That's why they kept sending me."

Tink thought of his bruises, the way he sometimes cried in his sleep in the cave, then rushed back to the ship.

"At first I tried making salves and potions with what I'd found here. I figured maybe that would break down their barrier somehow, get the others unstuck."

Tink thought about what Tiger Lily had said—the disturbed foliage, the overturned ground and torn roots. *Caiman* had been the intruder.

"But after talking to Tiger Lily, I realized it was bigger than that," Caiman went on, as if reading her thoughts. "Never Land itself was dead set against any pirate setting foot here. They'd never find a way. After all the bad things they'd done? It wasn't going to happen. Unless . . . I found a way to use the island's magic against itself."

Tink froze. "Caiman . . . what exactly did you do?"

"I'd heard you all talk about Prism Falls before you gave me that plant book. I knew it held the magic of the island so I went there one day after leaving the cay. Took a vial of water back to the ship and gave it to the captain and the crew." He swallowed hard. "I thought maybe the magic would get them onto the island, but it didn't. Instead, all those terrible things started happening—fires, dying trees, animals scattering."

Tink gasped. So the island's malfunctioning had nothing to do with her visiting the Mainland. It wasn't her restlessness. It was the pirates siphoning Never Land's magic. "You stole the water? Caiman, how could you?"

"I needed them to leave me alone, Tink! It was just a little bit at first, but when it didn't let them off the ship, I kept going back and getting more. That didn't work either." He ran a hand through his messy hair. "They were angry and I was desperate. And then you and the others gave me that plant book." He pulled it out of his back pocket and held it up to show her. He gave a small smile as he looked at the wrinkled cover. "This. This is what saved my life." He flipped to a page and pointed a dirty finger at some handwriting on it. "As soon as I read the entry, I knew the penumbra was the key." He looked out toward the cave opening again, watching the tide begin to rise, the *Jolly Roger* bobbing in the distance.

Tink tried to rub at the rusted bar with the pebble and felt a piece of the bar break. If she could break another piece, she'd be through. Caiman turned around again and she stopped.

"When I read about the sap nurtured by the magic of the falls, I started to wonder. If this plant truly had the ability to sever one's darkest parts, could I give it to the pirates? Would it rid them of their rotten pasts, their bloodlust? Make it so at least part of them could walk Never Land? Or, at the very least, stop tormenting me?"

Tinker Bell swallowed hard, watching as Caiman started to pace. "But the Forbidden Side sounded more terrifying than the pirates so I thought maybe I'd find a way to get you there. I told you all that stuff about the penumbra being able to save the island." He swallowed hard.

"And I offered to go with you," Tink said, putting the pieces together. "And when you took the sap . . ."

"I thought it'd be harmless, but I'd misinterpreted the book's meaning. It severed my darkest parts. Meaning *my shadow*."

Tinker Bell paled. "Wait—that creature, the one that seemed to be tearing you apart—that was *your* shadow?"

Caiman's eyes looked hollow. "One and the same. It detached itself. Flew away on its own accord."

She gasped. "And made you sick."

Caiman shook his head, avoiding her gaze for the first time. "Well, no, not exactly. Even if the penumbra didn't work as I thought it would, it seemed it would still fit the bill for what the pirates wanted. Maybe they couldn't get on land. But I was guessing their shadows would. So I may have exaggerated the sap's effects. That way, you would take me and the penumbra back to the *Jolly Roger*. . . ."

"You tricked me!" Tink shouted angrily, realizing her mistake. "You made me believe you were dying." Tink couldn't decide on what emotion tugged harder at her—hurt or anger. Her heart started to beat faster now, her brow perspiring. "And you gave them all the penumbra sap while I was on the Mainland, didn't you? Those other shadows—the ones all over the island we've been seeing—those belong to the pirates?"

"Yes." Caiman bowed his head a notch lower. "They've been wreaking havoc all over Never Land—stealing things they deemed valuable, burning the rest. They enjoyed it at first, but then it still wasn't enough for the captain. He wanted to pillage Never Land like his shadow did. He was the one who thought we should try getting more water from the falls. A lot more. If their shadows could roam the island, he figured maybe we could collect enough of Never Land's magic so the rest of them—their whole bodies, entire beings—could, too." He swallowed hard and looked away again. "I was just so tired of being afraid all the time, Tink. I had to make the madness stop, so I did what he asked."

Tink was so horrified she couldn't focus on her breakout. Caiman, her sweet friend, had become as wretched as the other pirates in his desperation to be free of them. Anger pulsed through her veins as she pressed the pebble harder against a second bar and felt it break free. Were two enough to slip through? It would be close, but possible. She stepped to a new section of the cage so she wouldn't draw attention to the opening. "You should have known it wouldn't be enough. Nothing is ever enough for the pirates."

"Yes," he admitted guiltily, looking at her again. "I didn't want any of this to happen, but once it started, I couldn't stop it. The captain made the pirates start carrying as much of Prism Falls water back to the *Jolly Roger* as they could so they could bathe in it. Drink it. Consume it so the magic of Never Land would course through their veins." His face was filled with anguish. "I didn't think they'd try to take it all."

Tink dropped the pebble, her fury taking over. "So you're the one the Never Fowl were trying to warn me about. You've been trying to outwit this place, trying to steal the island's magic this whole time! And now you've drained the falls till there's nothing left! Don't you see what you've done? You're killing Never Land! This place that *saved* you." She was shaking now she was so incensed.

"But it didn't save everyone. Never Land let my mother die!" Caiman fell in front of the lantern now and wept. "I had nothing to live for but her work after that. That's all that mattered to me. It's all that still matters. I like the Wanderers well enough, but I can't live like this anymore. Captain

Bartholomew won't stop till Never Land is his and he knows you and Tiger Lily won't let that happen, Tink." His eyes were wild again. "He knows you're here and he's going to try to kill you both. That's why I wanted you to leave. I was going to warn Tiger Lily, and the others, if I could. You have to believe me."

In the distance, she heard the clicking sounds and shrieking of the shadows again. Her heart filled with terror.

Caiman rose slowly and held up his lantern. He let out a sharp breath before turning back to her. "It's too late. They're here."

TWENTY-SEVEN

TINK HAD TO GET JAMES OUT OF THERE. SHE PUSHED HARD ON THE BROKEN bars, knocking them loose, and started to climb out as Caiman stared at the shadows approaching. She was almost free when a creature whisked by and snatched the cage, lifting Tink high in the air. She fell backward, landing in the cage again.

"No!" Caiman cried.

The shadow screamed and clicked its nonexistent tongue as it dropped the cage over the cave's waters. Tink plummeted, knocking against the back bars. She knew in a moment she'd be underwater, sunk to the bottom of the Never Sea in a Mainlander's bird cage. And then what would happen to the Wanderers? To the Lost Boys? To James? No. She wouldn't let a little life-threatening situation get in her way.

She darted toward the opening, zipping through the cage as it hit the water with a huge splash. She flew to the nearest ledge and pressed herself against it, hoping she wasn't spotted.

"You killed her!" Caiman wailed, watching the cage sink beneath the water. "I told you I'd take care of them! They wouldn't be a problem." One of the shadows surrounded Caiman, looking as if its mist was trying to choke him. She heard Caiman struggle for air. "All right. Stop!"

The clicking sound grew louder and Tink watched as the cave lit up like a flame as the shadows took over, carrying lanterns in their hands. The ominous shadows creeped along the walls, showing off the moss and vines that had grown like spiderwebs across the damp rocks. She watched as they carried in two familiar figures and dropped them into the water below.

"Blair and Mimic," she whispered, horrified.

Her friends were tied back-to-back. Mimic was in his human form, his hair matted to his forehead, his arms bruised and bloody from straining against the ropes. Blair's hair was now plaited and in knots, a strand of seaweed woven through it looking as if she'd put up a fight before being dragged away. The pair shimmied their way to a rock in the middle of the water and pulled themselves up on it. Tink felt rage building inside her as she watched the shadows circling them. Mimic's body flickered, revealing the seal he must have been before transforming back and getting captured.

If Blair was anxious about the situation, she didn't show it. Instead, she was her usual cool, detached self, chin held high and her arms folded over her chest as if this whole situation was one big inconvenience. Tink's heart warmed for the mermaid. She needed to find a way to let them know she was here.

"You can't keep us here!" Blair shouted at the shadows. "All of Never

Land will realize I'm missing. Believe you me! People will come to rescue us!"

"She's right," Caiman told the shadows. "You're being rash. First Tinker Bell, now the other Wanderers. You're going to get caught."

"Caiman!" Blair said happily. "You're alive! You're— Wait. Why are you talking to the shadows?"

"Caiman?" Mimic's voice echoed in the cave. His tone was darker. "What happened to Tinker Bell?"

Caiman looked over the ledge, his face cast in shadows making him look wicked. "I'm sorry. I didn't want it to come to this." He stepped away again.

"Caiman? Caiman!" Blair yelled, but he ignored her.

The shadows' clicking sounded like snickers. They seemed emboldened by what was happening in the Rock and continued swirling through the small cave, back and forth, a few hovering near the entrance. It occurred to Tink they were waiting for something . . . or someone. This was her chance to get her friends' attention.

Tink picked up a pebble and threw it at Blair. It rapped off her head, leaving an angry red mark.

"Oww!" the mermaid shouted at the shadows. "That was uncalled for! What if you bruised my face?"

Mimic, however, turned his head. Tink knew the exact moment he saw her—a flicker moved across his face. Tink put her finger up to her lips and he nodded. She watched as he whispered something to Blair. Her eyes widened.

"Never mind!" Blair said cheerily to the shadows. "I can see from my reflection my face is fine. You're lucky."

The shadows swirled together now, forming a vortex, and their shrieking grew louder. Tink watched them hover near the cave's entrance; they seemed excited now, which only added to the fairy's mounting dread. Still, she took advantage of their distraction to fly to Mimic and Blair on the rock.

"Tink," Mimic said as the water lapped at his torso. "Am I glad to see you."

"That's a change," she jingled dryly, unable to help herself as she went straight to work on the ropes binding them.

"I know. I'm sorry. We could've been a little more understanding back at the cay." Mimic winced as she yanked at the knot hard. "Is Caiman really working with the shadows?"

"He is," Tink whispered, working the rope loose. She almost had them. "There's no time to explain. We have to get out of here. I have dust, but I don't know how we'll fly past all these shadows, plus James is up on that ledge. Caiman knocked him out."

"He is?" Blair looked up, her lips pursed. "We cannot leave that handsome Mainlander behind."

Tink glared. "I wasn't going to. But we need a diversion. Something to get the shadows away from the cave so we can fly past." She pulled at the rope again and it came loose. "There! You're free."

"Thanks, Tink," Mimic said, stretching his arms. "Let's make for the opening."

"Wait, have you been listening? I can't go without James," she said again.

"We can't risk Never Land for a Mainlander," Mimic argued. "Blair can swim out and get help from the mermaids. Maybe they can do something to the ship to hold the *Jolly Roger*. And you and I need to get to Tiger Lily and tell her what's happening with the shadows."

James or Never Land. Tink's heart was pounding now. She looked up at the ledge again. She could only see James's calloused hand—lying terribly still.

The shadows all started screaming as one and suddenly two new beings entered the Rock. These were different from the others. Tink could see that immediately. They weren't gray so much as they were almost spectral in appearance, an outline of a pirate in a large hat and a small squat man wearing short pants. The creatures flickered, from human to shadow, over and over as if they were neither one thing nor the other, but something in between. They hovered in front of Caiman, clicking their tongues.

"Yes, Captain," Caiman said automatically. "I have a new batch for you right here." Shakily, he held up two spoons full of glittering water.

"What are they doing?" Blair hissed.

"Shhh!" Tink jingled. Her heart was pounding now as she watched in horror.

The shadows snatched the spoons and drank greedily, then dropped the utensils onto the ground, the metal clanging. The shadows shrieked louder and louder as they flickered once more before transforming into Captain Bartholomew and his trusty mate, Mr. Smee, in the flesh.

"How? It isn't possible. . . ." Mimic stuttered.

Captain Bartholomew looked at his hands in delight, wiggling his fingers and spinning around, his jacket twirling behind him in the cave. "My boy, you did it. You did it! At last—we're free!" he shouted, his voice echoing.

"He did it, yes he did," said Mr. Smee, patting his belly and his backside, looking delighted at being whole again. "I feel good as new, Captain. Other than my sea legs."

"That will go away, Smee. That will go away." The captain threw his arm around Caiman. "My boy, you've done good! Very good!"

Caiman's voice was strained. "Thank you, Captain."

"You have more waters, yes?"

"Yes, sir." Caiman held up the small glass vial. His hand was shaking hard.

"And that's the last of it? The water of the falls?" he pressed. "We need every last drop. I'm sure of it. If Never Land is to be ours, we need all its magic."

"My gods," Blair whispered. "Never Land is doomed."

"We need to get that vial." Mimic looked at Tink. "Fly up there!"

Tink's eyes narrowed in on the vial and she tried to think of the best approach. She couldn't be foolhardy. "If I go now, they'll grab me before I can do a thing. We need a plan."

"But—" Mimic cried.

The captain stared at the vial as if in a trance. "Good. Good. Excellent. And the Wanderers . . . you've dealt with them, too?"

Caiman nodded, his expression anguished. "Haven't found Tiger Lily, but I got the new Mainlander that just flew in." He nudged James with his foot. "Blair and Mimic are down there."

He motioned to the water below and Tink hid herself in the folds of Mimic's shirt. Blair inched closer to block the fairy as best she could.

"Let us go!" Mimic shouted as the shadows tittered nosily.

"I'm afraid that won't be happening, boy," Bartholomew said cheerily. "You'll drown when the tide comes in soon enough. I'd enjoy what time you and the mermaid have left."

"You're a wicked fool," Blair seethed.

The captain tipped his hat to her. "I'll take that as a compliment!" He looked at Caiman. "And our dear Miss Bell?"

Caiman swallowed hard. "In a watery grave, sir. The shadows did it."

The captain laughed, the sound echoing in the space, bouncing off the walls and making it seem as if Captain Bartholomew was all around them. Caiman looked pained. "Then we've nothing else standing in our way! Men, Never Land is truly ours for the taking!"

All around the cave, pirates and shadows began to cheer. It was deplorable.

"It's now or never," Mimic instructed. "We have to try. I'll transform into a bird, and we can get that vial together. Blair can go for help."

Tink knew he was right, but she hesitated, looking at the ledge. What about James?

She shot a look in his direction. Her heart leapt when she saw James slowly start to sit up. "Tinker Bell?" she heard him say, his voice echoing down the dank cavern walls before he realized what was happening.

"Who's this?" the captain asked sharply.

"Tinker Bell's Mainlander, sir," Caiman said as a few of the ashen shadows surrounded James.

"Ahh . . . Let him join Miss Bell in the fathoms," Bartholomew said dismissively. The shadows picked James up and prepared to drown him.

"Put me down!" James demanded, kicking furiously.

"No!" Tink jingled, flying up to stop them as Mimic transformed into a bird and headed straight toward Caiman while Blair dove underwater. "Stop!"

Her cry was the last thing she heard before a blast rocked the cave.

TWENTY-EIGHT

The sky turned black, rocks raining down on the cave and sending the pirates and the shadows running in all directions. Tinker Bell felt her body sail through the air, narrowly avoiding a collision with falling debris. She couldn't see Mimic, Blair, James, or Caiman. All she heard was screaming. The last vial of Prism Falls water. Where was it? Did Caiman still have it? Did he lose it in the blast? Tink couldn't stop her mind from whirring. Her eyes scanned the waters for the vial and instead she saw a body, floating face down.

Tink descended fast and landed on his back. "James! James!" she cried, throwing dust on him as quickly as she could. His body started to rise out of the water, and she heard him gasp and choke, water flying out of his mouth. Thank the fairies. He was all right.

He shook his head and looked around in surprise as he saw himself in midair again. She flew in front of him. "You have got to stop doing that," he joked in a raspy voice, but his expression was strained. "Where are we? Where are the boys?"

Before she could answer, a second blast rocked the cave. Tink and James dove out of the way, pressing themselves against the wall as a cannonball sailed through the air. It landed right on a shadow that clicked and screeched trying to get out from under the heavy object.

Tink looked up in surprise. Two holes had been blown through the side of the cave. They almost matched the shadows' haunting, void-like eyes. As she stared, a new figure flew into one of the openings, examining the wreckage below. Tink heard a familiar voice.

"Did someone call for a rescue?"

"Peter!" James cried.

The pair rushed over to greet him. She'd never been so happy to see the redheaded boy.

For his part, Peter looked equally thrilled. "James! Tink! You'll never believe what we've done!" He puffed up his chest. "We took over the *Jolly Roger*."

"The *Jolly* what?" James asked, confused as he shook his wet hair.

Tink almost forgot how to fly. Her wings stalled. "You took over the *Jolly Roger*?"

"Yes," he said proudly, hands on hips again. "It was Tiger Lily's idea."

There was a screech and Tink looked up to see Mimic, in the form of a pelican, flying through the cave. Tink prayed he had found the vial of Prism Falls water. She didn't see the captain or Caiman anywhere. Rocks kept pelting down on them as the shadows screeched, their cries bouncing off the cavernous walls.

"Tiger Lily said you and James had been captured by the shadows, and she came and got us boys for a rescue mission," Peter went on. "We staked out the cave and I wanted to ambush it, but Tiger Lily said this isn't a game. Which, obviously, I *knew*. It's war. She said we needed a plan; so that's when we took over the *Jolly Roger* since all the pirates abandoned ship." He grinned. "The pirate ship is a way better hangout than the tree, but Tiger Lily said no." He sighed. "Anyway, we needed a distraction to save you all and the cannon was just sitting there so . . ."

"You could have hit one of us!" Tink reprimanded him at the same time James said, "A cannon?! We do not play with weapons!"

Peter looked slightly baffled. "It worked, didn't it?"

"Where are the other boys?" Tink asked.

"The boys and Tiger Lily are all back on the ship," Peter told her.

"Did you just say the rest of the boys are on a *pirate ship*?" James asked aghast.

"Brilliant, right?" Peter smiled slyly. "Now let's fly." He grinned mischievously. "Might have pinched a bit of your dust for myself back at the tree, Tink. Sorry. Thought it might come in handy with all those shadows around and it did. I can fly as good as I can walk, can't I?"

"Peter!" James groaned.

Tink shook her head, vacillating from impressed to horrified. This boy was going to be trouble, wasn't he?

Just then, a new commotion below them stole her attention. Captain Bartholomew and Mr. Smee were fleeing in Caiman's dingy, with the young pirate rowing them away.

"Get to the ship!" the captain barked as he stood at the bow of the small boat, one foot perched up on the ledge, casting it at a dangerous angle while Mr. Smee struggled to right them. "That cannonball came from the *Jolly Roger*! There is a mutiny, Smee!"

"Wait! Watch this," Peter said to Tink and cupped his hands. His voice was suddenly deep, and it echoed thanks to the cave. "Captain, beware of the mighty sea spirit. Beware!"

The captain startled. "Did you hear that, Smee?"

"Yes, Captain," Mr. Smee blubbered. "Must be an evil sea spirit! Row faster, Caiman!"

Caiman looked like a shell of himself. Blood was running down his forehead from a gash and his eyes were hollow and wide. In the glint of the setting sun, Tink saw a flash. The glass bottle was in Caiman's pocket.

"There's the vial!" She pointed to the rowboat. "We have to get that before the pirates drink it. Peter's right. We need to get to the ship!" Tink didn't wait for James to protest. She took flight and the others followed, flying out of the two round holes in the side of the Rock and over the Never Sea to the *Jolly Roger* in the distance. Below, she saw a tail splash in the water and she hoped it was Blair getting help.

Lightning flickered, backlighting the ship against a stormy sky. Tink was so busy worrying about the vial in Caiman's possession, she almost didn't see what was coming till it was right in front of them.

"Watch out!" she jingled.

She, James, and Peter dove out of the way as another cannonball whished past them toward the cave. It smashed just below the two other blasts, creating a third hole, right above the jagged opening that made the Rock transform before their very eyes.

"Is it me, or does that boulder now look just like—" James started.

"A skull! It's a Skull Rock!" Peter proclaimed. "Brilliant."

Tink wasn't sure about brilliant. The place looked even more perilous than it did before. With the dark sky around it and all the seagulls, the place now looked more nefarious—like the pirates were indeed remaking Never Land over in their own image.

The battle was already raging when the three landed on the *Jolly Roger* deck. Shape-shifters and birds of Never Land faced off against shadows and pirates alike on the deck, while in the waters below, Blair had called on mermaids, who were now drowning shadows and pirates who were knocked overboard. Claws and swords were being brandished about, pirates shouting, shadows clicking, and children cheering, as if, contrary to Tiger Lily's warning, this really were all one big game. An arrow shot through the air and Tink watched it sail dangerously close to the group of boys dressed as animals on the upper deck.

Tink zoomed forward, kicking it off-course.

"Boys!" James cried, landing beside them. "We need to get you out of here. It isn't safe."

Peter flew past him and grabbed a rope from one of the sails, swinging round and knocking out pirates as he went. "Safe? It's time to battle, James. I'll get you, pirates! Each and every one of you!"

"Peter, no!" James scolded, but Peter didn't listen.

The boy's right foot kicked into a pirate's stomach and the pirate flew backward, a tiny dagger falling out of his hands. Tink watched as Peter reached down and picked it up, looking at the shaft and blade from all angles. He swung at the air, gleeful.

"Hey, this is even better than a sword. Look at me, Tink! I'm like a pirate. Not an evil pirate, mind you. A good one, ready to fight till the end." He brandished the dagger in the air, almost cutting off his own rope.

"Peter, stop that!" Tink scolded. "You'll hurt yourself!" But the boy ignored her, too, and swung into the air again, dagger held at the ready.

More arrows flew past them and pinned two shadows to masts where they wriggled and clicked trying to get loose. Tink looked up to see where the arrows were coming from and saw Tiger Lily perched in the crow's nest. Her friend was shooting as quickly as she could. Tink flew up toward her, dodging shadows left and right.

"Tinker Bell!" Tiger Lily kept her eye on targets below. "You're all right." She pursed her lips. "Caiman is behind this all, I'm afraid. I saw him with the captain."

Tink's stomach rolled. "I know. He did all of it—Never Land's disturbances, the falls emptying. Our home is dying because of him."

She filled her friend in on the rest as best she could as Tiger Lily fired another arrow. It shot straight through a shadow, which plummeted into the sea where a mermaid . . . *Oh.*

Tink watched in horror as the mermaid grabbed the shadow and dove, drowning it in the waters below the surface.

"We must get that last vial of Prism Falls water from Caiman. It's our only chance to save the magic. You know that, don't you?" Her dark eyes searched Tink's. "I know he's our friend, but if we don't stop him, there will be nothing left."

Their island. Never Land. Tink looked out at the small boys she'd brought from the Mainland to save and then to the shore of the cay she'd called home for so long. With certainty, she knew this island was where she belonged. That restlessness she'd been feeling was gone. Her place was here. The boys' was, too. She wouldn't let the pirates take this land she loved away from them.

"I know," Tink jingled, her voice thick. "I'll get it from him. Even if I have to fight him for it."

Tiger Lily's face softened. "Good luck, friend. I'll do all I can from here. Go! Now! While I cover you."

Filled with resolve, Tink dove, weaving around pirates and their shadows. She headed across the deck, flying low and narrowly avoiding colliding with a pirate that had caught fire. She'd just dodged a pirate's grasp when a shape-shifter in seal form slid across the deck into the pirate, taking a bite out of his leg. Screaming, the pirate threw himself overboard.

"Back, get back!" Mr. Smee shouted, as Tink flew around a flock of seagulls that were trying to steal his beanie hat.

Tink flew on, her sight set on Caiman. He was brandishing a sword against the pelican she knew was Mimic.

"I don't want to fight you!" she heard Caiman yell as he swung a sword through the air.

Blast. When had he gotten a weapon? Tink rushed forward and flew to his pocket, where the small vial was bouncing around. Moving fast, she yanked the cold, hard glass.

"I've got it!" Tink cried, holding the bottle tightly to her chest. Pixie dust scattered around her in her haste, forcing Caiman to look down.

He felt the pockets on his pantaloons, and his eyes widened when he realized what Tink was holding. "No!"

"Yes!" she jingled triumphantly, flying upward to get away.

A hand swooped in front of her and closed tightly around her waist.

"So, Miss Bell," Captain Bartholomew trilled. "It seems you haven't drowned after all. What do you have in your possession? Could that be the last of the magic water from Prism Falls?" The captain looked manic as he laughed with delirious glee. His wide nose and mustache were so close to her face, they tickled her arms. Captain Bartholomew narrowed his eyes and started to squeeze.

Tink could hear shouting, the boys crying out for Tink to get away, but the captain's hold tightened.

She had trouble inhaling. *Breathe, Tink.* But she couldn't. She was sure he was going to crush her.

"That vial is mine, Miss Bell. Mine!" he said, his face reddening. "Did you really think you could take it from me? It's all that's left between me and this confounded island. And now it's between me and *you.*" The captain squeezed tighter, and Tink felt the life drain out of her.

"No!" Caiman cried, running across the deck to reach the captain, his sword held high. "Don't hurt her!"

But the captain had a sword, too, and he raised it in defense as Caiman rushed toward him. With Tink in one hand, and his weapon in the other, Bartholomew lunged forward. The blade struck through Caiman's heart.

TWENTY-NINE

"CAIMAN!" TINK CRIED AS THE YOUNG MAN DROPPED LIKE AN ANCHOR, hitting the deck and clutching his chest, which did nothing to stop the bleeding that was quickly spreading across his white shirt. In surprise, Captain Bartholomew released her.

All across the deck of the *Jolly Roger*, creature and pirate grew quiet. Tiger Lily dropped down from the crow's nest. Blair pulled herself up to the railing. Mimic transformed into his human form and fell to the ground by Caiman.

Thunder rolled low and long across the Never Sea, and the rain came fast and hard like pellets, landing straight on Caiman. He was dying right in front of them.

Caiman looked as shocked as anyone else. His eyes flitted back and forth from Tink to Mimic. Tears filled Tink's eyes as she glanced at the upper deck and saw James try to pull the boys away so they wouldn't see what was happening. Peter, however, was undeterred. He pushed his way forward. He'd found a green cap somewhere on the ship and stuck a feather in it. The feather was wilting in the rain, but not the boy, who still had his dagger and was now racing across the deck toward them. But Peter was too late. By the sound of Caiman's breathing, Tink knew he'd be gone in moments. He'd betrayed them all, but he'd also been betrayed by the pirates. He'd been battered and tortured, and she knew in her heart, Caiman didn't want to hurt the land he'd begun to call home.

The captain, however, didn't show an ounce of remorse.

"Now give me that water, fairy!" he said, reaching down and prying the bottle from Tink's weakened arms. She hadn't realized she was still holding it.

Shouts sounded and arrows flew, and Tink clung to the bottle as best she could, but she was no match for the Mainlander in her grief-stricken state. Bartholomew held the vial up in triumph.

Tink knew she should take flight immediately and wrestle that precious water back from the captain, but before she could react, there was a flash. Pixie dust flooded the air and Tink looked up in surprise to see Ash zoom into view, shooting the bottle with dust and sending it high into the air, right out of the captain's hands. Tink couldn't believe her eyes. Ash had come back.

"No!" Bartholomew cried. "Get that bottle and trap that fairy!"

All around the ship, pirates and their sentient shadows jumped and clawed the air. Caiman let out a pained gurgle, and Tink placed a hand on the young pirate's cheek. "Caiman," she whispered, tears falling down her cheeks. "You saved me."

"I . . . I couldn't let him hurt you, Tink," Caiman said, the words coming fast as he struggled for breath. "This is all my fault." He winced in pain. "I'm sorry I was so frightened of the captain that I ruined everything. I don't want to be a coward anymore."

"You're not," Tink insisted. "You're a Wanderer." She glanced at Mimic, who was holding Caiman's other hand, his face ashen.

Caiman's eyes found hers and fluttered open and closed. "Find a way to save Never Land. Please? I don't want it to die like Mum. She wouldn't have wanted that. She would've loved Never Land." He swallowed hard. "Goodbye, Tink," he said, and began to close his eyes.

"No!" Tink was sobbing now. She felt so helpless. She didn't want to see Caiman die.

Ash dropped to the deck, the vial of Prism Falls waters in his arms. All around him, the pirates and captain were shouting. ("Where did that blasted fairy go?" she heard Bartholomew cry.)

When Ash saw what was happening, he paled. "Caiman . . . I'm too late." He bowed his head.

Even Blair was teary.

"Tink?" Tiger Lily said, urgently drawing the fairy's attention. "The water." She motioned to the bottle in Ash's hands. "What if you take a drop for Caiman? Not all of it, of course. But a drop. Maybe the island will find favor with him for saving you."

Tink didn't think. She just acted, hands trembling as Ash handed her the vial and she popped the cork. She forced the water into Caiman's wound. *Please*, she thought, recorking the bottle for safety and wishing her thoughts into reality, *save him. We will use the rest of the water to restore the falls, but save our friend. He made a terrible mistake.*

Tink sat back with the vial, watching the wound and looking at Caiman's chest to see if he was still breathing. For a moment, nothing happened. Then, Caiman began to shimmer, his body waffling. Tink held her breath, wondering if Tiger Lily's plan had worked. Suddenly, Caiman's whole body disappeared right in front of their eyes.

"Caiman?" Tink panicked. "Caiman?" She looked at Tiger Lily, whose expression was grim.

Mimic seemed equally stunned. "What just happened? Where did he go?"

"Captain! The vial!" Mr. Smee pointed wildly to the deck floor. "Miss Bell has it!"

"WHAT?" Captain Bartholomew whirled around and rushed for her, kicking over barrels and knocking over chairs in his efforts to reach her. "Give that to me, you bloody fairy!" He ripped the bottle out of Tink's hands just as she heard a ringing voice shout.

"Stay back, pirate!"

James! She looked up in surprise to see him jump over the upper deck railing as Peter swung through the air again, high over the pirates' heads, the dagger in his hand swinging wildly. The Lost Boys cheered at his bravado, and that only made Peter show off more. He lifted his dagger higher and swished it through the air, making pirates duck. James lunged for the captain, connecting his fist with Bartholomew's jaw. Tink gasped as the captain started to fall backward, arms flailing wildly at his side. Peter swung over him at that same moment, his dagger colliding with the captain's left hand, which was holding the vial. It sliced his hand clear off. Tink covered her mouth in shock.

The captain fell to the ground, howling.

The vial bounced and rolled off the side of the ship.

"No!" Tiger Lily cried, rushing for it, but it was too late. It went over the side. "Mimic! Get down there! Blair! Someone! Get that water!"

Bartholomew was still screaming. He held his arm out in front of him, staring aghast as his left hand lay on the deck. Crimson blood issued from his limb, and the pirate hopped around in horror. Mr. Smee rushed in with a rag, tying it around the captain's appendage.

For a moment, all the chaos stopped, as everyone paused to watch the pirate captain, agog.

Even James couldn't hide his horror, immediately dropping to the deck. Peter looked alarmed for a moment. . . .

And then the boy started to laugh . . . shakily at first, then more loudly, as though trying to convince himself this was all part of the game. It was the first time Tink had ever seen the boy unnerved. But then he seemed to shake himself out of it, standing tall, hands on his hips, like Tink. "That's what you get for messing with Tinker Bell and me!" he declared. "You dirty old pirate!" And with that, Peter picked up the bloody hand by the fingers and flung it off the ship. The other boys started to cheer as James and Tink looked on, aghast.

"No!" the captain cried, stumbling to the side of the ship as pirates dove out of the way, afraid of Bartholomew's fury. "My hand! My hand! SMEE!"

"I'll get it! Don't you worry, Captain!" Smee said, running to the side of the ship where he stopped short and gasped. "Oh my."

"Tink! Mimic! Look!"

Blair? Tink flew to the side, the others right behind her. She looked below and saw the mermaid swimming next to a crocodile as if it were the most normal thing in the world. Blair was crying. "It's Caiman! He's been saved."

It took Tink a moment to understand. But of course, she knew the water could grant a great transformation. Perhaps it had done it for Caiman. Was it possible? How did they know for sure it was him?

The crocodile opened its jaw and out floated the vial of water.

Tink gasped. The last of Prism Falls waters had been saved.

Tink's eyes welled with tears. In his new form, Caiman could navigate every part of Never Land, land and sea. He could live among the plant life he loved so much in both. Besides, the crocodile was one of Never Land's most fearsome creatures. She smiled to herself. As a predator, he would have to be afraid no more.

Never Land had granted the poor boy's greatest heart's desire.

Blair snatched the bottle and held it up for Ash. The fairy swooped down low and grabbed it, then turned back to the others. "I'll meet you on shore."

Tink wasn't even sure the captain noticed. He was still looking down at the crocodile and his hand, floating nearby. Seeing it now, the crocodile rushed forward, and with its wide jaws, swallowed the pirate's hand whole.

"Nooo!" the captain cried out, as though the appendage were still attached to his person.

Tink saw the captain's mutinous expression and turned to Tiger Lily. "We need to get out of here."

"Agreed," Tiger Lily said, and climbed over the side of the ship, prepared to dive. "I'll meet you on shore. Don't forget your Lost Boys."

Tink flew fast now to Peter, sprinkling pixie dust on him in case he finally had run out, before gathering more from her pouch and spreading it over the Lost Boys and James on the upper deck. The smaller boys cheered, while James was green, either from the sight of the severed hand or the thought of flying again. In any case, they all took to the air and no one tried to stop them. As they swooped through the clouds, the captain, still clutching his arm, looked up. Tink could hear him screaming.

"I will get you for this, Peter!"

Peter didn't seem all that concerned. "Nothing will ever be as scary as being sick," Peter muttered to himself, almost too quietly for Tink to hear.

The pirate's threats echoed across the Never Sea. "I will get you, you insolent child, or my name isn't Captain James Bartholomew—feared by all on the seven seas!"

Tink looked back. James—her James—had gone from green to ashen white. Perhaps he, too, was shocked to hear he had something in common with one so nefarious.

There was a sudden movement beside her. Peter somersaulted in the air, interrupting her thoughts. He looked at Tink and smiled slyly. "You know, I'm looking forward to it."

THIRTY

The group reconvened at Wanderers Cay. As Tink and the Lost Boys came in for a landing, Tiger Lily rode up on Pony, Ash was waiting with the vial of Prism Falls magic, and Blair and Mimic—now a whale—gathered in the waters. The Lost Boys were all in a tizzy, talking at once and chattering about fighting pirates and Peter's brave turn on the *Jolly Roger*.

"He won't mess with me again, or any of us. Though I wouldn't mind another tussle on that ship of his," Peter declared, still waving his dagger in the air.

Tink would have to find a way to get it away from him, or at least give him some rules for safety's sake.

"Boys, you all could use a good washing after all that excitement," she heard James say. "Why don't you rinse off in the water? You're beginning to smell." There were protests all around and some bargaining. James shook his head.

Tink left him to it and flew over to the water's edge where Mimic had transformed into a human once more and was wading in the water next to Blair. Tink was sad to see Caiman was not with them. "Is he . . . all right?" she jingled hesitantly as Tiger Lily approached as well.

"He will be," Blair said, understanding her meaning at once. Her tail flipped in the water behind her.

"It will take Caiman time to adjust, of course," Mimic added. "But he will learn to love it. How could he not, living both by the sea and plant life?"

"And you're certain it was Caiman?" Ash asked.

Tink didn't blame him. She wondered the same thing.

"I could feel it. We both could," Mimic said, gesturing to Blair, who nodded. "It was him. And now that he's gotten a taste of the captain, I suspect he'll be trailing the *Jolly Roger* forever to get another bite. Even though those pirates can walk on land, I'd bet he'll never let the captain get anywhere near Prism Falls again."

Tink shuddered at the thought, and yet . . . there was some satisfaction in that outcome. *Good*, she thought. *The captain deserves to be afraid of the pirate he tortured for so long.*

"Speaking of"—Ash held the vial out to Tiger Lily—"I think you should get this back where it belongs."

Tiger Lily took the bottle from him. "Thanks, Ash. Pony and I will get this up to Prism Falls at once." She looked at Tink. "The waters should replenish themselves after a little while." She smiled. "And our home will be good as new."

Home. Tink understood what that meant now. Never Land was where she belonged, and with the boys beside her, it felt complete. Tink looked over at the boys running happily around the beach. James had started a small fire and was watching them from a rock nearby. He, however, looked lost in his own thoughts.

"Before I go, I should give you this." Tiger Lily placed a book on the sand. "I grabbed it as we fled the *Jolly Roger*. It was lying on the deck."

"Caiman's book!" Blair said. "He loved those plants so much."

Tink touched the leaf-paper lovingly. "I'm glad you found it." She used all her strength to open the book and smiled at the familiar handwriting. Caiman had written notes in the margins since she'd seen the book last, but she also realized he'd added something new on the blank pages—stories. Stories about . . . Never Land? The Wanderers? She inhaled sharply when she saw one titled simply: Tink. She looked up at the others tearily. "I want to say something."

"Here we go," Ash said with a sigh. "Haven't you said enough?"

Tink stopped crying and bristled. "*No.*"

"Let Tink speak," Tiger Lily told him. She smiled at her friend. "I suspect she wants to apologize again, even though I'm not sure an apology is necessary—you left for the right reasons."

Tinker Bell beamed. Tiger Lily always understood. "But still, I could have told you all where and why I was going beforehand. And then maybe you would have known where to find me when I didn't return right away."

"Well, we can see why you stayed so long," Blair said, staring now at

James in his wet, white shirt, half-unbuttoned, his pants, stained and dirty, now cuffed to his calves. "He is a delicious snack, isn't he?"

Tink felt a flash of jealousy. *"Hey."*

Blair laughed. "Sorry! I can't help myself." Her electric-blue eyes were warm. "But Tiger Lily is right—you don't need to apologize again. We're Wanderers, aren't we? That's what we do. We wander. You just got to do it on the Mainland."

"In a way, I think maybe we were envious," Mimic said, and looked shyly at Tink. "You got to go beyond the Never Sea. Blair and I have wanted to do that forever, but we didn't want to break up the group."

"You have?" Tink gasped. "Why didn't you say something?"

"Despite what you might think, I have feelings and I was thinking of you," Blair said as she pushed a lock of her hair behind her ear. "You loved the Wanderers more than any of us."

"I have a confession to make," Ash said suddenly, his eyes pensive. "I don't think I am a Wanderer." He looked at Tink worriedly. "I tried to be. I wanted to be one for you. I didn't like the idea of you out of the hollow on your own."

Tink's cheeks warmed. "You've been a good friend, but you miss the fairy tree."

Ash nodded. "Being back there, I just knew it was where I was meant to be."

Tink grasped his hand. "Then that's where you should be. No one should live a life they don't want to," she said, thinking of James. "You should go back."

Ash hesitated. "Are you sure I can't convince you to come with me?"

"Peter, no fair!" Tink heard Cubby shout, and they all looked over to where the boys were using downed tree twigs as weapons. "Why does he get a dagger and a sword?"

"Because I am the king of Never Land!" Peter said, using whatever pixie dust he had left to hop onto a large rock so that he stood taller than the others.

Tink shook her head and smiled. "No, I think this is where I'm meant to be. With these Lost Boys. I care about them, and well, they could use some guiding."

"I'll say. That boy's ego might be bigger than the pirate captain's." Mimic motioned to Peter.

"Yes, but he has a good heart," Tink said fondly. "It feels like he belongs here. They all do. And so do I, for that matter." She looked to Tiger Lily.

"You will always have me around the corner," Tiger Lily said. "I am not going anywhere."

The friends smiled at each other.

"So, is that it? Are the Wanderers no more?" Blair asked.

"Maybe, but we will always be family. And if you ever need us, we'll come," Mimic promised and Tink knew he meant it. They all did.

SQUAWK!

Just then a flock of Never Fowl descended on the beach. Tink had never seen so many of the large blue birds in one place before. Even the Lost Boys silenced at their appearance. The birds moved as a pack, stopping at the water's edge by Tinker Bell and the other Wanderers. Tinker Bell flew forward to greet them.

"We have the last water of Prism Falls and plan to take it to the waters to replenish the island's magic," Tink told them.

Tiger Lily stepped forward as well and showed them the bottle.

The Never Fowl looked at one another, squawking quietly. Then the largest blue bird spoke to Tinker Bell. The deep voice seemed to reverberate inside her mind.

"*THE DANGER IS NO MORE. THE ISLAND'S MAGIC WILL BE RESTORED.*"

Tink felt like her heart might burst. "Thank you," she whispered. "We all thank you."

And with a small nod, the Never Fowl took flight once more.

THIRTY-ONE

Tiger Lily left first with promises she'd be back to check in at the hideout (where Tink planned to relocate with the boys), after her work at Prism Falls was done. Then Tink stood at the shore, waving with Ash till Blair and Mimic were nothing more than a dot in the distance of the Never Sea. Finally, she hugged Ash goodbye, even though she knew she'd see him, too, sooner than later.

"Promise you won't be a stranger." He pulled back and looked at her, his blue eyes hopeful. "You know you'll always be part of Pixie Hollow."

"Of course," she said feistily, her eyes sparkling. "I'm a fairy. The hollow is in my blood. And I'll need to restock my pixie dust." They both chuckled. "I'll come by soon once we're all settled," she said with more seriousness. "I promise."

She watched Ash take flight against the orange sky. The clouds had moved out already, which was a good sign, as if the island knew it was in good hands once more. Tink stood and listened to the sound of laughter behind her. She sensed something, just like she could feel a charge in the air before a storm or a change in the wind.

Breathe, Tink. Just breathe.

"Tinker Bell?"

She turned around to face James. She couldn't help but still feel a flutter at the sight of him. He had dark stubble coming in on his face, and there was something daring about the small cut he had above his right eye. She could stare at him for hours, but she wouldn't. This moment would have to be enough. He'd saved her, and she'd saved him. They'd be forever tied to each other, even if—

"I think it's time for me to go home," he said gently.

Tink steeled herself for the truth she already knew was coming. She wouldn't cry. Instead, she nodded. "I know. You don't belong here. I do."

"I don't belong here," he said, his habit of echoing her as uncanny as ever. "I can see that you do." He looked back at the boys playing on the beach near the bonfire. "And I understand now that they do, too."

Tink smiled at the crew of Lost Boys she'd be watching over on Never Land. She was sure sometimes this would be trying, but it would also be just what she needed. They were her boys and they always would be now. "I'll take good care of them."

"I know you'll watch out for them. I'm not worried." James looked down at his bare feet buried in the sand and then up at her again. "But I will miss them. I'll miss you too."

"I will miss you forever," she said softly.

"It's not that I'm not grateful for all you've done. If you hadn't taken us here when you did, they wouldn't have survived. Here, they're thriving." James looked back at the boys playing with pride. "But me . . ." He looked at her sorrowfully. "I have to go back and finish what we started. Our invention. I don't know what it is, but I feel like I have something there that could be great. Something that could go beyond the sewing machine and hospital. I want to see it through."

Tink understood that itch. She'd had it herself many times. Finding an item that she wanted to tinker on and not being able to stop thinking about it till it was completed and functional. Till it had reached its full potential. James was the same way. Keeping him here, stifling him from his potential, would only be selfish. That vial of Prism Falls water was not meant to transform the young inventor. Not really.

"I know you're going to do great things," she said, smiling bigger than she felt so he understood. Because she was happy for him, even if her heart hurt so very badly.

If there was one thing she'd learned from this whole ordeal, it was that every one of them—Caiman, Mimic, Blair, Ash, James, and herself—had to forge their own paths. And that's exactly what they would do. James's future was meant to be on the Mainland, and hers was here with the boys who were lost no more.

But since she couldn't say all those things to James, she did the one thing she knew he'd understand. She flew slowly toward him, hovering in front of his face and touched his cheek. James raised his right hand and held out his pointer finger and Tink turned and flew toward his hand, pressing her fingers against his as the boys' laughter lifted high into the sky, carrying on the breeze.

Tink moved away, brushing a rogue tear from her face.

"You should say your goodbyes, and I'll fly you back," she said.

James blinked. "I should say my goodbyes and then . . . You'll help me get home?" She nodded. "Thank you."

Tink gave James and the boys some privacy, hovering at the water's edge, then resting on Caiman's flora guide. She watched the sun set and finally heard James's approach. She rose to greet him and found the boys standing beside him.

"Look out for everyone while I'm gone," she jingled to Peter. "I won't be long."

Peter stood taller, but not that tall. On Never Land, he would always look as he did right then—an impish, precocious boy forever caught between childhood and adulthood, and proud of it. There was something she loved about the confidence Peter had in himself. He wasn't in a rush. He was happy right where he was.

"You got it, Tink!" He turned to the other boys. "Tink says I'm in charge while she's gone. Back to the treehouse, boys! We have some decorating to do."

James looked tearful then. "I guess it's time to go."

The fairy nodded, swallowing the tightness in her throat. For the last time, Tinker Bell sprinkled pixie dust over James, wondering what his happy thoughts might be as he rose into the air. He followed her silently into the night sky. The journey felt too quick. Before she knew it, they were descending over the city, the fog covered the sky and she saw . . . What was it Peter called it? Big Ben? She could see the clock tower, reminding them of the time passing right before their eyes. The pair descended in the middle of a quiet street, the ground wet from recent rain.

James landed softly. She watched as the last of his pixie dust fluttered into the air and disappeared.

"I guess that's it then," James said, his voice quiet as he watched her hovering like the lightning bug the boys once thought she was. She saw him hesitate. "Will I . . . ever see you again?"

Tink felt her heart break just a little. *Just breathe.* She forced out a smile, not letting her sadness be the last thing he remembered of her. Instead, she smiled. *Some might say it's impossible*, she jingled with a slight shrug. *But you know what they say about that.*

And with that, Tink took off again, into the night, headed for the second star to the right where she'd go straight on till morning.

Peter was waiting for Tinker Bell when she returned. He was sitting on a rock near the water, looking out at the *Jolly Roger*, and she could tell from the look on his face he was plotting something incorrigible.

"Tink!" he said, jumping up at the sight of her flying down to greet him. "What took you so long? You've been gone *forever*."

Tink faltered. "I have? It was barely a day!"

"It was not a day," Peter said with a scowl. "It was way longer. I think. Who can tell? There's no Big Ben here." He smiled.

She did too. "No there's not."

"Do you think we could go flying?" he begged.

Tink sighed, secretly thrilled. She sprinkled some pixie dust over Peter and he rose into the air.

"Thanks! We missed you," he said. "Tiger Lily took us to her village to learn how to catch fish. That was the fun part. The not so fun part? Cooking it. Oh, and someone made Cubby a new outfit. They said they'd make us all new clothes. I'm thinking of something green, like the grass here. There's so much of it and the color just speaks to me, you know?"

Tink nodded, letting him ramble. "I know."

"Otherwise, everything is good. The hideout is coming along, too, and Tiger Lily said Prism Falls looked a little fuller when she checked it this morning."

That was a good sign.

"And I maaaaay have flown over to see the *Jolly Roger*. Just for a little bit."

Tinker Bell shook her head, exasperated. "Of course you did."

Peter flew closer, his mood shifting. She could see him thinking hard about something. "Are you sad? About James leaving?"

Tink was afraid to answer as they lifted higher into the air. "A little bit," she admitted. *A lot.*

He swallowed hard. "Me too. But don't you worry, Tink. I'm not going anywhere. I'll never leave you or Never Land."

He looked over the Never Sea far below, and the forest in the distance, Prism Falls hidden away and hopefully starting to replenish again, the smoke from Tiger Lily's village nearby telling them friends were waiting, and Peter put out his hand mid-flight to touch her with his fingers. "You and I will have adventures forever. I know it."

At that moment, she knew with certainty, Peter was right.

"I do, too." Tink shot ahead. "Come along, Peter. I'll race you."

EPILOGUE

Many (many) moons later . . .

"Aha! I have you in my clutches now!"

"You may think so, sir, but I promise you don't!"

Thwack! Thwack! The sound of the two boys' wooden swords connecting again and again pierced the air.

"Take that! And that!" said the smaller child as he backed up to the edge of his bed. "It's time for you to walk the plank!"

"Never!" the older boy vowed, swishing his sword through the air before connecting with the other wooden weapon again.

Thwack! Thwack!

"Boys, please!" an older girl admonished as she sat in bed. She wore a blue nightgown that touched her toes and she was reading a worn leather book by the light of a small lamp. Her hair was tied back in a blue bow. "You're giving me a headache!"

"What is that racket?" someone bellowed from a floor below.

The children's eyes widened.

"Please keep it down," the girl whispered. "You don't want Father or Mother to come up here and—oof!" She ducked, narrowly avoiding getting hit by the younger boy's sword as he swung wildly. "Do be careful, will you? You know you're not supposed to be standing on your beds. Boys? Boys?"

The boys continued to ignore her completely. Instead, the older of the two—a dark-haired child wearing spectacles that kept sliding down the bridge of his nose, and a top hat he'd borrowed from his father, hopped from one bed to the other, narrowly avoiding knocking the younger child off in the process.

The girl reached out a hand just in time and kept the little boy from falling. He was lucky he didn't hit his head in those pink footie pajamas. She picked up the boy's worn teddy bear that had fallen onto the floor and placed the bear carefully on her own bed before returning to her book.

It amazed Tink that none of the Mainlander children noticed the two figures watching them from an open window.

"Are you sure this is the place?" Peter whispered.

"Well, I'm not certain," Tink had to admit, her wings aglow in the darkness of night. "But I think so. That Mainlander tome said it was number fourteen."

"I don't think this is it."

Tink's heart fluttered, then sank wondering if Peter might be right. After all, so far the only humans she'd seen were these children running around what looked like a large bedroom filled with toys. The home seemed stately, and the area charming. *This has to be it,* she thought.

"A buccaneer is not a pirate!" said the older boy, as he jumped off the bed. He slipped into oversized black dress shoes and clomped off to the window seat to look out over the city. "I don't want to play anymore."

Tink and Peter immediately scattered, flying to another window. London twinkled through the clouds in the distance.

"That isn't fair, John!" The smaller boy in pajamas hopped up and down, making his bed creak and his whole body wobble. "Come back and fight!" the little one begged. "You promised we'd play! You're cheating!"

"Michael, please! Lower your voice!" the girl told him, putting down the book once more. "Pirates . . . buccaneers . . . whatever you choose to call them, you were both being quite loud. I thought I heard someone shouting. And if Mother and Father heard you—"

"They won't," the little one interrupted, his pink lips puffed out making him look like, well, a codfish.

"But they could and they have, and they will again if you two aren't quiet," she reminded him, helping the little boy down and walking him over to the window by the other child. "You know they already aren't happy about me still being up here."

The older boy stiffened at mention of this.

"If they hear everyone fighting, it will just make Father want to move me sooner," she said. "He says it's about time to grow up and leave the nursery."

"You can't leave us!" said the boy named John. "Wendy, please don't go yet! You can't grow up. Not yet."

Tink felt a tingling sensation at mention of these words.

"Grow up?" Peter looked affronted. "Who would want to do that. You know, Tink, we could—"

Absolutely not! she warned. Then she heard footsteps right next to the pair's new hiding spot.

"Mary! Have you seen my cufflinks?" a new voice rang out. Tink and Peter followed it to a different window. Then Tink froze.

"No, George, I haven't," said a woman.

"I know I left them on this table. Did that confounded dog move them again? Honestly, I'm starting to wonder if she should spend so much time in the house." The man continued up the steps and flicked on the light in the room.

Tink inhaled, her heart leaping to her throat, wondering if she'd been spotted.

But the man simply went on with his business, searching under papers, behind a paperweight.

"He looks old," Peter whispered.

Shhhhh! she scolded.

"*Someone* must have moved them," George continued now, yelling louder.

That's when there was the sound of giggling. The child in the pink pajamas came from around the corner.

The father's expression changed, understanding dawning in his eyes. "Ah, Mary, never mind." He crouched down now, peering at his youngest son. "All right, Michael, hand them over."

"Do I have to?" the tiny one asked. He clutched his bear tightly in his arms.

"Yes, I need them for the award ceremony tonight. Don't you want your father to bring home a plaque with his name on it?" George asked.

"Yes," Michael decided. He held something up that he'd been hiding behind his back.

"Your cuff-pinks."

George barked out a short laugh. "Cufflinks, Michael."

"Well they look like gems . . . maybe *treasure*." Michael's eyes sparked, as if stowing that information for a later game. "What do the letters on them mean?"

George showed him the small, round items that looked like jewels. "G.J.D. G stands for George. James is my middle name. I used to be called that as a boy, though I go by my father's name now . . ." he trailed off, his thoughts clearly elsewhere.

When had he changed it? Directly after his return from Never Land? Later?

"And then, of course, there's Darling. I must say, that's the most important of the lot. A surname I chose myself. One I share with you four. It reminds me we can always make something worthwhile, even in the most impossible of circumstances. It reminds me of, well. . . ." He cleared his throat loudly, looking uncomfortable and all the more grown up.

Darling. Tears sprung to Tink's eyes. *I remember it fondly, too, James.*

"George, dear. We must get going!" the woman called.

"Right, yes, coming, dear!" George said, and picked Michael up, carrying him up the stairs to the large room where Wendy and John were waiting.

"Can't you read us a story, Father, before you and Mother go? Please?" John asked, and that's when Tink realized what the book was in his hands, the one Wendy had been reading from. It was Caiman's plant book. She gasped. When had James pinched that? She'd always wondered where it went.

"No time, John, no time." Then James paused at the top of the steps. His eyes flickering to the journal. "But maybe Wendy will read one. That book . . . I haven't dipped into that one for a very long time."

Wendy thumbed through the journal, flashing the back pages. They were full of elegant handwriting. Tink's heart fluttered faster. She remembered Caiman's hastily scrawled notes in the margins. Had James added stories of his own about their time together? Tink reached for the windowsill to hold on and steady herself.

"Yes, Father," Wendy responded.

"Good. Just the one. And then it's lights out, straight to bed," James said, continuing on his way. "And don't give Nana too much trouble."

"Yes, Father," John said.

"Aye, aye, Father!" Michael said.

Tinker Bell tugged on Peter's tunic. It was time to go.

"A few more minutes?" Peter whined just as there was the sound of barking. A small fluffy brown-and-white dog bounded into the room. "The girl's gonna start a story. Don't you want to know what it's about?"

Yes and no. Tink sighed. "I'll be waiting at the window ledge. Don't let them see you! And if you're not back in five minutes, I'm flying home without you."

Peter crossed his arms over his chest. "Fine." He grinned slyly. "I'll listen from the other window." He flew off and disappeared.

Tink headed back to the window to wait. She wouldn't really leave him behind. Who knew if he'd get lost? Peter needed her. He would always need her and she would always be there for him. Looking out at Big Ben, feeling the cool night air, Tink didn't feel unsettled being back on the Mainland like she thought she would.

Maybe a small visit now and then wouldn't be the *worst* thing.

She heard the sound of footsteps again and looked into the window once more. She inhaled sharply.

There he was. Her James.

Now George James Darling.

She saw him pause and she quickly ducked back into the shadows as James came to the window and looked out. Had he seen her?

"Ready, Tink?" Peter called, startling her as he flew toward her after hovering outside the other open window.

Tink shushed him as she flew to meet him, a trail of pixie dust extending behind her. She had the strange feeling she was being watched, but she wouldn't turn around.

"Ready," she jingled to Peter, and prepared to take off.

She'd seen enough. Tink smiled to herself. Together, the pair took off into the night, headed to the second star to the right where they would fly straight on till morning.

ACKNOWLEDGMENTS

Getting to play in the Disney sandbox is a dream come true for a self-professed Disney Girl like myself. I feel so fortunate to explore so many Disney characters, and getting to write about Tinker Bell has been a personal favorite. I have been a fan of Tink and seen her fly over Cinderella Castle on trips to Walt Disney World more times than I should probably admit. I've always found her to be such an intriguing, complex character, so I feel privileged to have been given the chance to explore a new take on her story, during the fairy time period that comes right before *Peter Pan*. Special thanks to J. M. Barrie for creating this beautiful world and for his story *Peter Pan in Kensington Gardens*, from which I took inspiration.

I'm so thankful to have worked on Tink's story with my wonderful editor, Brittany Rubiano. Like Tiger Lily is to Tink, Britt is the perfect partner for both creating magic and collaborating on ideas that send me off and running in a new, inspired direction. I feel so lucky to have had Britt sprinkle pixie dust on this project.

I'm also incredibly thankful to everyone at Disney Books for entrusting me with the Enchanters Tale series and for giving Tink so much love. Special thanks to Cristina Casas, Kelly Forsythe, Ariana Denebeim, Crystal McCoy, Lisa McClatchy, Augusta Harris, Holly Rice, Cassidy Leyendecker, and Jody Corbett. I'm grateful to Chris Koehler for his gorgeous art (London and Never Land in one beautiful image!), and to book jacket designer Marci Senders. This series' look and design gives me all the Disney feels.

To my agent, Dan Mandel, thanks for always being up for an adventure with me. I'm so thankful for the magic in the world that gave me you as an agent. I'm also grateful to my writer friends, especially the ones I talk all things Disney with. Thank you to my wonderful Twisted Tale family: Liz Braswell, Elizabeth Lim, Mari Mancusi, Keila Kendall, and Farrah Rochon for all the love and encouragement. I love our group emails!

Finally, to my Disney-loving family—my husband Mike and our two boys, Tyler and Dylan—thank you for putting up with me when I'm watching Disney movies on a loop, singing Disney tunes in the car, and explaining why another trip to the Parks is crucial for "research." If I had all the wishes in the world, I'd still wish for a life with you three every time.

JEN CALONITA is one of the authors of the *New York Times* best-selling A Twisted Tale books and the author of the award-winning Secrets of My Hollywood Life and Fairy Tale Reform School series. She lives in New York with her husband, two boys, and a rebellious chihuahua named Ben Kenobi. A huge Disney fan, Jen dreams of moving the whole family into Cinderella's castle at Walt Disney World. Visit her online at www.JenCalonitaOnline.com.